75

SMKE SCREEN

SMOKE SCREEN

A NOVEL BY

TRACI HUNTER ABRAMSON

Covenant Communications, Inc.

For Tiffany

Cover images: *Circuit* © Edfuentesg, *Playing With Fire* © Susandaniels, courtesty istockphoto.com

Cover design © 2011 by Covenant Communications, Inc.

Published by Covenant Communications, Inc.
American Fork, Utah

Printed in the United States of America
First Printing: January 2011

18 17 16 15 14 13 12 11   10 9 8 7 6 5 4 3 2

ISBN-13: 978-1-60861-183-6

ACKNOWLEDGMENTS

MY SINCERE APPRECIATION GOES TO Rebecca Cummings and Samantha Van Walraven for all of your help and insight throughout the editing process. Thank you to Zeda Abramson for sharing your knowledge of the artistic process and for your willingness to entertain my little ones when I most needed quiet time alone with my computer.

Thank you to my family and all of the incredible people at Covenant who have continued to support my writing career.

And, finally, I want to thank Mom, Tiffany, and the smoothie guy for making my trip through Palm Springs truly memorable.

FIVE MEN. FIVE TARGETS.

Quinn Lambert visualized the mission once more in his mind, a mission the whole world was watching on the evening news. Once again pirates had commandeered a vessel in the Indian Ocean, only this time the two Americans on board weren't just a couple of innocent bystanders who happened to get caught in the wrong place at the wrong time. No, these two hostages had been specifically chosen because of the ransom they could command.

Hotel tycoon Monte Eastman and his wife, Georgia, had boarded a friend's yacht in Sri Lanka for an extended vacation. Four days into their voyage, pirates had intercepted them and had taken control of the vessel. The ransom demands began within hours. If all went as planned, another hour would be all that was needed to end those demands permanently.

Quinn checked his air gauge as he continued to breathe the canned air currently strapped to his back. The submarine that delivered him and his teammates within a mile of the yacht had submerged into the dark water beneath them. Slowly, steadily, Quinn moved toward the surface, constantly checking for his swim buddy and best friend, Tristan Crowther.

As expected, Tristan was a few feet to his right, and just beyond him was the rest of the Saint Squad, the elite five-man unit from SEAL Team Eight. Newly promoted Lieutenant Commander Brent Miller was in the center of the group. Beyond him was Jay Wellman, the newest addition to the squad. On the far side, his dark skin making him almost invisible in the dark water, was Seth Johnson.

They were within ten feet of the surface when they reached the side of the yacht. It was motionless in the water largely due to the fact that two destroyers were currently flanking its position. A standoff was coming, the deadline for the demanded wire transfer looming over them. Twelve hours was all they had left before the pirates would begin killing their hostages, starting with the only woman on board, Georgia Eastman.

Quinn didn't take the time to consider what this woman's husband must be going through right now, the panic and helplessness that was certainly consuming him. Instead, Quinn continued forward and watched for the signal.

* * *

She was hiding, whether she wanted to admit it or not. With a large painting in her hands and her supplies weighing down her backpack, Taylor Palmetta would hardly consider herself inconspicuous as she walked down the street in Paris, but she was hiding nonetheless.

An art program in Venice had lured Taylor to Europe shortly after she had graduated from college. At one time she had considered sharing her love of art in the classroom, but she knew now that teaching would never suit her. She needed the freedom to create, to paint what she wanted, when she wanted, and where she wanted. She had spent the past several months completing her studies in Venice and doing exactly that, traveling throughout Europe and stopping to paint whatever caught her attention.

At only twenty-four years old, Taylor had found her freedom, and she was using it to hide. She couldn't be certain if she had extended her stay in Europe so she wouldn't have to see Quinn Lambert again or if she was still trying to pretend that he hadn't really broken her heart.

Their long-distance relationship had been casual for the first six months after she moved to Europe, and now Taylor wished it had stayed that way. Everything had changed when Quinn had come to visit her in Venice. At least she thought everything had changed. Those few days together had been incredible, and Taylor had been convinced that they had moved from casual dating to exclusive, maybe even serious. A month later, only a few short weeks after seeing him again at her sister's wedding, her illusion crashed against an alternate reality when she found out he was dating someone else.

That tidbit of information had changed everything for her. She supposed she was more embarrassed than anything. She had fallen for Quinn completely and thought he felt the same for her. She had even started imagining a future with him in it. The news that he was still dating around had unraveled her dreams and left her feeling vulnerable.

Instead of moving back to Virginia Beach to be close to her family and Quinn like she had planned, she shifted her focus and energy to her work. Ironically, just as her personal life was falling apart, her professional life was flourishing. She had always dreamed of being a professional artist but had never truly believed it was possible. After an unexpected offer to sign with a New York agent, Taylor's professional dreams were now reality.

She glanced down at her most recent handiwork, still a little awed by the fact that she had created it. According to her favorite art professor, her gift was in the way she translated light onto the canvas. Her agent, on the other hand, insisted that the detail and realism in her work made it stand out. Regardless of what had prompted her success, Taylor was always amazed by the sense of wonder that rushed through her after she completed a painting.

As she approached her hotel, the doorman spotted her and reached for the door in anticipation of her arrival. Taylor greeted him and uttered her thanks as he opened the door wide for her.

A handful of people were sitting in the reception area of the lobby, but Taylor didn't pause to wonder if they were coming or going. Instead, she crossed to the elevator and stepped inside. The moment the elevator doors slid closed, reality washed over her again. She was in one of her favorite cities, the weather was stunningly beautiful, and she was doing what she loved. And she was painfully alone.

Another sigh escaped her as she entered the hall and approached her room. She leaned the painting against the wall so she could dig out her key. Then she reached for the door, only to see that it was already cracked open. She stared at the slightly open door and focused on the sign hanging from the doorknob that read Do Not Disturb in three languages.

A rush of images flashed in her mind, beginning with the absolute certainty that she had heard the door latch behind her when she had left her room a few hours earlier. Her heartbeat quickened as she considered why she had put the Do Not Disturb sign on her door. Her paintings. Had someone broken into her room? Surely her limited success couldn't have warranted someone wanting to steal her work.

Certain that there must be some rational explanation, Taylor took a deep breath, pushed the door open, and took three hurried steps inside. She could see two of her paintings across the room where she had left them to dry. The scent of paint and turpentine still lingered in the room, almost overpowering the newer, more subtle scent. Taylor started to take another step so that she could look past the bathroom into the bedroom area where several more of her paintings were drying, but a sudden thought stopped her. What if someone was still inside her room? Her heartbeat quickened, and she edged back toward the door. Her breathing became shallow even as she assured herself that her sudden fear was irrational.

Her hand was shaking when she backed into the hall and instinctively closed the door behind her. There must be a logical reason why the door was open. Quickly, she picked up the painting she had set down in the hall and moved back to the elevator, relieved when the doors instantly slid open.

Less than two minutes later, she approached the front desk. "I'm sorry to bother you, but I need hotel security to check out my room. I think there's someone inside."

The desk clerk, a light-haired man of about thirty, looked at her with disbelief and disdain rather than concern. "Why do you think that, miss?"

"My door was open when I got upstairs," Taylor explained, her words coming out rapidly. "Something's not right."

The man's eyebrows lifted. "Perhaps you left your door open."

"I didn't leave my door open." Taylor let out a frustrated sigh. Then her eyes narrowed. "Are you going to call security, or do I need to ask the manager to do it?"

The clerk let out a sigh of his own. "Fine. I'll call security."

"Thank you."

He picked up the phone and started speaking rapidly in French. Taylor didn't understand much of what he said, but she couldn't miss his condescending tone.

Taylor stood up a little straighter, her annoyance with the desk clerk beginning to help fight away her fears. Then she had the sudden realization that if something like this had happened to Quinn, he wouldn't have let it shake him up. He would have taken charge of the situation. Annoyed that she was thinking of him again, she tried to steady her nerves as two men from the security office approached.

After ascertaining that they spoke English, she explained the situation to them. "I'm sorry to bother you, but I really think someone was in my room. I would appreciate it if you could check it out for me."

"*Oui, mademoiselle,*" the taller of the two men said. His expression was unreadable as he escorted her to the elevator. No one spoke as they rode upstairs, and Taylor began to second-guess herself. Could the maid have ignored the sign on her door and gone inside to clean anyway? Was it possible that perhaps she hadn't closed the door all the way when she had left that morning?

Already preparing herself for the embarrassment that would surely follow when the security guards discovered that she had indeed overreacted, she set her painting down once more in the hall and handed her key to the shorter guard who had yet to utter a word to her.

She had expected them to draw their weapons or at least announce themselves when they entered her room, but they did neither. Instead, they simply walked inside, leaving her in the hall to wait for them. Seconds ticked by slowly. Then a minute stretched into two. Another minute passed, and finally Taylor edged closer to the door. She glanced inside to see one man examining the balcony door. The taller guard wasn't anywhere in sight, but Taylor guessed he was around the corner in the bedroom area.

Cautiously, she crossed the threshold and moved into the room. She noticed that one of her paintings on the far end of the room was tipped onto its side and wondered why the guard would have moved it. "Did you find anything?"

The taller guard stepped into her path before she could move all the way into the bedroom. "Mademoiselle, it might be best if you wait in the hall."

"Why?" Taylor asked. Instinctively, she leaned forward to look past him.

Then she saw it. And smelled it. A pool of dark red on the floor next to the bed, the splatter of blood on the wall.

* * *

Quinn shifted his weapon, his target clearly in sight. The man stood on the aft deck, his AK-47 lifted to ward off any invaders. Little did he know that Quinn and his teammates were already aboard. The timing had been flawless, all five men managing to climb aboard during the last confrontation with one of the nearby destroyers. The staged altercation had been the perfect distraction to give the SEALs the precious few minutes they needed to board the yacht undetected.

Quinn held his position on top of the pilot's cabin, waiting for his teammates to get into position. Brent and Tristan were even now moving toward the cabin where they believed the hostages were being held below deck. Seth and Jay had been tasked with finding the other men on board, presumably in the dining cabin. That left Quinn with eliminating anyone topside.

As much as he hated killing, Quinn silently wished that more of the pirates would reveal themselves on the open deck. From his position he was well hidden by the darkness, and his skill as a sniper would give him the advantage even if the odds weren't in his favor. He also knew that the fewer pirates there were with the hostages, the greater the likelihood that everyone would survive the encounter.

As though reading his thoughts, a second man emerged on deck and stepped beside the pirate standing guard. Quinn barely had time to mentally readjust to this second threat when the silence of the night was broken by a burst of gunfire as the other SEALs opened fire on the pirates below deck.

Quinn squeezed the trigger, and his first target dropped lifelessly to the deck. The second had time to turn and take a step forward before Quinn's second shot rang out and he too fell to the floor.

2

TAYLOR STOOD IN THE HALL outside of her hotel room, her body still trembling. Who had been in her room? Were her paintings okay? Whose blood had that been, and where was the injured person now? She reassured herself that maybe the maid had ignored the sign on the door and had somehow gotten injured on the job. Or maybe it had been a maintenance man.

She had tried to push her way back into her room to demand some answers, but the security guards refused to let her past the threshold. Instead, she could only wait helplessly as curiosity and worry combined into a jumble of nerves. Several minutes passed before an older man in a business suit stepped off the elevator and hurried toward her. There was a bead of sweat visible on his brow, and he looked as shaken as she felt.

"Mademoiselle, I am Norris Pelletier, the hotel manager."

Taylor accepted his outstretched hand automatically but didn't bother to respond.

"I am so sorry about your inconvenience," Norris told her nervously. "I want to assure you that nothing like this has ever happened here before. Please allow me to escort you to another room where you will be more comfortable." He motioned to the elevator. "The police will arrive any minute. I will bring them to you as soon as they have some information to share."

"Thank you," Taylor managed and followed him to the elevator. A few minutes later, he unlocked the door to her new room. He held the door open for her and then handed her the passkey.

Norris waited for Taylor to step over the threshold and then motioned to a cart positioned farther inside the room. "I had room service send up some food for you in case you are hungry. If you need anything, just call the front desk. Everything is complementary for the rest of your stay."

"Thank you," Taylor managed, even as she felt her legs go weak. "I think I just need to sit down for a bit."

"Of course, mademoiselle." Norris bowed slightly. "Please accept my apology once again."

He stepped into the hallway and pulled the door closed between them.

Taylor let out a jagged breath, flipped the lock, and moved farther into the room. She dropped into the closest chair, not taking the time to appreciate that her new room was actually a suite, complete with a plush living room and a stunning view of the Eiffel Tower.

Instead, she stared blankly at the wall, the image of blood stains vivid in her mind. Again she tried to make sense of the events of the afternoon and who could have possibly been in her room. A horrifying thought flashed into her mind, a new fear that perhaps the police would think that she had somehow been involved or had done something wrong.

Surely whoever had been injured would be found soon. He or she would go to the police. Taylor pressed a hand to her stomach as a wave of nausea washed over her. There had been so much blood, the smell so pungent.

Minutes passed as the same questions repeated over and over in Taylor's head. *Who? Why?*

Slowly, Taylor managed to convince herself that whatever had happened in her room couldn't have had anything to do with her. One of the security guards had asked her who knew where she was staying, but the answer was absolutely simple: no one. She didn't even know anyone in Paris except for the few art dealers and artists she had met at a showing several months earlier. In fact, it had been at that same show where she had been discovered by her agent, Felicia Davenport.

Taylor cringed inwardly as she thought of what Felicia would say when she found out about the incident. Despite all of Felicia's support and encouragement over the past few months, Taylor knew that she was a businesswoman first and foremost, and a rather intimidating one at that.

As much as Taylor wanted to get that phone call over with, she didn't think she could handle dealing with Felicia right now. Undoubtedly, her agent would want to know if Taylor's artwork had survived the intrusion. Taylor wanted answers to that particular question herself, but she was more concerned with what had taken place inside her room.

Her stomach ached with nerves and the now ever-present sense of invasion. She also couldn't shake the underlying fear that perhaps whoever had been in her room had intended to hurt her.

A knock came at the door, startling her out of her thoughts and causing a new wave of unease to rush over her. She took a steadying breath and cautiously looked through the peep hole.

Seeing the manager and a policeman on the other side, she disengaged the safety locks and pulled the door open. The policeman's face was unreadable, but the manager still looked shaken, even as he tried to present a professional air.

Norris's voice was apologetic. "May we come in?"

Taylor nodded and motioned them inside. Before she could ask for information, the police officer tapped his pen against the clipboard he held. "Can you tell me who knows that you are staying at this hotel?"

"No one knows where I'm staying."

The officer's eyebrows lifted. "No one?"

"No one," Taylor repeated. "My family and friends all have my cell phone number if they want to reach me, but all they know is that I came to Paris for a few weeks to paint."

"You came from the United States?"

Taylor shook her head. "I'm from the United States, but I've been living in Venice for more than a year."

Now the police officer's eyes narrowed. "And no one knew that you were staying here?"

"No." Taylor shook her head again.

Disbelief and a hint of sarcasm tainted the officer's voice. "You're telling me that you don't have any idea who could have broken into your room?"

Taylor stood rigid, her tone turning defensive. "That's exactly what I'm telling you. What did you find in my room?"

"All we are certain of is that the blood we found is human, but we have not found a body or any sign of anyone leaving the hotel who appeared to have been seriously injured."

"Maybe whoever was bleeding wasn't hurt that bad?" she asked hopefully.

The police officer's eyebrows rose skeptically. "With the amount of blood we found, I don't think that's possible."

Taylor tried to absorb his words, struggling to visualize the reality that the police officer had painted for her. "If whoever was hurt hasn't left, then I'm sure they'll turn up soon. Maybe whoever it was can tell us what really happened."

"Like I said, there was a *lot* of blood. If we find a body, I expect we'll be calling the coroner, not a doctor."

Taylor's eyes widened. "You think someone was *killed* in my room?"

He nodded.

"I don't understand how this happened," Taylor said more to herself than to the men standing across from her. Then she looked at the manager. "And why in my room?"

Norris only shrugged helplessly as a new layer of sweat beaded on his upper lip.

"We will continue to investigate. As soon as we know more, we'll let you know." The police officer asked her several more questions, including her contact information.

When the policeman finally pocketed his pen, Taylor asked, "Can you tell me when I can have my things back? I really want to make sure that all of my paintings are okay."

"We will be done with our photos and crime sketches shortly," the officer said.

The manager gave her a sympathetic look. "As soon as the police are finished, I will have someone bring your things to you."

A new sense of anxiety rushed through her. "Most of the paintings aren't completely dry yet."

"We'll make sure they're handled with care," the manager promised, his sincerity and concern evident in his expression. "I am very sorry for your inconvenience. Please let me know if there is anything I can do to make the rest of your stay comfortable."

Taylor nodded, but she already knew that she wanted little more than to leave Paris and return to her apartment in Italy where she felt safe.

* * *

"I am so glad to have that mission behind us," Tristan Crowther said as their plane touched down at the naval base in Italy.

Quinn nodded in agreement but didn't say anything. The mission had been successful. All of the hostages had survived, and all of the pirates had been neutralized. Quinn grimaced to himself as the word *neutralized* played in his mind again. He hated that in his profession "neutralized" normally equaled death. He had to remind himself that if he and his squad hadn't done their job, innocent civilians would have died instead of the men who had chosen piracy and death as their career.

He still couldn't believe that there hadn't been any civilian casualties. One of the crew members on the yacht had suffered a flesh wound when the shooting had started, but around the world the mission was being hailed as a complete success.

"You know, we're probably going to be in Italy for at least a couple of days for debriefings," Tristan continued.

"Probably," Quinn said casually. He stood up and grabbed his gear in the hopes of getting off the airplane before the conversation could continue. In front of him, Seth reached for his duffel bag, his enormous frame effectively blocking Quinn's path.

Behind him, Tristan continued. "You should give Taylor a call. I'm sure she'd love to see you." Tristan gave him a friendly pat on the back. "Better yet, you should take a day or two of leave while we're in Europe."

Quinn shot him an impatient look, his voice edged with annoyance. "Stop pushing. I already told you it's over with me and Taylor. We're looking for different things in our future."

Seth took a quick glance behind him and apparently sensed Quinn's tension. He sent Quinn a sympathetic look before turning to Jay. "Come on, Jay. Let me show you around the base."

The moment the rest of their squad exited the plane, Tristan dropped his duffel bag on the seat beside him and turned to face Quinn more fully. "What happened between you two at my wedding?"

"Nothing."

"Don't give me that. You've been crazy about that girl for more than a year, and then all of a sudden even the mention of her name gets a rise out of you."

"I just realized that our lives aren't heading in the same direction." Quinn shouldered his duffel and motioned to the front of the plane. "Are you going to move?"

Tristan didn't answer him for a moment, instead just standing there intently studying Quinn. "Let me guess. She's looking for a future with you, and you're too scared to give it to her."

Quinn's jaw clenched. Only years of friendship prevented Quinn's fists from following suit.

"What are you so afraid of?" Tristan asked, apparently aware that he'd found the source of the problem. "What is it that's holding you back?"

Quinn took a steadying breath. He felt his emotions threaten as he fought back the memories of his past. Slowly he shook his head and spoke, his voice low. "Don't ask me that when I know perfectly well that you know the answer."

Tristan hesitated briefly. Then he touched Quinn's arm and said simply, "It's time to let go of the past."

* * *

Taylor looked over her shoulder and hesitated slightly before rounding the corner toward her apartment. Since the moment she had left the hotel in Paris, a feeling of being followed had settled over her. It had started when she had ventured out the day before to pick up some packing supplies and had noticed a car that appeared to be following her taxi. Then she had noticed a middle-aged man staring at her right after she dropped her paintings off to be shipped to New York.

Her time at the Paris train station that morning had been unnerving, and even on the train, Taylor felt on edge, like someone was staring at her. The uneasy feeling was the reason that she had asked the cab driver to drop her off three blocks from her apartment instead of driving her the entire distance from the station.

She shifted her suitcase, suddenly grateful that she had asked for her latest order of art supplies to be shipped to her apartment instead of following through with her original plan to pick them up in France while she was there.

The hair raised on the back of her neck, and she glanced behind her again. It was just her imagination, she assured herself as she crossed the last few feet to her building. She was just being paranoid after the incident in her hotel room.

Ignoring the ache developing in her shoulders from carrying her luggage, she hurried up the stairs and dug her key out of her backpack. The moment she had the door unlocked, she stepped inside, dropped her luggage, and quickly closed and locked the door behind her. Leaning back against it, she let out a shaky sigh.

The ringing of her cell phone startled her, and she lifted a hand to her chest where she could feel her heart pounding. She reached into her pocket to retrieve her phone, checked the caller ID and saw that it was her sister, and took a steadying breath before hitting the talk button.

"Hi, Riley."

"Hey, sis. I hope I'm not interrupting anything, but I wanted to let you know that Mom and Dad are leaving for Brazil next week to pick up Landon."

Taylor smiled, finally relaxing enough to move farther into the room. "I can't believe it's already been two years. Our little brother is growing up."

Riley laughed. "He's been grown up for a while now."

She dropped her backpack on the couch and kicked off her shoes. She hoped her voice sounded casual when she asked, "How is everyone in Virginia?"

"Everyone's good. I think Mom and Dad are already packed, even though they aren't leaving until a week from Friday," Riley told her with humor in her voice. "I got an e-mail from Tristan tonight telling me that he and the guys will be heading back home in the next day or two."

"How long were they gone this time?" Taylor asked, her thoughts automatically shifting to Quinn.

"Not long. Only about a week." Riley hesitated for a moment and then asked, "Have you heard from Quinn at all?"

"Nope."

"I don't get it," Riley said, a touch of annoyance now lacing her voice. "At my wedding, everyone was so sure that you two would be the next ones getting married. I mean, you even caught my bouquet."

Taylor's memory was instantly crowded with scenes from that day: the good-natured teasing of Quinn's buddies asking when they were getting married, the way Quinn always seemed to be within arm's reach no matter where she was in the crowd, and even the stunned look on his face when Riley's bouquet had landed neatly in her arms. Obviously, she had read more into their relationship than he had.

She shook those memories away, hoping to downplay how mortified she was when she realized that Quinn hadn't really been as interested in her as she was in him. She hoped her voice was steady enough to respond. "Riley, I don't want to talk about it."

"I'm sorry," Riley said, instantly apologetic. "I've just been kicking myself for telling you I saw Quinn with someone else. I mean, he could have just been having dinner with an old friend or something."

"Riley, it's not like we ever said we weren't going to date other people. You're reading more into this than you should," Taylor told her. "Besides, it's not like I've spent the past few months trying to contact him, either."

"Honestly, I don't know what to think about you two. You would make the perfect couple."

"Riley, just let it go." Taylor let out a sigh, her eyes wandering to the building across the street. She noticed a man standing in the doorway, her eyes narrowing as she tried to figure out why he looked familiar.

Riley was silent for a moment. Then she responded, "I guess I'll talk to you later. Just make sure you call Mom and Dad this week. Otherwise you won't be talking to them for the next month."

"They're going to Brazil for a whole month?"

"That's what they said," Riley told her. "I'll talk to you later."

"Okay. Thanks for calling." Taylor hung up the phone and glanced out the window again. The man across the street was still there, his body angled as if he was watching for someone to come out of her building. Could he be looking for her? Did he look familiar because she had seen him on the train from Paris?

It's just my imagination, Taylor thought to herself. She edged away from the window and turned to look around her apartment. Then she sighed. Whether she was imagining things or not, she knew what she had to do.

3

QUINN LAMBERT STRODE ACROSS THE grass, a bouquet of flowers in his hand. He made his way through the lower section of the King Street Cemetery in Alexandria, reading each grave marker he passed even though he could have recited the names from memory. Oblivious to the light breeze ruffling his short dark hair, he stopped and knelt down beneath the clear blue sky.

It was a perfect September day, just like that day six years ago when Emily had lost her battle with cancer. Quinn stared down at the simple block letters on the bronze marker, his heart squeezing a bit as he remembered vividly the first time he stood here at the tender age of twenty-two. A temporary awning had been placed over the open grave to block the sun that filtered through the trees.

The number of people at the graveside service would have surprised Quinn if he had taken the time to notice. He vaguely remembered standing beside Emily's parents when the bishop had said a few words. His own parents and his sisters had also been close by, as had Tristan Crowther, the man he thought of as a brother.

Tristan had offered to come with him today just like he did every year on the anniversary of Emily's death. And like always, Quinn had chosen to come alone.

"I miss you, Em," Quinn said quietly, his voice nearly lost in the wind as he lowered the flowers to her grave. He felt that rush of warmth he always felt here, the same feeling that always made him want to give in to the urge to cry.

He blinked hard, fighting the sensation as he stood and took a step back. He let himself feel the crisp fall air, but his eyes stayed on the ground as his heart ached. Rarely did he let himself indulge in the thoughts of what might have been had Emily survived, but today those thoughts dominated his very being. At twenty-eight years old, he was simply too young to be standing over the grave of the woman he loved, just as she had been far too young to die.

His throat tightened, and he took a steadying breath. "I'll always love you," Quinn whispered. Then with one last look, he turned and walked back the way he had come.

* * *

Taylor rolled down the window of her new SUV, delighting in the wind whipping through her hair. She looked out at the water and, for the first time since leaving Paris, found herself looking forward to getting back to work.

Her agent had taken the news of the break-in much better than Taylor had expected, actually expressing some concern about Taylor's emotional state as well as her artwork. Of course, the fact that none of Taylor's paintings had been stolen or seriously damaged had certainly made the conversation less stressful than Taylor had originally imagined. One painting had been stained with blood, but Felicia had promised to have it cleaned and restored if needed. Felicia had also given Taylor that last little push of encouragement she needed to move out of her apartment in Venice and go somewhere new to work.

Taylor looked out at the water once more and hoped that her heart was ready for the changes she had decided to make.

* * *

"Are you sure you're okay?" Tristan asked for the fifth time since he had picked Quinn up from the airfield in Norfolk.

Quinn clenched his teeth together for a brief moment, long enough to make sure his emotions were indeed under control. "For the eighteenth time, I'm fine."

"Sorry, man, but I'm worried about you," Tristan said in his western drawl.

Quinn rolled his eyes, hoping to lighten the mood. "You say that every year."

"And every year it's true," Tristan told him. "I guess I don't understand why you're so adamant about keeping Emily a secret from the rest of the squad."

"I just don't want to talk about it, okay?" Quinn shook his head. "Besides, look at how many times you've asked me today if I'm okay. Do you really think I want to have the rest of the guys checking up on me too?"

"Eventually someone is going to notice that you take the same day off every year, especially since you hardly ever take leave."

Quinn didn't respond, letting them lapse into silence for several minutes.

When Tristan finally spoke, his voice held a quiet understanding. "One of these days you're going to have to move on. Emily wouldn't want you to sit around and mourn for her for the rest of your life."

"Just stop worrying about me, okay?" Quinn said with a hint of frustration.

"Whatever you say." Tristan shrugged. "Do you at least want to come over for dinner tonight? Riley was talking about making lasagna."

Quinn looked at him suspiciously. "Did you tell Riley where I was today?"

"No, but she's been asking about you a lot lately. I think she worries when you go for more than three days without showing up at our place looking for free food."

"Are you saying your wife wants me to impose on you all the time?"

Tristan flashed him a grin. "No, I'm saying that I think she wants our help with something."

Quinn smiled automatically. He and Tristan had met Riley more than a year earlier when their squad had worked with her on developing a course for law enforcement officers. Since then, Riley had ventured out on her own and opened her own company. "Is she planning a new course, or does she just want our feedback?"

"She hasn't told me yet." Tristan's eyes sparked with mischief. "But if she's making lasagna, we should probably be worried."

Quinn nodded in agreement. "What time is dinner?"

"Come by whenever you're ready for some company," Tristan told him as he pulled up in front of Quinn's apartment complex. "We'll probably eat around six."

"Sounds good." Quinn opened the door and climbed out of Tristan's truck. "Thanks for the ride."

Tristan simply nodded.

Quinn slammed the door shut and watched Tristan drive away before heading into his apartment. The furniture was sparse. The couch and single chair were well worn, and the dining area was empty. Rather than a table to eat at, there was a single stool next to the kitchen counter. He glanced over at the lone bookcase next to the television set, his eyes landing on the photo albums on the bottom shelf. Normally he would have indulged himself and taken the time to stare at those images of the past, of the life that still had Emily in it.

Knowing that his emotions would likely hold him captive for hours once he opened those albums, he forced himself to continue moving through the small living room into his bedroom. He changed his clothes, kicked on some sandals, and headed back out the door in search of some fresh air and a chance to clear his head.

As he walked the few blocks to the beach, he let his mind wander back to when he had met Emily. After coming home from a mission in Caracas, Venezuela, for The Church of Jesus Christ of Latter-day Saints, he had found himself at a crossroads. With his dad's help, he had gotten a summer job at the Defense Intelligence Agency to help save money for college. Of course, he wasn't really sure he wanted to continue with school, but he was willing to explore his options at the local community college.

Then Emily had come into his life, and nothing had mattered as long as he was with her. His mother had introduced them at their home one morning when Emily had come over to help his mom prepare food for the ward's Fourth of July picnic. Quinn had noticed her fragile beauty immediately, but what had drawn him in was her warmth and sweetness. She found humor in everyday things, but she also had a way of seeing the good in people, both individually and as a whole.

Within weeks, they had become inseparable and couldn't imagine being with anyone else. Quinn's future had hinged itself to Emily's plans. She had finished her freshman year at George Mason University, the same school Tristan was attending. Although he still didn't know what career he wanted to pursue, Quinn had enrolled in junior college and had started making plans to transfer to GMU the following year, hoping that eventually he and Emily would graduate together.

Then she had gotten sick. Non-Hodgkin's lymphoma. Suddenly school and future plans didn't hold any importance. Everything was about living in the moment and finding a way to help Emily beat the disease. But she didn't beat it. Less than a year after the doctors had given them the news, Emily's body lost the battle. And Quinn had been struggling ever since.

Quinn made his way down to the water's edge and stared out at the Atlantic. Boats skimmed along the water in the distance. Seagulls swooped down crazily in search of their evening meals. A wave splashed up over his feet, dragging sand into his sandals and between his toes.

Tristan's words ran through his mind, and he tried to take them the way they were intended. He knew Tristan meant well when he said that Quinn needed to move on, but Quinn knew that even if he wanted to, he simply didn't know how. It wasn't that he hadn't dated over the years. In fact, he had dated a lot, enough that the other SEALs he served with never would have guessed that he was still nursing a broken heart. Unfortunately, he was rarely tempted to take a relationship beyond a few casual dates.

The only time he'd really considered pursuing a more serious relationship had been when he'd dated Taylor Palmetta, Tristan's sister-in-law. Of course, Tristan hadn't been related to her at the time. Quinn had met Taylor when Tristan had started dating Riley. In so many ways, Taylor was the complete opposite of Emily. Em had been so fragile physically and often soft-spoken when she was in a big group. Taylor was vibrant and strong, and she was one of those people who was drawn to crowds. Or perhaps it was more accurate to say that crowds were drawn to her.

For nearly three months Quinn dated Taylor, enjoying the way she made everything seem lighter. She was fun to be around, and the cloud that had been hanging over him since Emily's death had started to lift for longer than just a few days. They had kept everything casual after Taylor had left for Europe, calling and e-mailing on occasion to keep in touch. Then he ended up in Europe and had thrown caution to the wind. A few days leave, an incredible weekend with Taylor, and suddenly he found himself more interested in reading e-mails from Taylor than asking someone else out on a date.

Then Tristan and Riley had gotten married, and everything changed. He had tried to ignore all of the expectations that he and Taylor were destined to end up at the altar together. Then she had caught the bouquet, and he had panicked. He saw her holding those flowers, saw the speculation on everyone's faces and the delight on hers. And he knew he wasn't ready to move forward in his relationship with Taylor. In fact, he had seen that moment as a sign that he needed to take a significant step back.

She was looking for marriage. Quinn wasn't ready to make that commitment at this point in his life. With a shake of his head, Quinn tried to push aside the images of Taylor and Emily.

He stepped out of the frigid surf and started down the beach. Maybe a few hours with Tristan and Riley would help him forget about life for a while and the fact that he had finished living his future so many years ago.

4

Tristan pulled the door open, an odd expression on his face. "Hey, Quinn. Glad you made it."

"Did you figure out what Riley is up to yet?" Quinn asked, his voice low.

"Not yet." Tristan stepped aside to let him in. His tone was a little apologetic when he added, "I hope you don't mind that we added one more to the party."

"Don't tell me Jay is pulling the poor bachelor routine again," Quinn said, referring to the only other unmarried member of their squad. Then his eyes landed on Taylor as she swiveled around on her stool. Surprise and a touch of embarrassment lit her dark brown eyes.

Quinn felt an unexpected lurch in his stomach and was suddenly unsure of himself. Then his jaw clenched, annoyance with Tristan bubbling up inside him. It was one thing to spend some time with Tristan and his wife on the anniversary of Emily's death, but he definitely wasn't prepared to be around another woman, especially Taylor. He also wasn't prepared to deal with Taylor's expectations or why he had been unable to live up to them.

Her posture tense, Taylor pushed her red hair back from her face in a habitual gesture. The medium-length curls looked windblown, as though she too had just come in from the beach. Her eyes were unreadable as she stood up and faced him. "Hi, Quinn."

"Taylor," Quinn managed to say. "I didn't know you were in town."

"Neither did we," Tristan flashed him an apologetic look. "She only got into town a few minutes ago."

Quinn's eyebrows rose. "You didn't tell anyone you were coming?"

Taylor shook her head.

"How long are you staying?"

Taylor took a deep breath and stared at him for a long minute. "I'm moving here."

Quinn took a steadying breath himself, not sure how he felt about this new development. Then he surprised himself by saying, "I'm glad you'll be close by again. We all missed you while you were gone."

A timid smile lit her face, and some of the tension between them eased.

Before she could respond, Tristan told Quinn, "She'll be staying with us for a few days until she can find her own apartment."

Riley entered the adjoining dining room and set a salad bowl on the table. "Is everyone ready to eat?"

"I'm always ready," Tristan said.

Quinn followed him to the table and took his seat beside Taylor. He glanced at her and wondered what Emily would think if she could see him now. Then he had the odd realization that if Emily and Taylor had been given the opportunity, they would not only have liked each other but they would also have been friends.

His thoughts were interrupted when Tristan blessed the food. Then Riley served the lasagna and waited for the salad to be passed around before revealing her real reason for making them dinner. "Do you guys remember the dorm scenario we did at Oswell Barron University last summer?"

"Yeah," Tristan and Quinn both answered simultaneously, and Quinn couldn't stop the grin that crossed his face.

Taylor's eyebrows lifted. "I'm sensing an inside joke here."

Tristan nodded. "One of the mock scenarios we set up when we did the training course last year was in the dorms at your old college. We went in dressed like something out of a war zone and shot blanks at the participants while they were in their rooms sleeping."

"They must have loved that," Taylor laughed.

"Believe me, I heard about it every time," Riley told her. "It's like each class would elect someone to come yell at me about how unfair it was that they had been caught unprepared."

"And I'm sure you yelled right back at them about the rights of victims."

"In my own way," Riley nodded. "Anyway, I just received a proposal from the police department in Charlotte, North Carolina. The chief down there was one of our participants last year, and he wants us to conduct a course for his department. He specifically asked if there was any way we could add something like the dorm scenario into the training."

"Which is something you would need us for," Tristan finished for her.

Riley nodded. "Running fake hostage scenarios is one thing, but this is definitely out of my league."

"Even if we do agree to help, there's no guarantee that we'll be here when you're running your class," Quinn commented, knowing all too well that as Navy SEALs, he and Tristan could be called on a mission at any time.

"I can find people to play the fake terrorists if I have to. What I really need help on is how to set up security to make sure everyone is unarmed. Cops have a tendency of wanting to keep their weapons with them," Riley told them. Then she gave them a sheepish grin. "And I also need to figure out how to pull this off in a hotel without having someone call the cops on us."

"You expect an awful lot for some lasagna," Tristan said, even as he took another bite.

Riley's eyebrows lifted, and her eyes sparked with challenge. "Did I mention that I made cheesecake for dessert?"

Taylor laughed now. "Boy, did I pick the right day to show up at your house."

"You sure did," Tristan agreed, his gaze flicking over to land on Quinn for a brief moment. Then he shifted his attention to his wife and reached for Riley's hand. "Have I told you lately how much I love you?"

"It's been at least fifteen minutes," Riley teased and then leaned over to kiss him.

Watching them together, Quinn was reminded abruptly of what day it was. He listened to the friendly banter for a moment, but he knew that he needed to get away from the happily-ever-after life his best friend was living, the kind of life he was mourning for today. Logically, he understood that life had to go on even though Emily's had ended, but at moments like these when everything was so simple, so normal, Quinn found himself floundering.

"Just let me know what you need me to do," Quinn managed to finally say to Riley. Then he pushed away from the table. "Thanks for dinner, but I need to get going."

"Didn't you want to have some dessert?" Riley asked, surprised. "If you want, I can send some home with you."

"I guess that would work," Quinn agreed, even though he didn't particularly care about anything at that moment but finding some time to himself.

"Save me a slice," Taylor told Riley, also standing up. "I need to go unload my car before it gets too dark."

"Did you need some help?" Tristan asked before Quinn thought to.

"Yeah, if you don't mind." Taylor nodded.

As much as he needed to escape, Quinn found himself volunteering to help. "I'll give you a hand too."

"Thanks," Taylor said, following Quinn to the door. "There isn't much, but the paintings are awkward to carry."

Tristan called out to them, "I'll meet you guys downstairs. I need to find the visitor parking pass for Taylor so she can move her car into the garage."

Resigned to spending a few more minutes with Taylor, Quinn nodded and escorted her through the door and out to the elevator. "Where are you parked?"

"At the seafood restaurant across the street." Taylor stepped into the elevator and then looked over at him. She was silent for a moment. Then she asked quietly, "Are you okay?"

"Yeah, I'm fine," Quinn said a little too quickly.

Taylor gave him an odd look, but then she let the conversation drop as they reached the lobby. They stepped outside, their senses immediately assaulted by the sound of a car alarm. Quinn's attention focused on the blue SUV across the street with its temporary tags. He noticed someone behind the vehicle, but then an older man came out of the restaurant and yelled something, and the man ran off.

"Oh no. Not again," Taylor mumbled as though talking to herself as she pulled her keys free from her purse and ran for the street.

"What's wrong?" Quinn asked, running to catch up with her.

"That's my car."

5

TAYLOR PAUSED ON THE CURB long enough to check for traffic and then darted across the pavement and hit the button on her remote to disengage the alarm. Her heart was in her throat as she considered whether her artwork was okay. Of all of the paintings she had created over the years, only four had meant so much to her that she hadn't been willing to let her agent show them. All four of them were currently in protective cases in the back of her SUV. At least she hoped they still were.

"Is this your car, miss?" a man asked as Taylor approached.

"Yeah." Taylor nodded as she reached the back of the vehicle to find the back door hanging open, the lock clearly damaged. "Did you see who did this?"

The man gave her an apologetic look. "I didn't get a very good look at him. He ran off as soon as I came outside."

Quinn stepped beside her, his voice both calm and authoritative. "Taylor, take a look and see if anything's missing. I'll call the police."

Taylor nodded and elbowed the rear door open wider. Her luggage appeared to be untouched, and three of her paintings were still in their shipping containers. The fourth one had been opened and the top layer of bubble wrap peeled away. Taylor reached for it, pulling the next layer off. She let out a sigh of relief when she saw that the painting was still intact.

She stared at the blues and greens and browns that filled the canvas, remembering all too well the days she had spent near Palermo staring out at the Mediterranean. The beach scene could have been a snapshot, and she couldn't say why she had grown so attached to it. A couple of families had been picnicking in the sand, a sailboat a short distance from the shore. In the distance were a few other vessels making their way to and from various ports in the Med.

Taylor heard footsteps behind her and shifted to see Quinn approaching. He glanced at her and started to say something but was immediately distracted by the painting in front of her.

"Wow, Taylor. That's incredible. Did you paint that?" Quinn looked at her artwork, and she felt his sense of wonder.

"Yeah. I spent a week in Palermo about a month ago." Taylor nodded, his praise invoking an odd sense of satisfaction that nearly overshadowed the fact that her car had been broken into.

He stared at the painting a moment longer. "Your time in Italy sure paid off." He looked at her and seemed to remember why he was there. "The police should be here any minute. Is anything missing?"

"It doesn't look like it." Taylor shook her head. "This painting was opened, but it doesn't look like anything else was touched."

An odd expression crossed his face, and he took a closer look at the unwrapped piece of art. "Why would someone break into your car and open up a painting? If he was interested in the artwork, you'd think he would have just taken it and looked at it later."

"I don't know." Taylor shrugged. "Honestly, I can't believe anyone would break into my car in the first place, especially on such a busy road at this time of day. I mean, it isn't even that dark yet."

Quinn gave her a speculative look. "Who all knows that you're in town?"

"Just you, Riley, and Tristan."

Quinn squatted down beside the vehicle and looked underneath it.

"What are you doing?"

"I just want to see if there are any other signs of tampering." Quinn moved to the driver's side and checked beneath the car again. He continued the process until he had circled the car and then returned to the back of the vehicle where he had started. "Have you touched anything?"

"I pulled the rest of the bubble wrap off of that painting, but I don't think I touched anything else." Taylor's eyes narrowed. "Why?"

"We need to have the police dust for fingerprints."

Taylor's sense of violation multiplied. "No one's putting any dust or chemicals on my paintings."

"Don't worry. I'll make sure nothing happens to them," Quinn told her as a police car pulled into the parking lot, its lights flashing. He fished out his cell phone and handed it to her. "Do me a favor and call Tristan; tell him to drive over here with his truck."

A police officer approached them. "What seems to be the problem?"

"Someone broke into my car," Taylor told him.

"Taylor, go call Tristan." Quinn put a hand on her back and nudged her toward the restaurant. "I can talk to the police."

A little surprised at the way Quinn dismissed her, she stared at him for a moment before taking a few steps and opening up his phone. She quickly found Tristan's cell number in the list of his recently called numbers and hit the talk button. After giving Tristan a brief explanation of what had happened, she hung up and walked over to where Quinn was standing with the policeman.

She listened to them debate for a moment about whether it was really necessary to dust for fingerprints. Then her focus shifted, and she felt it again—that sensation of being watched. Taylor looked around the parking lot and at the street in front of her. Then she glanced back at the restaurant entrance where a couple of people had gathered and were talking among themselves. No one seemed to be paying any particular attention to her, but she couldn't shake the feeling that someone was watching her.

Then she saw Tristan pull up in his truck with her sister by his side. They both climbed out, and Riley rushed over to her.

"Taylor! What happened?"

"All I know is that someone broke the back door of my car." Taylor shook her head, trying to fight back the sudden reality that her brand new car was already damaged. "I can't believe this. I just bought it yesterday."

"Don't worry. We'll get it fixed up as good as new," Riley assured her.

Tristan gave her shoulder a comforting squeeze as he passed by her and joined Quinn and the policeman.

"What did the police say?" Riley asked.

"I don't know. Quinn's been talking to him," Taylor told her. "Come on. Let's find out what's going on."

Taylor and Riley joined the three men behind her vehicle.

"Well?" Taylor asked, letting the question linger in the air.

Quinn spoke first. "We're going to load your paintings into Tristan's truck so we can get them into the condo. Then after the police dust for prints, we'll bring the rest of your stuff over."

"What about the car? Will the back door even close?"

"I doubt it," the policeman said. "You'll want to get it into the dealership tomorrow and have the service department take a look at it."

"I can't believe someone broke into my car." Taylor shook her head.

Quinn and the policeman exchanged looks. Then the policeman said, "Hopefully we'll be able to lift some fingerprints and figure out who did this."

Taylor nodded. "I hope so."

"Come on." Tristan picked up the opened painting. "Let's get these someplace safe."

Taylor let out a sigh and took the painting from him. She stared at the colors once more and found herself with more questions than ever.

* * *

"What are you thinking?" Tristan asked Quinn the moment Taylor and Riley drove away in his truck. Another policeman had arrived and was now dusting the vehicle for fingerprints.

"I don't know, but something doesn't feel right about this."

Tristan looked at the damaged back door. "I know what you mean. Why would someone break into the back of the car? If they were trying to steal it, they would have gone for the driver's side door."

"And why was someone snooping through her paintings? I mean, the one I saw was great, but it's not like she's famous or anything."

"It was probably just some kid looking for something he could turn into some quick cash."

"You're probably right." Quinn nodded, but the uneasiness in his stomach didn't lessen.

6

IT WAS NEARLY MIDNIGHT WHEN the events of the evening came back to him with sudden clarity. Taylor had said two words that hadn't made sense, and now they were eating at Quinn uncomfortably. He still had her number but didn't consider why as he punched it into his cell phone.

He also didn't consider the time. Taylor's phone rang five times before rolling over into her voice mail. Quinn hung up, not quite sure what he wanted to say.

Restless, he walked into the kitchen and opened the fridge. He stared aimlessly for a moment at the lack of food there and then closed it again. Pulling his phone from his pocket again, he pressed redial. Again, it went to voice mail.

Resigned that Taylor was probably sleeping, he sent her a text message asking her to call him. Then he moved into the living room and stared at the bookshelf.

He closed his eyes for a moment, letting his mind transport him back in time. Emily would have been right there talking to him late at night. He could almost pretend she had fallen asleep on the couch again watching television, the scent of her favorite perfume still lingering in the air.

Quinn forced his eyes open and leaned down to retrieve the photo album that contained those memories. He set it on the coffee table and sat down, flipping it open at random. A smile crossed his face when he looked down at a photo his mom had taken of him and Tristan arm wrestling. Emily was laughing in the background.

He flipped through page after page, letting the memories keep him company until he came to his favorite photo. It had been taken in her parents' backyard on Easter morning. Emily's last Easter. He could remember the way he had picked her up, the way she had weighed little more than a child. He had carried her out under the clear blue sky, insisting that she needed some fresh air. He had sat down on the bench in front of a flowering dogwood tree, holding her on his lap. Then she had looked up at him with such joy in her eyes. Someone had snapped a picture in that instant, that single moment that had been a fleeting escape from reality.

"Emily, I don't know if I can do this again," Quinn muttered to himself. He thought of Taylor, of the way his protective streak had kicked into overdrive when he saw her racing for her car. He was also a bit unsettled that Taylor hadn't demanded any kind of an explanation from him about why he had never called or e-mailed her back after Tristan and Riley's wedding.

He stared down at the picture of Emily a moment longer. Then, slowly, he closed the album and put it away. With a last glance at the bookshelf, he walked out of the room.

* * *

Taylor kicked off her sandals and stepped onto the cold sand. With her shoes in her hand, she crossed the beach until she reached the edge of the surf. As she watched the sun breaking out over the water, she tucked her free hand into the front pocket of her hooded sweatshirt and let herself enjoy the moment, the familiar smells and sounds of a quiet beach.

She still wasn't sure what to think about Quinn's reaction to her arrival the night before. After the initial awkwardness between them, he had acted like everything was still normal between them. As much as she wanted to ask why he had broken off contact and if he was still dating someone else, part of her wanted to pretend that the last few months had never happened.

The feeling of being watched was yet another reason she wanted to erase her recent memory. The two weeks she had spent in New York had been necessary to make sure that her career was progressing the way she wanted, but unfortunately, she had continued to feel like someone was watching her while she was in the city. She supposed it was that sensation of being followed that had prompted her to buy a car in New York instead of waiting until she arrived in Virginia.

The night before, Riley had helped her unpack her paintings so she could make sure they were all unharmed, but it had taken nearly two hours for the police to release her vehicle. Quinn and Tristan had been great, transporting everything from her car up to Tristan and Riley's guest room. By the time Taylor had headed to bed, it had been after midnight, but then she found herself unable to sleep as the events of the past few weeks kept replaying in her mind. Even if her recent stress hadn't been weighing on her, seeing Quinn so unexpectedly would definitely have kept her up anyway.

He had looked as stunned as she felt when he walked into Riley and Tristan's apartment the night before, and Taylor still wasn't quite sure what to think about their relationship. Had he grown tired of dating her and that was why he had broken off contact? Or had he just been unwilling to continue such a long-distance relationship? Either way, they were both living in Virginia Beach now, and Taylor had no idea what to expect.

She definitely hadn't anticipated seeing Quinn within minutes of arriving at home, but looking back now, she knew she had been lucky that Tristan and Quinn had been home rather than out on some assignment. She was sure she could have handled dealing with the police, but she had felt so much safer last night knowing that Tristan and his small arsenal of weapons were in the next room. If only that feeling of security had translated into a decent night's sleep.

The water washed up over her feet, the icy cold wetness taking her breath away as Taylor took a step back on the sand. She sensed someone approaching and turned to see Tristan heading toward her.

Tristan started to say something and then seemed to think better of it. Instead, he said simply, "You're up early."

"I still have a bit of jet lag," Taylor told him, relieved that he hadn't mentioned Quinn. She noticed that he was dressed in jeans and a sweatshirt rather than his uniform. "So what are your plans for today, other than picking me up from the dealership at noon?"

Tristan grinned. "The usual."

Her lips curved into a smile. "I know better than that. Navy SEALs don't even know what the word *usual* means."

"I think our morning plans come close, though," Tristan told her. "It isn't until this afternoon that we're planning on jumping out of moving vehicles."

"I won't even ask what kind of vehicles," Taylor laughed. "You guys give a new meaning to trains, planes, and automobiles."

"We tend to avoid trains." He winked at her. "Too boring."

"I'm sure."

They fell into a comfortable silence for a moment as the waves crashed in front of them and seagulls called out as they searched for their morning meal.

Taylor glanced back at the building behind them, realizing that watching her surroundings was becoming a habit. "Have you ever felt like someone was watching you, but when you look no one's there?"

Tristan nodded. "Once or twice."

"How do you make that feeling go away?"

"With or without a gun?"

Taylor laughed. "Okay. Maybe I'm asking the wrong person."

Tristan looked down at her, his expression becoming serious. "Do you feel like someone's watching you?"

Taylor hesitated a moment, wondering what Tristan would think of her newfound paranoia. "Not right now." Taylor shook her head. "I'm sure it's nothing."

"Maybe, but after what happened yesterday, if you keep feeling like that, let me know. People's instincts about that kind of thing are right more often than not."

Taylor nodded, not knowing whether she should feel comforted or alarmed by the thought.

"I have to go get ready for work. I'll give you a call as soon as I can get away for lunch so we can go drop off your car," Tristan told her. "Your cell phone number is still the same, isn't it?"

"Yeah. My phone's in my room, but I'll go get it in a little while."

"Okay. I'll see you later."

Taylor took another step back as the surf continued to rise. Not five minutes after Tristan went inside, she heard someone call her name.

"Don't you ever answer your phone?" Quinn asked irritably as he closed the distance between them.

Taylor looked at him, confused. "How did you know I was down here?"

"When you didn't call me back, I called Tristan looking for you."

"Sorry, my phone is upstairs charging. The battery died yesterday afternoon." She looked at him with curiosity and wondered briefly why she had felt compelled to explain herself. "Why were you looking for me?"

"Something you said last night has been bugging me."

Taylor's eyebrows drew together. "What?"

"When you realized it was your car alarm going off, you said, 'Not again.' What did you mean by that?"

She crossed her arms. "It's nothing."

"Don't give me that," Quinn pressed. "What else happened? Has your car been broken into before?"

"No, nothing like that." Taylor shook her head. "It's probably just a string of bad luck."

Quinn's eyes darkened. "Define 'bad luck.'"

Realizing that Quinn wasn't going to let it go, Taylor sighed. "A few weeks ago in Paris, I came back to my hotel room and the door was open. Someone had been inside."

"What happened?"

"We're still not sure. No one was there when security checked it out, but there was a lot of blood on the floor."

"Blood? Whose blood?"

"I don't know."

Quinn's eyes narrowed. "You really don't know who was there?"

Taylor shook her head. "No one can explain it. I'm sure it was totally random that my room was the one that was broken into."

Quinn studied her for a minute. "What aren't you telling me?"

Taylor shrugged her shoulders and forced herself to say the words. "I was scared, Quinn." She blew out a breath. "When I started to walk into my room, I was suddenly terrified that something bad would happen if I didn't leave right then."

"You think someone was in your room when you got there?"

"Maybe." Taylor's shoulders lifted. "I sure didn't wait around to find out." She shook her head as she let herself remember those first few moments when she entered her hotel room. "I'm still not sure what caused me to go get security instead of checking out my room for myself."

"Maybe your heard something. Or smelled something," Quinn suggested.

Taylor looked at him with new understanding. "I think there was a different smell. Like a really faint scent of a man's aftershave." Taylor looked at him now and shook her head. "Why didn't I realize that before?"

Quinn shrugged a shoulder and pushed on. "So your hotel room in Paris turned into a crime scene, and now your car has been broken into here in Virginia. Anything else you're leaving out?"

"Just that I keep getting the feeling that someone's watching me."

"Like when?"

"I don't know. Lots of times." She blew out another breath. "Like when I got off the plane in New York two weeks ago. On a train to Marseille. Outside my apartment in Venice. Even yesterday when we were waiting for the police to arrive."

"Taylor, what did you do in Europe besides paint?" Quinn asked, his voice holding a combination of sarcasm, curiosity, and concern.

"Nothing!" Taylor ran her fingers through her hair and then forced herself to look at him. "Quinn, I don't know what's going on. I mean, maybe all of this is just one huge string of coincidences. What would anyone want with me?"

"I don't know," Quinn said. He stared at her for a moment and then asked, "Have you told Riley and Tristan about what happened?"

She shook her head. "I didn't want to worry them."

"They need to know," Quinn said with understanding. "And I don't think you should be here alone today."

"I'm sure I'll be fine," Taylor said, not sure whether to be comforted or annoyed by his concern. "Besides, I'm probably going to spend most of my day at the dealership trying to figure out what to do about my car," she told him. "I'm going to head over there when Riley leaves for work."

"How are you getting back home?"

"Tristan is going to pick me up at lunch."

Quinn nodded his approval. "I need to head over to the base in a few minutes. Did you want me to walk you back up to the condo?"

Taylor managed a smile, but she shook her head. "I'm sure I can make it on my own."

"I'll wait here and make sure you get inside okay."

"Thanks, Quinn," Taylor said. She hesitated, wanting to ask him what happened between them, why he had turned away from what they had together. The look of pained expectation on his face made her reconsider. Instead, she reached for his hand and gave it a squeeze. "And thanks for listening."

"No problem."

7

QUINN THREW HIS GEAR INTO the back of the truck, his mind still mulling over the events of the past twenty-four hours. Yesterday at this time he was kneeling over Emily's grave, and now he was obsessing about whether or not someone was after Taylor.

Seth Johnson stowed his gear beside Quinn's and spoke in his Southern drawl. "What's eating at you?"

"Nothing." Quinn shook his head.

Seth didn't respond except to stare at him. Seth's dark skin glistened with sweat from the day's workout, and he stood a full seven inches taller than Quinn's six feet. Rarely did Seth press anyone for personal information, but when he wanted it, he obviously knew that his stare could make just about anyone talk. Quinn assured himself that Seth's tactics weren't going to work on him.

"What?" Quinn demanded. "Don't pull that look with me. I'm not some informant you need to break in order to save the world."

"No, but something's definitely eating at you," Seth persisted. "Did something happen when you were on leave?"

"Not really." Quinn shook his head. He glanced up at Seth's dark eyes and let out a short laugh. Apparently, Seth's stare had worked on him after all. "Taylor got back into town yesterday."

"Really?" Seth looked at him speculatively. "And how did that reunion go?"

"Her car was broken into."

"That's a lousy welcome-home present."

"I know. Tristan and I spent our evening waiting for the police to dust for fingerprints."

"I'm surprised they even bothered," Seth told him. "Usually they don't break out the dusting kit unless they're dealing with a major crime."

"I kind of strong-armed them on that one."

Seth's eyes narrowed. "Why?"

"The guy broke into the back door of her SUV, so we know he wasn't just looking to steal the car."

"Right." Seth nodded in agreement.

"And then he didn't take anything. He just unwrapped one of Taylor's paintings."

Seth cocked his head to one side and seemed to mull over the oddity of the situation. "What was the painting of?"

"It was some kind of beach scene," Quinn told him impatiently. "What does it matter?"

"I don't know. But maybe it matters to whoever broke into her car."

Quinn shook his head. "This is Taylor we're talking about. I mean, I could see something weird like this happening to Vanessa," Quinn continued, referring to Seth's wife. "She's CIA so she's used to weird things happening. But Taylor's just an artist. And a relatively unknown one at that. Who would even know to look for her paintings, much less know where she was yesterday?"

"Sounds like we may have a new mystery on our hands."

"I'm starting to think so."

* * *

"It's a mystery," Officer Harbison told Taylor and Riley that evening when he stopped by the condo to give them an update. "Nothing was stolen, and no one is sure what this guy was after. There weren't any fingerprints other than yours, so we know that whoever did the damage to your car was wearing gloves. The bottom line is that this is nothing more than an unfortunate case of vandalism."

"A very unorthodox case of vandalism," Riley amended.

"I'll agree with you there, but I'm afraid there isn't much more we can do," Officer Harbison told them. "No one saw the perpetrator clearly enough to identify him. We only know that a man with dark hair ran away from your vehicle after the restaurant owner yelled at him."

Taylor suppressed a sigh. "Well, thanks for all of your help."

"Sorry we couldn't do more," he said, holding out a manila envelope to Taylor. "Here's a copy of our report. You'll probably need this for your insurance company."

"Thanks." Taylor took it from him and then walked him to the door. After he left she turned to face Riley. "What a day."

"How long did the dealership say it would take to fix your car?"

"At least a week. Maybe two." Taylor moved to the couch and flopped down on it. "The worst part is that the insurance company won't pay for a loaner car."

"I wish I could lend you mine, but I'm going to be out on location a lot this week for work." Riley sat down in the chair across from her. "I know. Why don't we go borrow Mom's car? They won't be back from Brazil until after your car is fixed. I'm sure she wouldn't mind."

"That's a good idea." Taylor nodded, cheered by the thought. "You know, I'm sure they wouldn't mind me crashing at their place too. That way you and Tristan can have your privacy back."

"Don't be silly." Riley shook her head. "I've hardly seen you for the past year. It's great having you here. Besides, after what happened yesterday, we'll feel a lot better having you stay here with us."

"Are you sure?"

Riley nodded. "I think Tristan should be home in a little while. Why don't we go pick up the car now, and then we can order some Chinese food for dinner."

"Sounds good." Taylor shifted to stand up just as the front door opened.

The scent of cashew chicken and lo mein drifted into the room as Tristan walked in followed by Quinn.

"Hi, honey. I'm home." Tristan crossed to where Riley was sitting and greeted her with a lingering kiss. "And I brought company."

Quinn set the paper bag he was carrying down on the kitchen table. "And the company brought food."

Riley laughed. "We were just talking about ordering out. You guys read our minds."

Quinn gave her a wry smile. "We decided it was my turn to cook."

"If you insist." Riley reached a hand out to Tristan and let him pull her up. "Let's eat."

Taylor crossed to the kitchen as Quinn unpacked the food and then, clearly at home in their kitchen, went to one of the cabinets to retrieve some plates. Within minutes, they were all sitting at the table, sharing Chinese food and laughing about the practical joke Tristan had pulled on Seth during their most recent training mission. They talked about their respective days, lingering for several minutes on Taylor's misfortune the day before. Quinn also prodded her into telling Riley and Tristan about the incident in Paris.

Other than the discussion about her recent dealings with the police, though, it felt like old times. Taylor could almost pretend that Tristan and Riley were still dating and that Quinn was there because he wanted to spend time with her as much as he wanted to enjoy Tristan and Riley's company.

Beside her, Quinn pushed back from the table and picked up his plate. "Thanks for letting me invite myself over again."

"Anytime." Riley grinned at him. "Especially when you decide to feed us."

Taylor lifted her plate from the table and started to stand as well, but Quinn laid a hand on her shoulder. "I can take that."

Taylor glanced up at him, warmth spreading through her at the simple touch. She fought back her frustration that he could still effect her like that and tried to remind herself that any interest Quinn had in her was only casual. She managed to smile up at him and let him take her plate from her. "Thanks."

Tristan took his cue from Quinn and stood to help clear the rest of the dishes. He set his and Riley's plates in the sink and then came back to start clearing away the leftovers. He winked at Riley. "Since Quinn brought dinner, does that mean it's our turn to take care of dessert?"

"I would say that we could have some leftover cheesecake." Riley looked pointedly at Tristan.

He gave her a sheepish grin. "Yeah, well, the guys said to thank you for that."

"What guys?" Taylor looked from Riley to Tristan. "What did happen to the cheesecake? I was looking for that earlier."

Riley shifted her attention to Taylor. "My darling husband decided he wanted some for breakfast and then had the brilliant idea that the other guys in the squad would probably like some too."

"For breakfast?" Taylor asked, shifting her attention to Quinn who now represented "the guys" in her mind.

Quinn nodded. "Energy food."

"You know, it's all coming back to me," Taylor said. "When we were all living in North Carolina, you and your buddies had a tendency to show up at our apartment a lot around mealtimes."

"You can't exactly make it into the SEAL teams without having some intelligence," Quinn reminded her.

"Really?" Taylor's eyebrows lifted.

Quinn gave her an innocent shrug.

"Tell you what," Riley pushed back from the table and looked over at Tristan, "why don't we go run down to the grocery store and get some ice cream for dessert, and then we can swing by my parents' house and pick up mom's car for Taylor? We thought she could borrow it until hers is fixed."

"I guess we can do that." Tristan nodded. Then he grinned and wiggled his eyebrows at Quinn. "Ice cream is pretty good for breakfast too."

Riley laughed as she reached out and gave Tristan a playful slap on his arm. "Come on."

Taylor glared at Riley, fully aware that her sister's plan was nothing more than a poorly concealed attempt to leave her alone with Quinn. Riley glanced over at her, gave her a little smile, and then led the way to the door.

Tristan followed Riley and pulled the door open for her. Then he glanced over his shoulder. "We'll be right back."

"We'll be here," Quinn said, his voice cautiously neutral.

Trying hard not to be annoyed, Taylor stood up and gathered a couple of empty food containers. She tossed them in the trash and then leaned back against the kitchen counter, resigned to having to make small talk with Quinn. "Did you really have cheesecake for breakfast?"

Quinn's eyebrows lifted. "Seems to me that you're the one who taught me that little trick."

Taylor nodded at him knowingly. More than once Riley had gotten annoyed at her for eating unconventional things for breakfast. She never could quite understand Taylor's logic about the fact that cheesecake had as much dairy in it as a glass of milk but tasted a whole lot better.

"What was I thinking?" she asked now, her tension easing. "By the time I got around to eating breakfast, all that was left was some of Riley's healthy cereal and bran muffins."

"And the leftover lasagna from last night," Quinn reminded her.

Taylor's eyes widened. "How did you know that's what I had for breakfast?"

Quinn shifted and leaned back against the counter facing her. "Taylor, it isn't rocket science. There's no way you would ever eat your sister's health food, and we had already snagged the cheesecake."

"I guess you know me better than I realized." Taylor met his gaze. "Should I be worried?"

"I don't know." Quinn shrugged, then surprised them both by saying, "But maybe we should find out. Do you want to go catch a movie or something tomorrow?"

For a moment, Taylor could only stare at him. Then she surprised herself with her response. "Sure. I'd like that." The moment the words were out of her mouth, doubts shot through her. He had broken things off with her once without any warning. What was to keep him from breaking her heart again? She fought back a sigh as a single fact continued to cloud her judgment: She was still crazy about the guy.

8

"WHAT DO YOU MEAN YOU didn't find it?" Gregorio Amici's eyes darkened as he stared at the man standing on the other side of his desk. "This should have been a simple operation, one that you assured me was going to be finished weeks ago."

The slender man shifted his weight and glanced down at the thick beige carpet beneath his feet. "I'm sorry, sir. We've had some complications."

"Get it resolved," Gregorio ordered in his typical brisk manner. Then he leaned back in his chair, and his eyebrows lifted ever so slightly. "And remember, I don't like to be disappointed."

"I understand, sir." The man stood for a moment longer, apparently unsure if he had been dismissed. Then he took a step backward and then another. When he reached the door, he nodded awkwardly at Gregorio and quickly left the room.

Gregorio stared after him for a brief moment before opening the thick agenda on his desk. He flipped through a few pages, calculating dates and travel times in his mind. Everything was moving along smoothly except for this current dilemma. He shook his head, annoyed. He wasn't sure how this American girl had managed to complicate his plans, but he assured himself that it was only a matter of time before everything fell into place. And if his men couldn't take care of the American, then he would simply have to resort to more effective measures.

The phone on his desk rang, and Gregorio closed his book. A few more weeks, he assured himself, and he would be able to leave this office behind for good.

* * *

Quinn checked his gear one last time as he stood up in the back of the helicopter along with the other four members of his squad. He could smell the saltwater through the open door of the helicopter, and the whirring of the blades overhead was deafening despite the protective covering over his ears. No one spoke, already aware that communication would be difficult except through the use of hand signals.

Brent Miller, the commander of the Saint Squad, used one of those signals now, and his men sprang into motion. The twenty-twenty jump was a routine training exercise, but like everything they did, there was always a risk of injury or worse. The helicopter reached the proper speed and position, twenty knots and twenty feet above the water.

Then the next command came. One at a time, in quick succession, each member stepped through the open door of the helicopter and splashed into the water, weighted down with nearly a hundred pounds of gear. Quinn was the last to enter the water today. He stepped off, took a deep breath, and then held it as he plunged into the cold water. He let himself relax as gravity forced him beneath the pull of the waves, and then he fought the weight of his pack as he worked his way back to the surface.

Already, the helicopter had turned sharply and was headed back to base, but Quinn didn't look toward the shore. Instead, he counted the heads bobbing in front of him to make sure his team had all surfaced safely. When he was certain that everyone was indeed okay, Quinn let his training take over as he fell into position with the other men and they began swimming toward the beach.

On one level, he was going through his mental checklist as he moved through the frigid water. Check on Tristan, count heads, pick a focal point on land, adjust angle to compensate for the current. On another level, Quinn was already thinking about what would come later. After he and the squad worked their way to the beach and ran the two miles to their final destination for the day, Quinn would take the time to shower off the saltwater and sand and dress for his date with Taylor.

He still wasn't sure what had prompted him to ask her out. For the past few months, he had avoided her in every way possible, thoroughly convinced that it was best if he let her get on with her life without him weighing her down.

That concern seemed insignificant now, especially after finding out about the recent events in her life. Besides, it wasn't like he planned to let things get serious between them. The fact that she hadn't demanded any explanations from him about their previous relationship only seemed to prove that she wasn't looking for anything long-term either.

He was relieved that the expected reproach from Taylor hadn't occurred, but he also found himself annoyed that she hadn't seemed to miss him much. As quickly as that thought invaded his mind, Quinn pushed it aside. She was just comfortable to be around, he assured himself. And if she was with him, he could make sure she stayed safe.

He was certain that the only reason he had woken up thinking of her yesterday was because of his concern about the incident with her car. Sure, it was odd how easily they had slipped into their old, familiar friendship. He was a bit surprised that he remembered so many little things about her even though he hadn't seen her much over the past year. How had he known what she would eat for breakfast yesterday? Or the way he had sensed she was holding something back when she finally admitted to feeling like someone was watching her?

Maybe it was her willingness to confide in him that caused him to still feel connected to her after all of this time apart. Quinn glanced over at Tristan swimming beside him and wondered if he should invite Tristan and Riley along on his date to give him a safety net. They were nearly to the beach now, and a wave crashed over both of them. The water pushed them forward, and suddenly Quinn's feet brushed against the shifting sand beneath him.

As some of that sand gave way and he struggled forward, he realized he might not find his footing with Taylor no matter what he did.

* * *

Taylor finished loading the last of her paintings into the back of her mother's minivan and glanced around the visitor's section of the parking garage beneath her sister's condo. Satisfied that she wasn't being watched, she stuffed a few beach towels on either side of the paintings to make sure they wouldn't shift and then closed the door.

When she pulled out of the garage, she slowed, studying the people on the sidewalks as well as the cars on the street before entering the light flow of traffic. She checked her rearview mirror and then turned away from the ocean. She took the long way, circling several times to make sure she wasn't being followed. She knew she was probably being paranoid, but her instincts were still on overdrive after the incident with her car.

After taking more than an hour to drive what should have taken thirty minutes, Taylor pulled up in front of her destination. The house looked the same as it had when she had been in high school, except for the new white delivery van parked in the driveway. The father of a high school friend, Gary Holloway, had been framing her artwork for her since she won best of show at the state fair her junior year. Though his main source of income came from the furniture restoration business he ran out of his garage, he did custom framing as a side business. Taylor couldn't think of anyone else she would trust more to frame these newest paintings.

She pulled past the house and then cranked the wheel so she could back into the driveway. Even though she was only going to be away from the vehicle for a few minutes, she locked the van and then walked to the front door and rang the bell.

"Hey, stranger," Gary said the moment he pulled the door open. He looked the same, except that his receding hairline had receded a bit farther over the past year, and what hair he had left was cut military short. He took a step forward and gave her a fatherly hug. "You haven't changed at all."

"You mean I don't look older and wiser?" Taylor teased.

"Not a bit." He motioned to the van. "Come on. Let's get those masterpieces unloaded so I can take a look."

Taylor nodded and led the way to the car. "How long do you think it will take you to frame them?"

"I'm a little backed up right now, but I should be able to have them done for you in a few days." He grinned at her. "Put it this way. Your art will be ready to hang long before you have a wall to hang it on."

"You never know." Amusement sparked in her eyes. "I'm going to go check out a couple of places tomorrow."

"Anything promising?"

"It's hard to say." She unlocked the van and pulled open the back door. "I found one that's only a couple of blocks from my sister, so hopefully I'll like it."

"I'm surprised you don't go stay with your parents for a while."

"I haven't seen their place yet, but Dad said it's only a two bedroom. With Landon coming home from his mission in a couple of weeks, he'll need to stay there until he heads off to college next semester."

Gary pulled the first container out of the van and took a step toward the house as Taylor picked up another one. He looked at her, surprised when Taylor set it down and then closed and locked the van before moving to follow him.

A touch of sarcasm laced his voice when he commented on it. "You afraid someone's going to steal one?"

Taylor nodded. "Actually, I think someone tried to a couple of days ago."

"What?"

Taylor told him about the damage done to her car and the way one of her paintings had been opened. He helped her unload the other two paintings and rested a hand on one of the protective cases.

"I'll make sure I take good care of these for you."

"I know you will." Taylor smiled at him. She opened one of the boxes. "Now, how about helping me figure out what kind of frames would look best with these?"

"My pleasure."

9

QUINN ANGLED HIS CAR INTO a spot next to the curb a half block from Tristan's condo. He had considered walking the three blocks from his apartment to pick up Taylor, but he wasn't sure if she would be up for walking back to get his car. Another thing he remembered about Taylor was her love of high-heeled shoes.

Emily had liked high heels, too, before she got sick. She said they made her feel like she was more dressed up, and she had liked the way they made her taller. Of course, Emily had only been a couple of inches over five feet, while Taylor was probably around five six.

Quinn shook his head, annoyed at himself for comparing the two women. Taylor was alive. Emily was dead. The comparison needed to stop right there.

He knocked on Tristan's door, not fully prepared to see Taylor answer it. He glanced down instinctively. Sure enough, she was wearing heels.

"Nice shoes."

Taylor looked down at her feet as though she had forgotten which ones she had on. Then she lifted her eyes to meet his and gave him a hesitant smile. "Thanks."

"Are you ready to go?"

"I am." Taylor picked up her purse from a little table by the front door and called out over her shoulder, "Riley, I'm leaving."

Riley's voice rang out as Taylor stepped into the hall. "Have fun."

"Thanks." Taylor pulled the door closed and fell into step with Quinn as he started down the hall. "So where are we going?"

"Did you want to start with dinner?"

Taylor nodded and grinned. "Are we going to eat real food or just skip to dessert?"

The corner of Quinn's mouth lifted. "Maybe we should look at a menu before we decide that."

"Okay." Taylor slowed down as they approached Quinn's car and waited for him to open the door for her.

Quinn drove away from the beach and the few tourists who hadn't yet realized that summer had ended. A mile inland, he pulled into a parking lot next to a seafood restaurant. "Is this okay?"

A smile lit Taylor's face, and she nodded. "I love seafood."

"I know."

As soon as they stepped inside the restaurant, Taylor breathed in the scent of fried fish, fresh bread, and lemon butter. "It smells wonderful. What's good here?"

"I've liked everything I've tried, but we should definitely start with the crab-stuffed mushrooms," Quinn told her as a hostess led them to a table.

Taylor opened her menu and nodded. "I can live with that."

When their waitress arrived, Quinn ordered the appetizer and then watched as Taylor shifted in her seat to face the woman more fully.

She jerked a thumb at him and smiled. "He said everything is good here, but do you have a favorite? I can't decide."

Quinn watched as the older woman's features relaxed into a smile, appreciating anew how comfortable Taylor was with people. "Well, it depends on what you like." The waitress leaned closer to point at the menu. "But these two are my favorites."

Taylor looked down at the descriptions and then nodded. "I'll go with this one."

"I think you'll like it." The waitress smiled her approval before repeating back their order and heading for the kitchen.

Quinn looked across the table at Taylor. "So what did you do today?"

"I spent a little time on the computer looking for an apartment, and then I took my paintings to be framed," Taylor told him. "What about you? What did you do today?"

He shrugged. "I jumped out of a helicopter."

Taylor stared at him for a minute as though trying to decide whether to believe him. Then she let out a short laugh. "Okay, you win. Your day was more exciting than mine."

"I think that's a good thing," Quinn reminded her. "After the problem with your car and what happened in Paris, I think your goal should be to have normal days for a while."

"Maybe." Taylor nodded. "I know I'll feel better when I can get settled somewhere and start painting again."

"Why can't you paint now?"

"It's just a hassle to organize all of my supplies when I'm staying with someone else. Besides, my mom wouldn't be too happy with me if I got paint on the upholstery in her van," Taylor said. She fell silent for a moment, and then she leaned forward. "Now tell me about jumping out of a helicopter. I thought you guys normally parachuted out of airplanes."

"I never said I was wearing a parachute." Quinn grinned.

Conversation was surprisingly easy over dinner. Taylor pushed her nearly empty plate toward the center of the table as a waiter walked by with another couple's dessert order. She nodded at the waiter and then shook her head. "I can't believe I forgot to save room for dessert."

Quinn chuckled. "We can always stop somewhere and get dessert after the movie."

Taylor seemed to consider his suggestion and then nodded. "Did you have a movie in mind?"

"I figured I'd let you choose since I picked the restaurant," Quinn told her. "But I have a couple of ideas."

"Of course you do," Taylor laughed.

* * *

"So what did you think of it?" Quinn asked Taylor as they walked out of the movie theater.

"I think you should never be allowed to go to a movie about Navy SEALs again. Ever."

"Why not?"

Taylor's eyebrows lifted. "Because that was supposed to be a serious movie, and you spent most of the time laughing at it."

"Did I embarrass you?" Quinn asked, turning to look at her.

Taylor tried to keep a serious face, but she couldn't quite manage it. "Okay, so maybe it was a little unrealistic when those Navy SEALs were swimming in the water and trying to catch up with the cruise ship . . ."

"Yeah." Quinn nodded. "And when the bad guys were shooting at them with automatic weapons and no one got hit. Not to mention . . ."

Taylor held up a hand to stop him. "Okay. Okay. You're right. It was more of a comedy than a drama."

Quinn nodded victoriously. He took her hand in his and pulled her away from the theater entrance toward the food court across from it. "Did you want to get some dessert?"

Taylor nodded and pointed at a smoothie bar. "I love those."

"Are you sure? If you want, we can go find a place with cheesecake instead."

"I don't think I'm hungry enough for cheesecake," Taylor said. "I think I'll wait for that until tomorrow night."

Quinn's eyebrows lifted. "Did we have plans for tomorrow night?"

"*I* have plans for tomorrow night," Taylor corrected. "I'm going to have some cheesecake. It's up to you if you want to join me."

"So that's the way you're going to be about it." Sarcasm dripped from his voice.

"Hey, you're the one who ate the rest of the one Riley made."

"It's not like I did it alone," Quinn reminded her. "In fact, I'm pretty sure Seth ate a lot more of it than I did."

Taylor laughed as she stepped up to the counter. After they ordered their smoothies, Quinn asked, "What else did you have planned for tomorrow?"

"Just looking for an apartment. What about you?"

His shoulders lifted. "I should get off work around five. Maybe I'll come over and hang out afterward."

She smiled. "That sounds good."

The cashier placed Taylor's smoothie in front of her. "Here's the strawberry banana." He turned to Quinn. "I'll have yours for you in just a minute."

Quinn nodded and turned his attention back to Taylor. She picked up her smoothie, slid a straw into the top, and took a sip.

"Oh, that's good." She set it down on the edge of the counter, and a split second later it splashed onto the floor.

Quinn shook his head and rolled his eyes for effect. "So much for that being good."

"Oh no!" Taylor scooped the cup up quickly, but not before the lid split open and most of the frozen concoction pooled at her feet. She shook her head as she stared down at the red goo splattered all over her toes, shoes, and jeans. "I don't know how that happened."

The man behind her suppressed a grin and pretended to turn away. "I don't see a thing."

"I guess they shouldn't have counters with rounded edges," another man added.

Taylor glanced at the counter, noticing for the first time the way the edge curved. Her eyes narrowed fractionally. "Does that mean I can blame this spill on the counter?"

"I don't think so." Quinn shook his head. When the cashier moved forward to hand Quinn his smoothie along with the napkins, Quinn pointed to the spill. "We're going to need some more napkins."

"I'm sorry. I don't know how that happened," Taylor told the cashier as he leaned forward to survey the mess. Taylor jerked a thumb at Quinn with humor sparking in her eyes. "But I'm sure it was his fault."

"What?! I was way over here!" Quinn insisted.

"He has a point." The cashier chuckled and handed a wad of napkins to her. "I don't think you're going to be able to blame him."

Taylor looked at the cashier in mock disbelief. "You mean this is really my fault?"

"Yeah." The cashier nodded and gave her a knowing grin. "It's disgraceful."

Taylor tried to keep a straight face as she took the napkins from him and then leaned down to wipe up the worst of the damage to her jeans and shoes, wiggling her toes as she tried to get the sticky mixture out from between them.

Then the cashier leaned over, apparently taking pity on her. "Don't worry about the spill on the floor. I'll take care of that." He then pointed to the girl working with him. "We need another strawberry banana smoothie."

Taylor looked at him with bright eyes. "You're going to make me another one?" Then she stood up and smiled. "I knew I liked you."

A few minutes later, Taylor and Quinn both had their smoothies, and they said their good-byes to the small crowd that had gathered behind them at the smoothie bar. As Quinn led her to the car, Taylor took a sip of her new drink and then grinned at him. "Did I mention that this is *really* good?"

Quinn looked down at Taylor and couldn't help but laugh. He was still amazed by the way she seemed to take situations like this in stride, while so many others would have made a big deal out of them. Only Taylor could take what should have been an embarrassing incident and walk away with a half dozen new friends. He was still laughing when he pulled up in front of Tristan's building. He didn't have any trouble finding a parking spot now that the shops were all closed and the restaurant traffic had died down.

"Are you sure you don't want to take your shoes off?"

Humor was still in Taylor's eyes when she turned to look at him. "That's okay. They're only a little sticky."

Still grinning, Quinn climbed out of the car and joined Taylor on the sidewalk. "I'll walk you up."

Taylor pulled out the key that Riley had given her and unlocked the door to the lobby. Quinn pulled the door open wider to let her walk through and then strolled with her to the elevator.

"Are you sure Riley and Tristan won't mind if I drop by tomorrow?"

"You always hang out with them when I'm not staying here, don't you?" Taylor asked. "Why would that change now?"

Quinn followed her into the elevator, pressing the button for the fourth floor and then turning toward her. "I don't know." Hundreds of memories flooded through his mind, but at the heart of them was the way Taylor lived every moment to the fullest and always made him want to do the same. He took a step forward, effectively boxing her in against the wall. "Maybe because I haven't forgotten how much I liked to do this."

He leaned down until their faces were close, and he could see the awareness in her eyes. Then he laid his lips gently on hers. His heartbeat quickened as he drew her closer. He hadn't meant to do this, but now with her in his arms, he couldn't remember why. Time blurred, and their months apart seemed to melt away. When he pulled back, he looked down to see the confusion on her face.

Taylor took a deep breath, and her eyes were wary. "I don't understand you."

"What's to understand?" Quinn asked, even as he worried that the casual relationship he had planned with Taylor was already trying to point toward serious.

"Everything." Taylor let out a frustrated sigh as the elevator doors opened. "You completely ignore me for months, and now you act like everything is great between us."

Quinn stared at her for a moment, not sure what to say. He had hoped to avoid this conversation, at least until he figured out his own feelings. Then Taylor stepped out of the elevator and started down the hall, and he knew he had to clear the air with her whether he was ready for it or not.

"Taylor, wait." Quinn caught up with her and grabbed her arm. He waited for her to face him before he continued. "I'm sorry about before. I just had a lot of things going on that made it hard to keep up with a long-distance relationship."

Her body tensed. "So instead of telling me that, you just started going out with other people? I guess you figured that I'd find out about it and get the message that you lost interest."

"I never lost interest in you. Besides, I wasn't really dating anyone else," Quinn started. When Taylor simply raised her eyebrows, he let out a sigh of his own. "A couple of girls from the singles ward asked me out. I only went because I didn't want to hurt their feelings."

Taylor's voice was barely louder than a whisper when she spoke. "So you hurt my feelings instead."

Quinn swallowed hard, for the first time truly understanding the impact his actions had had on Taylor. He reached for her hand, slowly rubbing his thumb over the back of it. His voice was low when he spoke. "I'm so sorry, Taylor. I never meant to hurt you. In fact, a couple of months ago I started going to church with Tristan and Riley so I didn't have to deal with the dating scene anymore."

Taylor stared at him for a moment, her shoulders relaxing marginally. "Now what? I had a great time tonight, but I don't want to set myself up to get ignored again."

"I have no intention of ignoring you." Quinn ran his free hand through his hair. He knew if he told her about Emily, she would understand, but he couldn't do it. Impatience bubbled up inside him. How long would it take for him to be able to talk about the first woman he loved? Part of him wanted to start the conversation, but he knew he still wasn't prepared to dredge up those old memories, not even for Taylor. Instead, he asked, "Can we just start over? Can you try to forgive me for being a jerk and give me another chance?"

"Maybe," Taylor said hesitantly.

"If nothing else, you know that Tristan would love nothing more than a reason to beat on me if I screw up again."

She offered him a timid smile. "Are you afraid Tristan is going to play big brother to me?"

Quinn stared at her for a second, trying to read her emotions. Slowly, he smiled. "Tristan's been playing big brother to me since we were fifteen. And he's only six months older than me."

Taylor let out a soft laugh, and the tension in Quinn's stomach eased. "Maybe I should bring the cheesecake to you tomorrow night."

Relieved, Quinn shook his head, and his grin flashed once more. "That's okay. I kind of like the idea of getting a rise out of Tristan."

Taylor nodded, but she looked at him with new curiosity. "I just realized that I don't even know where you live."

"It's not like I'm ever there anyway." Quinn shrugged. He waved a hand toward the north. "But my apartment's a few blocks down the road."

Taylor moved down the hall until she was in front of her sister's door. "Thanks for tonight. I had a great time."

"Me too." Quinn hesitated briefly. Then he reached for her hand and gave it a squeeze. "I'll see you tomorrow."

Taylor nodded. She unlocked the door and pushed it open. With a last glance over her shoulder, she lowered her voice and said, "Good night."

"'Night." Quinn stood in the hallway, waiting for her to close the door and flip the lock. He stared at her door a moment, suddenly relieved that the conversation he had been dreading was now behind him.

He turned and headed for the stairwell, thinking back to the smoothie bar. Most women would have been mortified or at least embarrassed to have a crowd of people mulling around after making such a mess. But Taylor had turned the whole incident into a bright spot in everyone's night. Quinn had little doubt that those who had seen the spill and heard the good-natured ribbing would get home tonight and laugh about it. Perhaps it was that trait that made her so easy to be with. She just made everything seem so much lighter.

He pushed the stairwell door open and almost ran into someone standing on the landing.

"Sorry. I didn't expect anyone to be in here."

The dark-haired man appeared to be about Quinn's age, mid- to late twenties. He looked around nervously for a moment before he managed to find his voice. "That's okay."

Quinn's eyes narrowed suspiciously, but he immediately chided himself for being overly protective. His tried to sound casual. "Are you coming in here?"

"Uh, no." He shook his head and then hurried down the stairs in front of Quinn.

Quinn followed more slowly. By the time he walked outside, he found himself already looking forward to tomorrow.

10

Vernon Riesenour blinked hard as he stared down at the image on his laptop, at the innocent faces of his two sons smiling back at him and the joy radiating from his wife as she stood beside them in front of her childhood home outside of Baghdad. He remembered debating whether to let his family travel to Iraq without him so that his wife could visit her family. She had been so eager to attend a cousin's wedding and to see her parents and other relatives again.

The unrest in that part of the world had worried Vernon enough that he had originally denied her wishes, insisting that it simply wasn't possible, not when his work with the French government was keeping him at their home in Marseille. Then the news reports had started about the successes in Iraq. The Americans had succeeded in stamping out the local uprisings, and the area around Baghdad was finally secure.

Those news reports and his family's desires had swayed him—and had given him a false sense of security. After a lot of discussion, he had finally consented to letting his beloved wife take their boys to visit her family. The photo filling up his computer screen was sent only two days before their excursion into the countryside, an outing that had ultimately cost them their lives.

Vernon didn't consider that his family had been killed in the roadside bombing because they had left the safety of Baghdad or that he had gone against his better judgment in allowing his family to travel to Iraq in the first place. No, he placed the blame squarely on the shoulders of the American people who tricked him into believing that they could protect his family.

For months, his grief had consumed him, focused him. He had left his job, withdrawn from his friends, and let his hatred for the Americans grow and fester. Born from that hatred was an ingenious plan, a way for him to make sure the Americans would pay for all of the lies they had told.

* * *

Taylor's cell phone rang three times before she realized it wasn't a dream. She moaned out loud and squinted in the early morning light. Then she reached out and grabbed her cell phone off of her bedside table. Bleary-eyed, she hit the talk button without checking her caller ID.

"Taylor?"

"Yeah?"

"This is Felicia Davenport," she said with a faint European accent. "I'm so sorry to call this early, but I have some bad news."

"What's wrong?"

"There was a fire at the gallery's warehouse last night. I'm afraid we lost two of your paintings."

"What?" Taylor sat up abruptly, now fully awake. "Are you sure?"

"I'm afraid so. The alarms went off at three this morning, and we've had people down there doing inventory since then."

"Are my other paintings okay?" Taylor asked, her mind still spinning.

"Yes. The warehouse staff said all of your other work is still intact. I'm afraid they only gave me the inventory numbers of the two we lost, but the inventory manager said he would pull the photos we took of them so we can get them identified."

Taylor closed her eyes for a moment and let out a sigh. "Okay. Please let me know when you find anything out."

"I will." She hesitated a moment. "And Taylor, I'm really sorry about this."

"I know," Taylor told her. "I'll talk to you later."

Taylor climbed out of bed, aware that there was no way she would be able to get back to sleep. She grabbed a quick shower and dressed for the day, determined to find an apartment, something she hoped would help her find a new sense of security . . . and autonomy.

She retrieved the list of apartments she was scheduled to see that day and headed into the kitchen. Tristan was standing at the counter, a drumstick in one hand and a glass of ice water in the other.

"Interesting breakfast," Taylor said, eying the piece of chicken.

"There's more in the fridge," Tristan told her. "I saved you a piece."

"Thanks." Taylor smiled at him, but the smile didn't quite reach her eyes.

Tristan's eyes narrowed. "What's wrong?"

Taylor took a deep breath and let it out in a rush. "I got a call this morning from my agent."

"And?"

"Two of my paintings were destroyed last night in a warehouse fire."

"You're kidding!" Tristan straightened, concern crossing his face.

"I wish I were." Taylor let out a sigh. "Tristan, you don't think someone could be deliberately targeting my paintings, do you? I mean, I haven't even been featured in my own show yet."

"I don't know, but with everything that's happened, I'm starting to wonder." Tristan considered for a minute. "Do you have any sketches or photos of the paintings you've done?"

Taylor nodded. "Yeah, I always take photos of each piece before they're shipped."

"Where are those pictures?"

"I haven't printed them out, but I always keep my camera in my purse, and I downloaded all of the photos to my laptop," Taylor told him. "Why?"

"Go get your camera for me."

She gave him an odd look, but she nodded. "Okay." She walked into the guest room and pulled her camera out of her purse. When she walked back into the kitchen, she handed it to Tristan.

He turned it on and began browsing through the photos. "Do you mind if I copy these?"

Taylor shook her head. "What are you thinking?"

"I'm starting to wonder if you painted something that someone doesn't want the world to see," Tristan said warily. "I want to take these photos into the office and have them analyzed." He paused for a moment and then glanced over at her. "In fact, it would be a lot easier if you could go through them and make a list of where they were all painted."

"If you copy the files off of my laptop, they're already labeled," Taylor told him. "I'll get it, and you can figure out the easiest way to transfer the files."

Tristan nodded casually, but Taylor could see the worry in his eyes.

* * *

Gregorio stood by the window and stared out at the city. Today was the day. Finally, everything he had been planning for was going to come together. He had already received the call that the warehouse fire had been executed perfectly. Now he only had one more person who needed to report in, the same person who had failed him the last time.

On the street below, the city was already moving despite the early hour. Of course, this was the city that never sleeps, just as he hadn't last night. A slow smile crossed his face as he imagined what this city would look like once his collection was complete. He wouldn't be here to see it, of course. At least not long enough to see the results except on the news from the safe haven he planned to buy in his native Italy.

Only a little longer, he assured himself as the phone rang. He lifted it to his ear, answering with a simple hello. Then he listened to the latest report, the most recent failure.

"This is twice you've disappointed me," Gregorio said in an eerily calm voice. "Don't let there be a third."

He listened to the mumbled apologies and assurances for a moment before he cut the other man off.

Gregorio clenched his teeth together and took an unsteady breath before speaking once more. "Let me be perfectly clear. I don't care what you have to do or who you have to go through to complete this assignment. Get me that painting."

* * *

"What have you got there?" Quinn asked Tristan when he walked into the office they shared. An image of a painting filled Tristan's computer screen.

Tristan glanced over at him. "It's a photo of one of Taylor's paintings."

Quinn's eyebrows lifted. "It's not exactly what I would have expected you to use as a screen saver."

"It's not a screen saver." Tristan's voice was uncharacteristically tense. He glanced up at Quinn for a moment. "Two of Taylor's paintings were destroyed in a fire last night."

"What? Where?"

"They were in a warehouse in New Jersey."

"You think it was deliberate?" Quinn asked skeptically.

"I'm not sure, but too much has been going on with her lately for me to believe it was just a coincidence."

Quinn let out a frustrated sigh. "What has she stumbled into?"

"I don't know," Tristan told him, concern shining in his eyes. "But I think it's time we figure it out."

Quinn nodded. "What can I do to help?"

* * *

Taylor pulled into the parking lot of the small apartment building. She had already looked at four other units, none of them really standing out in her mind. Two were pretty run down, and a third didn't have a dishwasher, something Taylor considered a deal breaker. The fourth was relatively modern but was on the other side of town.

She climbed out of her car and looked at the white brick building in front of her. The building wasn't new, but it was well kept. It was also the one location that Tristan and Riley had both insisted that she look at before making a decision. It was only a couple of blocks from their place and was an easy walk to the beach.

Unlike the hotel-style building her sister lived in, the apartments in this complex were garden style with the doors of each apartment opening directly outside. A long concrete balcony ran the full length of the building on the second floor, with metal stairwells on either side of the building.

Riley found the manager's apartment on the first floor and knocked on the door. The man who opened the door was only an inch or two taller than her, and his blond hair was sun bleached. Judging by his deep tan, Taylor guessed he spent a lot of the daylight hours outside.

"Hi, I'm Taylor Palmetta. I'm here about the apartment."

"Max Ruddock." He reached out, gripping her hand and giving it a friendly shake. "Let's go take a look."

Taylor smiled and fell into step as he motioned to the stairs on the right. "The only one I have available is a one-bedroom up on the second floor." He pulled a set of keys from the pocket of his plaid board shorts. "The kitchen was remodeled about two years ago, and the carpets were just cleaned last week."

He pushed the door open and stepped aside to let Taylor enter the apartment first. She stepped onto the tile entryway and looked around. To her left was a decent-sized living room, the beige carpet a little worn but clean. To the right, the ceramic tile in the entryway continued into a dining area. She walked across it and looked into the galley kitchen.

As Max had said, the kitchen had the feel of recent remodeling, and the appliances all looked new, including the dishwasher.

She walked through the kitchen, out the doorway on the far side, and into a short hallway. Three doors opened off of the hallway. To the right was a combination laundry/storage room. The door to the left led into the master bedroom, with wide windows on the far wall that looked out toward the east.

Taylor wandered into the bedroom, turning in a slow circle as she placed her furniture in her mind. She checked out the walk-in closet and then the bathroom. They weren't terribly large, but they were definitely adequate. She also liked the way the bathroom had two entrances, one from the hallway and the other from the bedroom.

"So what do you think?" Max asked from the bedroom doorway.

Taylor turned to face him. "How much is it a month?"

He gave her the amount, one that was well within her price range.

"And how soon would I be able to move in?"

"All I need is your deposit, the first and last month's rent, and a signature. Then you can move in any time you want."

"Great." Taylor smiled at him. "In that case, let me write you a check. I want to start moving in this weekend."

"You do realize that today is Friday, right?"

Taylor grinned. "Oh yeah. But I also realize that my brother-in-law lives a couple of blocks away, and he has some really great friends."

Max chuckled. "In that case, let's get your paperwork started."

11

"WE NEED TO KNOW WHICH paintings were destroyed before we'll be able to figure this out," Tristan said, running a hand over his face.

"This one could be something." Quinn said, pointing at the painting currently displayed on his screen. He and Tristan had been pouring over paintings for hours, but this was the first one that jumped out at him. Taylor had painted a beach scene with several people in the foreground. Out on the water, several boats were visible, including two freighters. "Look at this."

Tristan stood and crossed the room so that he was looking over Quinn's shoulder. "What am I looking at?"

"She painted it near Palermo. It's similar to the one in her car that was opened up." Quinn pointed at one of the freighters. "Look at the detail on this. It's as good as a photograph. She has the date listed in her log, and the freighter is clearly flying under a Libyan flag. You can even see the waterline on the side."

Tristan's eyes sharpened. "You think she painted something that someone didn't want anyone to see?"

"I don't know, but it's possible." Quinn jerked a shoulder. "Think about it. If that freighter was supposed to be full, this would show that it's transporting something besides freight."

"Like people," Tristan surmised. "Or terrorists."

"Or the waterline could indicate that it was transporting more than it should have been into Libya."

"There's also the possibility that she caught someone on the beach that she wasn't supposed to. The Italian mafia is still very much alive and well in Sicily."

"That's true." Quinn looked at the picture more closely. "Maybe NCIS can run facial recognition on the people in the painting."

"I don't know if that's possible, but I suppose we can ask," Tristan said cautiously. "Do you really think they would do it for us? I mean, Taylor isn't navy. And there hasn't been a crime except for her car getting vandalized."

"And the break-in at her hotel in Paris," Quinn reminded him.

"Yeah, but that would definitely be out of their jurisdiction."

"Maybe we should try Naval Intelligence. I doubt they would pass up this kind of information," Quinn suggested. "Better yet, we should hand this off to Amy," he added, referring to Amy Miller, their intelligence officer.

A knock sounded on their open door, and both men looked up to see Brent Miller, Amy's husband and their commanding officer, standing in the doorway. "Grab your gear. We're heading out."

Quinn's stomach tightened. "Where to?"

"I don't know yet," Brent said as he turned to leave. "But we're supposed to be in Norfolk within the hour."

"It's four o'clock on a Friday afternoon," Tristan called out to him. "I hope you found us a ride."

Brent started down the hall, but he called out, "A chopper's standing by. Let's go."

"You heard the man," Tristan said as he powered off his computer and Quinn did the same.

As they left their office, Tristan slipped his cell phone out of his pocket and pressed speed dial to call his wife.

The helicopter was ready for liftoff when they arrived. Jay and Seth were already on board, and Brent was standing beside Amy signing off on some paperwork. Then Brent climbed into the chopper, and Amy walked toward them.

Quinn shouted over the thrumming sound of the helicopter blades when she closed the distance between them. "Are you coming with us?"

Amy shook her head. "And no, I don't know what's going on yet either." Then she pointed to the chopper. "You'd better get going."

Quinn and Tristan both grabbed their gear and hurried onto the helicopter. Quinn buckled in and looked down at Amy, who was standing a short distance away as they lifted off. If she was staying behind, it meant one of two things. Either this was just a readiness exercise, or they were going behind enemy lines where she couldn't go.

* * *

Quinn was only in Norfolk for ten minutes before he broke down and called Taylor. He still didn't know if they were going to be deployed on some mission or if they would be given the order to stand down and be sent home. Either way, he needed to make sure she was okay and figure out a way to keep her that way.

Her phone rang three times before she picked up.

"Hey, Taylor. Where are you right now?"

"I was just going to head back over to Riley's place," Taylor told him. Excitement filled her voice. "I just finished signing the lease on a new apartment."

"That's great," Quinn said, but he rushed on. "Listen, we got called up today, so I'm not sure when Tristan and I will be back in Virginia Beach."

Taylor paused for a minute before saying, "I guess I'll have to save you some dessert then."

"Actually, I wasn't even thinking about that," Quinn admitted. "I don't want you and Riley staying home alone tonight."

"What?" Taylor asked, and Quinn could imagine her eyebrows drawing together in that expression she always got when she was caught completely off guard.

"Until we figure out who it was that broke into your car, you need to be somewhere safe."

"You have to have a key to get into Riley and Tristan's building," Taylor reminded him. "I'm sure we'll be fine."

"Please, Taylor." Quinn lowered his voice, hoping that none of the guys were standing close enough to hear his pleading tone. It was hard enough for him to acknowledge that despite their months apart, his feelings for Taylor were just as strong as ever. "Please do this for me. If you don't hear from us by nine o'clock, go over and stay at my place. At least for tonight."

"I don't even know where you live."

"Riley does, and my spare key is around her place somewhere."

"You realize that you're being extremely overprotective right now, don't you?"

"Yeah," Quinn admitted. "I do."

"Fine," Taylor finally conceded. "But call me if you can so I know what's going on."

"Okay. And you stay safe."

The minute he hung up, he looked over to see Tristan standing a few feet away. "What was that all about?"

Quinn's tone became defensive. "I don't want Taylor and Riley home alone tonight."

Tristan stared at him a moment as though debating whether to say something. Then he nodded. "That's probably a good idea." He motioned to where Brent was standing a short distance away talking to Kel Bennett, the commander of SEAL Team Eight. "Let's go see if Brent and Kel know what's going on."

Quinn nodded, and for the first time since joining the SEAL teams, he truly hoped that they were going to be sent back home.

* * *

"Does Tristan ever get like this with you?" Taylor asked from her spot on the center of Riley's bed. Spread out in front of her was a big pile of laundry that she and Riley were slowly turning into several folded stacks.

"You mean does he get overprotective?" Riley nodded with emphasis. "Oh yeah."

Taylor folded a white T-shirt and set it into her pile. "I've never had anyone act like this with me before. What's even stranger is the fact that he wouldn't even talk to me until I moved back here."

"I'm afraid I can't explain that." Riley looked at Taylor with sympathy in her eyes. "Right after my wedding, he went on a few dates with some of the girls in the singles ward, but the last few months he hasn't seemed to socialize with anyone but us and the other guys in his unit."

"That's pretty much what he told me," Taylor nodded. "Still, I don't know what to think. When we went out on our date, he acted like nothing ever happened between us."

"I thought you said he explained why he stopped calling."

"He did, but now I don't know if he's hanging around because he's still interested in me or if he just thinks I need to be protected." She picked up another shirt and then glanced up at Riley. "I mean, Dad wasn't even this paranoid."

"I have a feeling Dad would be plenty paranoid right now if he were here to know what's been going on," Riley told her. "I'm not sure if it's a good thing or a bad thing that he won't be back for a couple more weeks."

"Knowing him, we'd not only be told we can't stay home alone, but he'd probably also sign us up for another self-defense class."

Riley laughed. "You're probably right. I don't know what it was with him and those classes."

"I just remember every time he got deployed, he made us take another one."

"He made Mom take one right before they left for Brazil." Riley lifted a pile of shirts off of her bed and slid them into a dresser drawer. "I keep thinking that they'll call us, but maybe it's just as well that they don't. They'd be really worried about you."

"You're probably right." Taylor pulled her cell phone from her back pocket to check the time. "I'm surprised Felicia hasn't called back yet. It's already six o'clock. How long can it take to figure out which paintings are missing?"

"Apparently a long time." Riley shrugged. "Why don't you call her and make sure she hasn't forgotten about you?"

"Maybe I should," Taylor agreed. She scrolled through her contacts and then made the call. Felicia answered on the first ring.

"Taylor, I was just about to call you."

"Do you have any news?"

"Nothing good, I'm afraid," Felicia told her. "We're having trouble locating the inventory photos."

"You're having trouble locating them, or they're missing?" Taylor asked suspiciously.

"I'm sure they were just misfiled. No one has used them since you met with us last week," Felicia assured her. "I did want to ask if there's any way you could come up here on Monday."

"What for?"

"If we can't find those photos, the gallery manager wants to know if you can come and identify which pieces are missing."

"I can probably do that," Taylor agreed.

"Good. I'll give you a call tomorrow when we have a better handle on the situation."

"Okay." Taylor disconnected the call and then relayed the conversation to Riley.

"I can't believe all of this." Riley shook her head. "It's been one thing after another since you got home."

"I know." Taylor nodded. "But at least I'll be able to get moved in to my own place tomorrow and start getting settled."

"We aren't going to have much help if the guys are out of town."

"I know, but it isn't like I have a lot of stuff yet," Taylor reminded her. "Especially since Mom and Dad got rid of so many of my things when they moved into their new place."

"What are you going to do for furniture?"

"I have a few things I got in Europe that should be arriving in a couple more weeks, and I already bought a kitchen table, a bed, and a dresser. I just need to pick them up."

"You mean you want Tristan to pick them up." Riley smiled at her.

"He does drive a truck." Taylor grinned back at her sister. "And I can always use a sleeping bag for a few days if I need to."

"I assume you want to borrow mine."

"Unless you know where Mom put mine." Taylor folded a pair of Riley's pants and wondered briefly if her sister would notice them missing for a few days. Then she caught Riley looking at her, gave her a sheepish grin, and placed the pants in Riley's stack of clothes.

After they finished putting away the laundry, Riley nodded toward her bedroom door. "Come on. Let's go get you all packed up, and then we can run down to the grocery store and get you that cheesecake you've been talking about all day."

"New York–style cheesecake?" Taylor asked hopefully.

Riley laughed. "Maybe with the guys gone, you can even have some for breakfast tomorrow morning."

"Now that's a plan."

12

"WHAT'S THE PLAN?" QUINN ASKED as they climbed out of Tristan's truck in the parking garage beneath his condo. "Did you want to head into the office tomorrow so we can do some more research on Taylor's paintings?"

"We probably should, but let's see what the girls have planned first, especially since you don't have a car this weekend," Tristan said.

Quinn nodded. When they had returned from their readiness exercise in Norfolk, Jay had discovered that his starter motor had gone bad. Knowing that Jay had plans for the weekend, Quinn had taken pity on him and let him take his car since he could walk home from Tristan's place. "You know, I'm half tempted to bring Taylor into the office and have her help. She can at least tell us if she knew the people in her paintings."

"That's not a bad idea," Tristan agreed. "Of course, we'd need to get permission to bring her in there since she doesn't have a security clearance."

Quinn walked past the elevator and pushed open the door leading to the stairs.

"What is it with you and elevators?"

"Walking the stairs is good for you."

"So you keep telling me." Tristan followed him inside, and together they jogged up the first flight to the main level. "Hold on a second so I can grab my mail."

"No problem." Quinn followed him into the lobby area and then out the lobby door and to the left where the mailboxes were located for the building. A movement caught Quinn's attention, and his eyes narrowed as he recognized the man coming toward them. "Do you know that guy?"

Tristan turned and looked at the dark-haired man Quinn had motioned to. "No, why?"

"I saw him in the stairwell last night."

"In my building?" Tristan asked suspiciously.

Quinn nodded. The man stepped into the alcove next to the building entrance where the buzzers were located to call up to the individual units. Quinn took a step toward him just in time to see him press several buzzers, one right after the other. "Hey!" Quinn called out from several yards away. "What are you doing?"

The man looked up at Quinn, his eyes flashing with guilt and awareness. Then he turned and raced down the sidewalk. Quinn sprinted after him, gaining with each step even as he heard Tristan's rapid footsteps behind him. Then without warning, the man darted into the street, barely evading a car as it slammed on its brakes.

Quinn followed him out into traffic, slamming his hand down on the stopped car to keep it from moving forward. He had only taken two steps before a dark blue van coming from the other direction slowed down right next to the man Quinn was chasing. The panel door opened, the man jumped inside, and then the van's tires squealed as Quinn came within a yard of it before it sped away.

Tristan came to a stop in the middle of the road beside Quinn, both of them ignoring the honking horns from the drivers who had been cut off. "Did you get the license plate?"

Quinn nodded. "Yeah, I got it."

"Let's get inside and make sure the girls are okay. Then we'll call the police."

* * *

Taylor looked up at the door as it opened. Her smile was instant when she saw Tristan walk in followed by Quinn. "Hi, there. I didn't think we were going to see you guys tonight."

"It was just a readiness exercise," Tristan said, but he looked past her to where Riley was sitting at the kitchen table with her work spread out around her. "Is everything okay here?"

"Yeah." Riley looked at him suspiciously. "Why?"

Before Tristan could answer, Quinn pulled out his cell phone and looked at Taylor. "Do you have the phone number for the policeman who took your statement?"

"Officer Harbison?" Taylor asked, her eyebrows drawing together. "Yeah. It's in my purse."

"Can you get it for me?"

Taylor didn't move. "What's going on?"

"We aren't sure yet, but I just chased a guy in front of the building. I think he was heading up here," Quinn said, his focus still on Taylor. "I saw him last night after I brought you home. I don't think it's a coincidence."

"You think someone's after me?" Taylor asked, instantly seeing the answer in his eyes.

"Or he could be after something you have," Tristan suggested. "Either way, you aren't safe here."

A chill ran through Taylor, but her voice was surprisingly calm and hopeful when she spoke. "If you chased this guy away, I doubt he's coming back."

"Maybe. Maybe not." Quinn shook his head slowly, and then he crossed to her. "But why take chances?"

"Look, I already have the keys to my apartment." Taylor held her hands out in surrender. "I can stay there tonight."

Quinn shook his head. "It's not a good idea for you to move straight from here to your new place."

"Taylor doesn't have that much stuff. She can stay over at our parents' place tonight," Riley suggested. "We can load all of her stuff up before she goes so she doesn't have to come back here."

"I'm not sure I want *you* staying here tonight either," Tristan told Riley.

Riley looked pointedly at Tristan. "Fine. We can all stay at Mom and Dad's place. I'm sure you can figure out some way to set up surveillance or whatever it is you do to see if anyone tries to break into our place tonight while we're gone."

"When do your parents get home?" Tristan asked.

"In two weeks."

"Then we can stay there for a few days until I can make sure our place is secure," Tristan told her. "Can you go pack a bag for us? That way Quinn and I can start loading up Taylor's stuff after we call the police."

Riley glanced over at Taylor and then nodded in resignation.

Taylor looked into Quinn's eyes, surprised by the intensity she saw there. She swallowed hard and then motioned to her room. "I'll get you that number."

* * *

"You know, it's been a while since I've done this kind of work," Vanessa Johnson whispered to her husband as she adjusted the backpack hanging from her shoulder.

"It's just like riding a bike." Seth winked at her. "It'll come back to you."

"It had better," Vanessa said wryly.

Seth dropped his pack onto the hard concrete in the parking garage of Tristan's building and removed the first of the surveillance cameras that he was planning to place there. When Tristan had called and filled him in on his concerns, Seth had volunteered to help and had effectively volunteered his wife as well. He would have asked Brent to come along, but he and Amy had headed up to visit Amy's parents in northern Virginia for the weekend.

Since it was already two in the morning, Seth expected that they could set the equipment up without anyone even knowing they had been there.

Seth calculated angles, and with Vanessa, he finished in the garage relatively quickly. They then took the stairs to the fourth floor, placing another camera inside the stairwell and yet another in the hallway near the elevator.

As soon as they activated the camera in the hallway, Vanessa whispered, "Okay, that should do it except for the lobby."

"Tristan wants one inside his place, too, at least until they come back home," Seth told her.

"Did he give you a key?"

Seth nodded, pulling a house key out of his pocket. He put his hand on the doorknob and immediately realized that the door wasn't all the way closed. Knowing that Tristan was being overly cautious, he came to the unwanted conclusion that someone else was inside. He quickly stepped away from the door and pushed Vanessa back against the wall.

Vanessa's eyebrows lifted, and she gave him a questioning look. He signaled to her the way he would to one of the other SEALs in his squad. He knew she wouldn't understand all of the hand signals, but he was pretty sure she would get the gist of what he was saying: Stay here. Someone is inside.

Seth reached down to the weapon he had holstered at his ankle and handed it to Vanessa. He then pulled his second weapon from the small of his back. Silently, he shifted to the other side of the door and nodded with approval when Vanessa slid closer in case she needed to back him up. Seth then crouched down and slowly pushed the door open.

He stepped inside cautiously, scanning the darkness for anything out of place. There wasn't the typical mess associated with a burglary, and nothing appeared to be disturbed. Padding across the floor, he checked the living room and kitchen before starting for the hallway. He reached the guest room first and peered inside. That's when he saw the slight movement on the far side of the room.

Seth aimed and spoke in his deep voice. "Hold it right there."

The figure spun quickly, and Seth jumped back behind the door frame automatically in case he had a weapon. The intruder held his hands out to his side for a brief moment. Then to Seth's surprise, he turned back toward the sliding glass door, quickly opened it, and ran out onto the small balcony. Seth dashed forward as the man climbed over the wrought-iron railing and tried to lower himself to the balcony below. Just as Seth made it to the edge and reached out to grab the intruder's hand, the hand let go and suddenly the man was plummeting to the ground below.

Vanessa rushed into the room, gasping when she saw the man sprawled on the lawn beneath them. "What happened?"

"I don't know. I tried to grab his hand, and he just let go." Seth shook his head and turned to look at her. "I'm not sure if he slipped or if he jumped."

"I hope he slipped," Vanessa murmured. "Because if he jumped, that means he was more afraid of getting caught than he was of dying."

The muscle in Seth's jaw jumped as he considered the possibilities. "Call the cops. I'm going to check out the rest of the apartment, and then I'm going down there."

Vanessa nodded, pulling out her phone. "Make sure you don't touch anything."

Seth nodded and then disappeared out the door.

13

QUINN DIDN'T KNOW WHY HE was here. He knew that Tristan could handle things at the Palmettas' place, but he also knew he wasn't going to be able to sleep at home anyway, especially without knowing who was after Taylor or why. After getting Taylor and Riley settled at their parents' house, Tristan had offered to take Quinn back to his apartment, but somehow he had already known that Quinn wasn't going home.

The license plate number he had given to the police had turned out to belong to a completely different vehicle than the one Quinn had seen on the street by Tristan's place. As a result, the police were jumping to the same conclusions that Quinn and Tristan were. Whoever they had chased off wasn't some random criminal off the street. It was someone who was smart enough to hide his tracks.

Quinn paced across the Palmettas' living room, stopping to look at the framed snapshots hanging on the wall. The photos ranged in age, from a framed photo of Riley and Tristan at their wedding to a picture of Riley and Taylor wearing tutus when they were young. The corner of Quinn's mouth lifted as he thought of Taylor as a little girl. He could only imagine that she had kept her parents on their toes.

Although the Palmettas' house was much smaller than the one Quinn's parents lived in, the feeling of it was similar. His own childhood home sported many of the same types of photos, all in mismatched frames of varying sizes. Many of those photos from his later teenage years had included Tristan, who had moved in with his family when they were both fifteen. Tristan's mother, an admiral, had let him stay with Quinn's family while she was deployed overseas and then had allowed him to stay to finish high school.

Then a few years later, Emily's photo had appeared often as well. Those photos had all been taken down at Quinn's request. Many were still at his parents' house, some in boxes and others in albums, but most were hiding in plain sight on the bookshelf in Quinn's apartment.

Quinn heard a sound behind him and turned to see Taylor step out of the hallway. She was wearing a pair of flannel pajama pants and a loose-fitting T-shirt. Her hair looked like she had combed through it with her fingers after a restless night's sleep.

"You should try to get some more sleep."

Taylor's eyebrows lifted. "I could say the same thing about you."

"I took a combat nap a while ago before Tristan went to bed."

"A combat nap?"

Quinn nodded, as though she should know that he had been trained to fall into a deep sleep at will in order to help him survive in combat situations. He watched her take a step closer and noticed the mascara smudges under her eyes. After growing up with three younger sisters, he knew immediately that she had been crying.

He stepped closer and put a hand on her arm. "Are you okay?"

Taylor shrugged a shoulder but didn't answer.

"Hey, come here." Quinn pulled her closer and wrapped his arms around her. He could feel her tremble, apparently still trying to fight the tears. "It's going to be okay."

"Quinn, I don't even know who is doing all of this. How can I defend against something when I don't even know what it is?" Taylor asked, shifting back enough that she could look up at him. Her eyes were moist, and Quinn could see the turmoil of emotions swimming in them. "Every place I go, something happens, and I have no idea why."

"You're safe now," Quinn promised, stroking one hand up and down her back. "We'll get you moved into your new place, install a security system if we need to. One way or another we're going to figure this out."

Her eyes still bright with tears, Taylor stared up at him for a minute, and then she turned to nod at the couch. "Do you mind if I lay down out here? I don't want to be in that room by myself."

Quinn nodded. He took her hand and led her to the couch, grabbing the afghan off of the back and spreading it over her after she lay down.

"Thanks, Quinn."

Again Quinn nodded. He sat down on the chair beside her, warmed by the smile she gave him as she reached out and took his hand in hers. Slowly, Quinn rubbed his thumb over the back of her hand, listening to the quiet of the house and to Taylor's breathing as it slowed into a steady rhythm.

For a moment he was transported back in time. He shook his head free of the image of Emily lying on the couch beside him, her hand in his. Instead, he stared down at Taylor as she gave into sleep and wondered just what he was doing here. Logically, he knew that he would have offered to help any of his or Tristan's friends in a similar situation. He also knew that his concern for Taylor went beyond friendship. How far beyond, he wasn't sure. Nor was he sure he wanted to know.

Quinn leaned back in the chair and let his eyes droop closed. He listened to the rhythm of Taylor breathing, still alert to anything out of the ordinary. When footsteps approached twenty minutes later, his eyes opened instantly and focused on Tristan coming down the hall. Tristan motioned for Quinn to join him in the kitchen and then led the way there.

"What's wrong?" Quinn asked in a hushed tone.

"Seth just called." Tristan's voice was grave. "He caught an intruder in my place. The guy was in Taylor's room."

Quinn's eyes widened. "What? Do we know who?"

"The cops haven't identified him yet." Tristan clenched his teeth before continuing. "And I'm afraid Seth wasn't able to ask him any questions."

"Then I gather he was armed."

Tristan nodded. "Yeah, but Seth didn't find that out until after he died. He fell from the balcony when he tried to get away."

"Taylor's going to freak when she hears about this."

"Maybe we shouldn't tell her quite yet," he suggested. "At least until we know more about who this guy is."

"What about Riley?"

Tristan shook his head. "She won't be able to keep something like that from Taylor. Besides, I was going to wait a few days before taking her back to our place anyway. We'll stay here until we're sure the condo is safe."

"Maybe we should hold off on letting Taylor move into her new apartment."

"She isn't going to go for that unless you tell her why." Tristan ran a hand over his face. "The fact that the guy at my place was in Taylor's room reinforces the fact that whoever he is, he was after something she has. Otherwise when he saw she wasn't there, he wouldn't have stuck around."

"Or he was after something he *thinks* she has," Quinn said. "We have to figure out who's behind all of this."

"Maybe once we identify the intruder, we'll be able to narrow it down."

"In the meantime, we need to set up security at Taylor's new apartment, and I'm going to see if Brent will let us start investigating. Or at least bring in NCIS."

"Taylor isn't navy. NCIS won't be able to help," Tristan said.

"But her dad is retired navy, and that was your place that was broken into today," Quinn reminded him.

"That's true. I guess it's worth a try." Tristan nodded. Then he waved at the living room. "Why don't you try to get some sleep? I'll stand watch for a while."

Quinn nodded. He crossed back into the living room, slowing as he passed the couch where Taylor was sleeping. Then he lowered himself into the chair beside her, took her hand in his, and forced himself to close his eyes and fall asleep.

14

QUINN ROLLED THE STIFFNESS OUT of his shoulders as he pushed away from the kitchen table. Riley had insisted on fixing everyone breakfast before they started moving Taylor into her new apartment. With the exception of an overnight bag Taylor had brought inside, all of her belongings were still locked in her parents' van. Tristan had offered to go pick up the furniture she had ordered, and Riley was making noise about doing some shopping with Taylor as soon as they dropped off her luggage.

By unspoken agreement, Tristan and Quinn had already determined that they weren't going to let Taylor or Riley go anywhere alone today. Quinn watched Taylor pick at the muffin in front of her for a few minutes. Then she finally picked up her plate and took it to the counter.

"Taylor, if you're ready, I can go with you and unload the van at your place," Quinn suggested.

Tristan chimed in immediately. "That's a good idea." He turned to look at Riley. "How about you come with me to pick up her furniture, and then we can meet them over at Taylor's apartment?"

Riley nodded her assent, but a hint of suspicion sparked in her eyes. "If that's what you want."

Taylor wrapped up the leftover muffin in plastic wrap and turned to face Quinn. "I'm ready whenever you are."

"Let's go then." Quinn picked up Taylor's overnight bag as she grabbed her purse and keys.

Together they stepped out into the crisp morning air. The sky was cloudless, contrasting against the mature trees in the Palmettas' front yard that were starting to hint at fall.

They climbed into the van, and Taylor began the drive toward her new place. She was silent for several minutes before she finally said, "You know, I was thinking . . ."

"About?" Quinn prompted.

"Maybe that guy you chased off yesterday didn't have anything to do with me." Her shoulders lifted slightly. "I mean, if I had two guys in uniform yelling at me, I'd probably take off too."

"You think Tristan and I are really that scary looking?"

Taylor rolled her eyes. "That's not what I mean."

Quinn was torn. He understood her need to find some explanation for recent events, some way to feel safe again. He also knew that after the incident with Seth earlier that morning, Taylor wasn't safe. "Taylor, there's no way to be sure if that guy was there because of you or if it was just coincidence that I kept seeing him around. Either way, he had to be into something he wasn't supposed to for him to run away from us."

"You can't be sure of that."

Quinn's eyebrows lifted. "He had a getaway driver."

"Okay, I admit that was weird."

"Everything has been weird lately," Quinn muttered. Then he shifted in the passenger seat as Taylor pulled into a parking lot. "This is where you're moving?"

"Yeah," Taylor nodded. "Isn't this a great location?"

Before Quinn could respond, Taylor climbed out of the van and moved to open the back.

"Exactly how did you find this place?" Quinn asked as he stepped beside her and tried to decide if he should be annoyed or amused.

"Actually, Tristan and Riley both told me to check it out." Taylor pulled a box of art supplies from the back of the van and balanced it on her hip as she looked at Quinn. "You know, it was kind of weird that they both suggested this place."

"You could say that." Quinn shook his head and smothered a laugh as amusement won out. He unloaded two suitcases, put them on the ground, and then closed the back of the van before lifting them again. "You'd better lock the van."

Taylor shifted the box she held and hit the lock button.

"What apartment are you in?"

"208."

"Of course," Quinn said, and this time his laughter escaped him.

"What's so funny?"

Before Quinn could answer, Max stepped out of his apartment and waved at them. "Hey, Quinn."

"Max."

"I see you met your new neighbor."

Quinn recognized the confused expression on Taylor's face. "You could say that."

"I'm heading out to run a few errands, but I'll be back by noon," Max said, directing his comment to Taylor. "Let me know if you need anything."

Taylor simply nodded and watched as he pulled a bicycle out of the bike rack in the parking lot and then headed down the street. With a shake of her head, she turned to face Quinn more fully. "Wait a minute. You live here?"

Quinn grinned at her. "Hi, neighbor."

"Unbelievable." Taylor shook her head, caught between laughter and exasperation. "You said you lived a few blocks away. It never dawned on me that Tristan and Riley were trying to get me to move into your complex."

Quinn started for the stairs, his mind still trying to wrap around this new development. "I'm starting to think that they're trying to set us up."

"You think?" Taylor asked, sarcasm dripping from her voice. She followed him to her front door, dug the key out of her pocket, and unlocked it. As soon as they walked inside and set everything down in the living room, she turned to face him again. "So which apartment is yours?"

"That one," Quinn said, pointing to the left. "207."

Taylor's eyes widened. "Next door?"

Quinn nodded. Then he motioned to the door. "Come on. Let's finish unloading, and then we'll figure out some way to get back at Tristan and your sister."

"That's easy," Taylor said. Her voice was casual, but there was vulnerability in her eyes. "Tell them you're dating someone else. That'll throw them off."

Quinn stared down at her, realizing that Taylor was fishing for information. She needed to know how he felt, and whether he was ready to admit it or not, he knew his feelings for Taylor were even stronger now than they had been when he had dated her the first time. He shook his head and managed a smile. "Like they'd believe I'm that stupid. I want to make *them* suffer, not *me*."

Now Taylor's eyebrows lifted with amusement. "Oh really?"

"Yeah, really." Quinn took a step closer and put his hands on her shoulders. He grinned down at her, and humor sparked in his eyes. "Don't worry. We'll think of something."

Taylor followed Quinn back out to the van and unlocked it once more. She lifted another box of art supplies and looked at him with a glint of mischief. "Isn't Tristan afraid of spiders?"

"Maybe I should just thank him for setting this up instead of getting back at him. I have a feeling once you get started, we may have a war on our hands." Quinn laughed. "Then again . . ."

* * *

"Hey, Tristan!" Taylor called as she stepped out of the bathroom into the hallway. "Can you come here for a minute?"

"Yeah, hold on," Tristan called from the bedroom where he and Quinn were putting together her new dresser. "What do you need?"

"I need you to kill the spider in the bathtub." Taylor looked up at him with innocent brown eyes. "You know how much I hate spiders. And this one is huge." She held two fingers wide apart to demonstrate.

Tristan looked at her for a minute and then turned back to the bedroom. "Quinn!"

Quinn's voice echoed out into the hallway. "Don't look at me. I already killed the one in the kitchen. Besides, she's your sister-in-law."

"And she's your girlfriend," Tristan countered.

"Nice try." Quinn sauntered out into the hall. "Family trumps boyfriend. Ask anyone."

Taylor tried not to goggle at Quinn. Did he really did think of her as his girlfriend? She felt a bubble of hope rise inside her, along with a sense of anticipation. What would it be like to feel secure in her relationship with Quinn? Even more, what would it be like to be allowed to hope for a future together?

Reminding herself that she had a role to play, she shook her head and stepped into the bathroom. Taylor leaned down and picked something up. Then she turned and tossed the prickly black object toward Tristan, only to see him jump out of the way.

"Hey!"

Quinn leaned down and picked up the rubber tarantula. Then he grinned at Taylor. "You were right. He's still afraid of them."

Tristan shook his head, half annoyed, half amused. "Very funny."

Taylor nodded and stepped forward. "Yeah, just like convincing me to move in next door to Quinn without me knowing about it."

"In my defense, I didn't know you were going to move into the apartment *next door* to him," Tristan said. Then he grinned. "That was just good luck."

Riley walked into the hallway and shook her head as she grinned at her husband. "You never should have let her know that you don't like spiders."

"Yeah," Tristan agreed. "Momentary lapse in judgment."

"While you guys finish putting the furniture together, I thought I could take Taylor out to get some groceries and pick up some lunch," Riley said.

"We're almost done here," Tristan said quickly. "Why don't you wait a minute, and we'll all go?"

Riley's eyes narrowed. "Since when do you want to go grocery shopping?"

"It's not like I've never seen the inside of a grocery store." Tristan shrugged. "Besides, I thought we could all go out for lunch before heading to the store."

Taylor looked from her sister to her brother-in-law suspiciously. "What's going on?"

"Nothing," Tristan insisted.

Taylor looked past Tristan now and focused on Quinn. "Quinn?"

Quinn shifted his weight from one foot to the other. "We just don't want you to be alone, okay?"

"I won't be alone. I'll be with Riley," Taylor said. Then she noticed the concern flare in Tristan's eyes. "You don't want Riley alone with me either."

Tristan shook his head. "I know we're probably being overprotective, but just humor us. Okay?"

Taylor looked from Tristan to Quinn, not sure how to feel about the fact that they didn't believe she would be safe if she went somewhere on her own. She understood their concerns, but she ached for a sense of normalcy and the knowledge that she could find it soon. Taylor let out a sigh. "Okay. If you want to go grocery shopping with us, I won't stop you." Then the corners of her mouth lifted. "But you're buying lunch."

15

QUINN STOOD NEXT TO TRISTAN'S truck in the parking lot, alternating between watching the door to Taylor's apartment and checking out the road. He gave a sideways glance to Tristan and asked, "Did Seth tell you anything about the guy from last night?"

"All I know is that he didn't survive the fall," Tristan told him. Then he pointed at the little black coupe headed toward them. "There's Seth now."

The car turned the corner into the parking lot with a sassy squeal of the tires and then came to a screeching halt next to Tristan's truck. A moment later, both doors opened. Vanessa nimbly climbed out from behind the wheel as Seth somehow managed to unfold his six-foot-seven frame from the passenger side.

Seth glared over the top of the car at his wife. "Why did I agree to let you drive?"

Vanessa gave him an innocent shrug and suppressed a smile. "Probably because you didn't have enough adventure in your life."

"Right." Seth shook his head and turned to look at Quinn and Tristan.

Before he could offer any information, Quinn asked, "What did the cops say?"

"Not much, but it's in NCIS's hands now anyway. Our old friend Larry Steinert is in charge of the case," Seth told them, referring to the NCIS special agent who had been involved in a case with them a few months earlier. "He asked me to have you both meet him at Tristan's place."

"Now?" Tristan asked, glancing up at Taylor's apartment.

Seth nodded. "I thought Vanessa could stay here with Riley and Taylor while we meet with him."

Vanessa rounded her car and stepped next to Seth. She seemed to sense Tristan's and Quinn's hesitation because she gave them a not-so-subtle look of challenge. "Would you feel better if I told you that I'm carrying?"

Quinn and Tristan looked at each other. Both men nodded. They understood her terminology perfectly. She was telling them that she was armed.

"Good," Vanessa said and patted her purse. "Then you should feel better."

Tristan's posture relaxed slightly. "Riley and Taylor don't know about what happened last night."

"Why not?"

"Taylor is already having a hard enough time with the idea that someone is following her," Quinn told her. "She doesn't need to know about this until we can give her some answers."

"Are you sure she doesn't know anything about why someone's following her?" Vanessa asked skeptically. "These kinds of things don't happen without a reason."

Quinn shook his head. "The only thing we know is that someone seems extremely interested in her paintings."

"But we don't have any idea why," Tristan added.

"I'll see if I can get any more information out of her," Vanessa offered. "Maybe I can put some of my CIA training to good use."

"I really don't think she's holding anything back from us," Quinn insisted.

"You're probably right," Vanessa conceded. "But I'll bet she knows more than she realizes. She just doesn't know what details are important."

"Good luck," Tristan told her. "At this point, we'll take all the help we can get."

Seth leaned down and kissed Vanessa good-bye. "Be careful."

"I will." Vanessa stepped away from the truck as all three men climbed in. "Call me when you're done so I know when to expect you."

"Will do."

* * *

"Vanessa!" Taylor stepped forward and hugged the dark-skinned woman standing at her door. "What are you doing here?"

"The boys wanted to go out and play for a while, so I thought I'd see if you need any help getting settled into your new place." Vanessa stepped inside amid the clutter of shopping bags, suitcases, and art supplies. She lifted a hand in greeting when she saw Riley standing in the kitchen doorway. "Hi, Riley."

"Hey, Vanessa." Riley smiled at her. "Did I hear you say you came to help out?"

"Sure. Where do you want me to start?"

"Help me convince my sister that she needs to set up her kitchen *before* she organizes her art supplies," Riley suggested.

Taylor rolled her eyes. "Riley knows more about where to put things in the kitchen than I do." She waved a hand at the heavy-duty shelves that were situated in the living room where an entertainment unit would logically go. "Besides, Quinn is going to be pretty annoyed that I convinced him to set my shelves up today if I'm not even going to use them."

"Fine." Riley let out an exasperated sigh. "Set up your art supplies, but I don't want you calling me in the middle of the night when you can't find your blender."

Taylor watched Riley disappear back into the kitchen, and she grinned at Vanessa. "I don't even have a blender."

Vanessa chuckled. "By the way, I have to tell you that Seth and I get so many compliments on that painting you gave us as a wedding gift. That was so sweet of you to give it to us."

"It was great that you ended up honeymooning in Europe where I could give it to you in person," Taylor reminded her. She hadn't met Vanessa before she had married Seth, but when Riley had told her that Seth was taking his new bride to Venice for their honeymoon, they had brainstormed together for the perfect gift. That gift had been a landscape Taylor painted near Seth and Vanessa's hotel.

Riley had made arrangements for them to meet Taylor in Venice and pick it up, and Taylor had instantly hit it off with Vanessa. They had been corresponding ever since.

Vanessa pointed at one of the open boxes filled with paints. "How about I start helping you put these away?"

"Actually, if you can just hand them to me, that would be great," Taylor told her. "Getting them organized is half the battle."

"Sure." Vanessa nodded. "So tell me about Europe. I want to hear about everything."

"Okay, but remember," Taylor grinned at her, "you asked for it."

* * *

Special Agent Larry Steinert was standing next to Tristan's front door when Quinn, Seth, and Tristan approached. "Gentlemen."

"Steinert," Seth said by way of a greeting. "Any news on the body?"

"Why don't we take this inside?" Steinert suggested. He lifted a section of yellow tape that read "Do Not Cross" in capital letters and waited for all three men to duck under it before following them inside and closing the door behind him.

"Well?" Quinn asked impatiently.

"We have an ID on the intruder," Steinert told them as they all sat down in the living room. "Nicholas Orton, twenty-nine years old. He did six months in a juvie facility for petty theft when he was seventeen, and then a few years ago he graduated to bank fraud."

"What about his weapon?" Seth asked. "Any leads on where he got it?"

"It was a Mark 23, unregistered." Steinert scratched at a spot just below his ear. "My guess is that he bought it off of the street somewhere."

"Or whoever hired him gave it to him."

"It's possible. This guy doesn't seem like the mastermind type," Steinert agreed. "We checked out his apartment in Yorktown, but that didn't turn up much except for a few weeks' worth of mail. None of the neighbors have seen him for the past three weeks either."

"Any kind of credit card activity that would tell us where he's been staying for the past few weeks?" Seth asked.

Steinert shook his head. "He received a money transfer of ten thousand dollars about a month ago, and then he made a large cash withdrawal about the same time he dropped off the map. We're guessing he's been paying for a hotel room somewhere with cash." He paused for a moment, the corner of his lips lifting slightly. "We did find a copy of a train schedule in his place though. Our best guess is that he spent some time in New York City."

"New York?" Quinn said tensely.

Steinert's eyes sharpened. "You have any idea why he'd be in New York?"

Quinn looked at Tristan, a chilling understanding passing between them. "Taylor made a stop in New York on her way back from Europe. She was there for about two weeks." Quinn did the mental calculations, and his lips drew into a thin line. "She would have arrived there about three weeks ago."

"Who's Taylor?"

"My sister-in-law, Taylor Palmetta," Tristan offered. "The intruder was in her room."

"Any idea why?" Steinert asked now.

"Whatever this guy was after has something to do with Taylor's paintings," Quinn told him impatiently. He and Tristan then proceeded to tell Steinert about the events since Taylor's arrival, beginning with the incident with her car down to the man Quinn had seen lurking around Tristan's condo.

Steinert punched a couple of buttons on his Blackberry and turned it so Quinn could see it. A photo of a man's face filled the screen, clearly taken at the morgue. "Is this the man you saw outside of this building yesterday?"

Quinn stared at the image for a long moment and then slowly shook his head as his eyes lifted to meet Steinert's. "That's not him."

"Can I see?" Tristan asked, reaching out to take the Blackberry so he could get a closer look. Then he too shook his head before handing it back. "It could have been the driver yesterday, but neither one of us got a good look at him."

"So we still have someone out there, and we don't know why," Steinert said bluntly. "My instinct would be to assign a protection detail to Miss Palmetta, but so far no one has threatened her with any physical harm. Not to mention the fact that she isn't navy or an immediate family member of anyone in the navy."

"Actually, her father is retired navy."

"That will help. I should be able to use that to help me access the files for the other incidents. Maybe we can find a common link."

Tristan nodded his approval. "Quinn and I started looking through photos of Taylor's paintings. We're starting to wonder if she inadvertently painted something she wasn't supposed to see."

"If the two paintings that were lost in the fire were similar, that's a good possibility."

"I don't think we're going to be able to narrow that down until Taylor goes up to New York to identify which paintings were burned. The photos at the gallery are missing."

Quinn looked over at Tristan with apprehension. "Taylor's planning on going back to New York?"

"Her agent wants her to come up sometime this week." Tristan nodded. "I thought I would put in for some leave so I could go up with her."

"But that would leave Riley home alone," Seth commented. "Unless she wants to stay with us."

Quinn interrupted before Tristan could respond. "I'll go to New York with Taylor."

Tristan looked at him, surprised. "You would do that?"

"It's no big deal," Quinn said casually. "You need to keep Riley safe, and no one seems to have tied me to Taylor. It makes sense that I be the one to go."

Steinert looked at each of the SEALs with interest and then moved to stand. He motioned to Quinn. "I'll want you to stop by my office to work up a composite sketch of the man you chased off yesterday," he said and offered his card to Quinn and then another one to Tristan.

"Can it wait until Monday? I don't want to leave Taylor alone for long."

"That's fine. In fact, I'll send our guy to you first thing on Monday."

"We'd better make it afternoon. We've got a training exercise in the morning."

"Monday afternoon then." He nodded. "For now I'll start looking into those other case files. Let me know if you all turn up anything on your end."

"Thanks. We'll let you know if we find any new leads." Tristan stood and turned to look at Seth. "But for now, I want to know exactly how this guy got into my place."

Seth stood as well. "Come on. I'll walk you through what I saw."

16

Taylor wasn't sure what was going on with Tristan and his buddies, but she had the distinct image of a bunch of early pioneers circling the wagons to guard their women. She felt both protected and stifled to see that they were apparently considering her one of their own.

With the exception of leaving them alone with Vanessa for an hour earlier in the day, Taylor couldn't think of a single minute that one of the Saint Squad hadn't been at her new apartment. She thought that after everyone finished eating the pizza they had ordered for dinner they would all take off for home, but that hadn't happened. Riley seemed determined to wash and put away every dish in her kitchen, and Vanessa was currently staring at Taylor's laptop screen with Tristan and Quinn as they scrolled through the photos of her paintings.

Seth had somehow finagled a local security company to come out on a Saturday evening and even now was overseeing the installation of her new security system, a security system she hadn't even planned on getting.

When her cell phone rang, she pushed that thought aside and pulled her phone out of her back pocket. She answered it to find Gary Holloway on the other end, letting her know that the paintings she had left with him were framed and ready to be picked up.

Taylor had been on the verge of asking him if he could hold onto them for a week or two for her until he commented that he was leaving town in a few days and was worried about leaving her artwork at his house without anyone home. After promising him that she would come over and pick them up in the next day or two, she hung up the phone in time to see Seth walk the security specialist out of the apartment.

Quinn abandoned his spot at her new kitchen table and wandered toward her. "Is everything okay?"

Taylor nodded, but she motioned to the keypad for the new security system. "Do you really think all of this is necessary?"

"Yes," Quinn said without hesitation. Then he reached out and gave her hand a squeeze. "Relax. I would have suggested this even without everything going on. When you live this close to the beach, it pays to have a security system."

"Do you have a security system in your apartment too?" Taylor asked, her eyebrows lifting.

"Yeah." Quinn nodded. "When you're gone for weeks, sometimes months at a time, it's nice to know that all of your stuff will be there when you get back."

"I guess I never really thought about it." Taylor shrugged. "I mean, who would be stupid enough to steal from a Navy SEAL?"

"Someone who knows I'm not home." Quinn gave her a wry grin, and then he motioned to the phone she still held in her hand. "Who was that on the phone?"

"An old friend," Taylor told him. She angled her head and considered for a minute. "Can I ask a favor?"

Quinn nodded. "Sure. What do you need?"

"I need to go pick up some paintings I had framed, and I was hoping you would come with me."

"Where are they?"

"Norfolk," Taylor told him. "I took them to a friend who used to frame all of my paintings when I was in high school. After everything that's happened, I don't want to leave them at his house for long."

"You really think you should bring them to your apartment?"

"I don't know." Taylor shrugged. "I'm starting to wonder if there's anyplace where they'll be safe."

Quinn considered for a moment. "I think I have an idea."

"What?"

"Did I ever mention to you that our offices are in a secure building with a bunch of armed men running around outside?"

"I kind of figured," Taylor said. "But what does that have to do with anything?"

"I was just thinking that our offices could use some redecorating," Quinn told her. "And your paintings might be safest if they are hidden in plain sight."

Awareness filled Taylor's eyes. "I think I like your idea."

"Good." Quinn motioned to Taylor's keys. "Let's go now before it gets too late."

Taylor pointed across the room where Tristan and Vanessa were still scrolling through the pictures on her laptop. "I hate to leave while everyone is still here."

"Everyone's about done here anyway," Quinn told her. He motioned to Seth. "Let's show you how to use your new security system, and then we'll get going."

"Okay," Taylor said, still a bit overwhelmed with all of the help everyone had offered. She crossed the room with Quinn to where the security keypad had been installed near the front door. As Seth began to instruct her on how to use it, she hoped that maybe tonight she would finally feel safe.

* * *

"I don't understand why we can't stay at our place tonight," Riley said for the third time as Tristan drove toward her parents' house. "Taylor is all settled into her new apartment, and none of her paintings are there. Besides, I thought you had Seth put in some kind of security system at our condo yesterday. Surely it's safe to go home."

"Just humor me, okay?" Tristan pleaded. "I'm not willing to take any chances with your safety."

Riley shifted in her seat and studied her husband more closely. Her eyes narrowed suspiciously. "What aren't you telling me?"

"What do you mean?"

"Tristan." Riley stared at him, waiting.

Tristan clenched his teeth and then gave a subtle shake of his head. "Seth ran into some unexpected problems yesterday when he was installing the security system. I'm not convinced we've worked out all of the kinks yet."

Riley's eyebrows lifted. She could tell he was still holding something back by the way he was avoiding specifics. "And?" she prompted as Tristan parked at her parents' house.

"And what?" Tristan asked, an uncharacteristic edge in his voice. He climbed out of the car and led her inside.

Riley waited until they were inside and the door was closed behind them before she reached for his arm, stopping him before he could put any distance between them. "Tristan, I know you're really worried about what's going on. I am too," she said. "You need to stop trying so hard to protect me. I do have a degree in criminal psychology. Maybe I can help."

Tristan stared down at her for a moment, and she could see in his eyes that he was debating. She reached up to kiss him, hoping to soothe away the worry. She was surprised when he pulled her tightly against him in a crushing embrace. His voice was barely louder than a whisper when he said softly, "I am really worried."

"Please tell me what's going on," Riley said, shifting away from him enough that she could see his face.

Slowly, Tristan nodded, taking her hand and leading her toward the couch. "But you're going to want to sit down for this."

* * *

"Would you like to sit down?" Gary motioned to the living room couch. "I just want to grab my camera so I can photograph the finished work before we pack everything up." He took a step toward the hallway off to the left before winking at Taylor. "I have a feeling that someday I'm going to want proof that I really did frame paintings for Taylor Palmetta."

"I doubt that," Taylor laughed, some of her earlier tension easing.

Quinn waited for her to take a seat before sitting down beside her. "How long have you known Gary?"

"About ten years. His daughter Zoe and I were friends all during high school," Taylor told him. "She's in grad school now at USC, but I usually pop in to say hi when I'm in town." Taylor smiled at him. "Even when I don't have any paintings I need to have framed."

"Does that ever happen?" Quinn asked with a shake of his head. "I still can't believe how many paintings you did last year. It must have cost a small fortune to ship them all back."

"Oh yeah. Especially when I was in Italy. " Taylor nodded. "I'm lucky my agent started taking care of all of the shipping arrangements after I signed with her; otherwise, I would have literally spent another thousand dollars to ship the rest of my pieces home."

"It sounds like you're going to have to sell a lot of paintings to pay for it all."

Taylor grinned at him. "I'm planning on it."

Gary walked back into the room carrying one of the newly framed paintings. "What do you think?"

Taylor moved closer to run a finger along the top edge of the frame. "You did a great job on this."

Beside her, Quinn could only stare. The dark wood frame was nice enough, he supposed, but he couldn't get past the paint that filled the canvas. Taylor had captured the movement on a crowded city street, cars competing for space on narrow roads, pedestrians moving along uneven sidewalks. To the left was a red and white striped awning over wrought-iron tables that made up a sidewalk café. He could almost smell the pasta the waiter was carrying, and he could imagine the blaring horns and the car engines sounding.

He was vaguely aware of Taylor talking to Gary, some discussion of preparing the paintings so they wouldn't be damaged when they were moved.

Taylor touched his arm and motioned for him to follow Gary, who had headed back down the hall. "Come on. Let's see how the other ones turned out."

"Hey, Taylor," Quinn said, reaching for her hand.

"Yeah?"

"You'll still remember me when you're rich and famous, right?"

Taylor's laughter rang out. "Quinn, I could never forget you."

Quinn nodded, an odd sense of satisfaction pulsing through him. "Just making sure."

17

THE SUN WAS BARELY UP Sunday morning when Taylor pushed off her brand-new comforter and climbed out of her brand-new bed. She had hardly slept despite the fact that Quinn had practically tucked her into bed the night before and was even now sleeping in the apartment next door. The security system was on. In fact, if activated, she had a feeling the entire building would hear it go off.

She stretched her hands over her head, trying to shake off the last lingering effects of a restless night's sleep. She took a quick shower and then pulled on an old pair of jeans along with her favorite sweater, one she had purchased in Milan last winter.

After packing up some supplies and grabbing her cell phone, she slipped on her sandals and stepped into the cool morning air. Instinctively, she looked around, relieved that no one was visible except for a few cars driving by. Part of her wanted to stay locked inside her apartment, but on another level, she knew she was going to go stir crazy if she didn't give herself some time outside, some time alone. She hoped an hour or two on the beach would help her relax and find the sense of normalcy she craved.

She glanced at the door she now knew belonged to Quinn and noticed that there weren't any lights on. She also had the odd realization that she had yet to be invited inside.

As she passed by his door, she found herself wondering how he lived when he was at home. When they had started dating more than a year ago, he had been on assignment in North Carolina where she had just finished college. At the time, she had been preparing to move overseas, and he had spent his days working with the other members of the Saint Squad, developing a course for law enforcement officers.

During their evenings, they had been together often, usually going out to dinner or dancing, bowling or to a movie. Sometimes Quinn and his friends had spent their free time in the apartment that Riley and Taylor had shared throughout college, and other times they had enjoyed the hiking trails and the lake nearby. But never could she remember going to hang out at his temporary quarters, even though Riley had gone there occasionally to see Tristan.

She supposed she would see the inside of Quinn's apartment soon enough now that they were neighbors. He had already asked her for a ride to church since he had lent his car to a friend for the weekend. Taylor pulled her cell phone out and checked the time. 7:04. Quinn had told her that their church wasn't until eleven. That would give her at least three hours to relax before she needed to head back and get ready.

When she arrived at the beach, it was quiet except for a few surfers a short distance away. Taylor looked over her shoulder, satisfied that she hadn't been followed. Then she walked onto the sand and sat down several yards away from the water. Pulling her pad out of her bag, she grabbed a hunk of charcoal and let herself get lost in the simplicity of the moment.

* * *

Panic skittered along Quinn's spine as he pounded on Taylor's door again. He had come over nearly an hour earlier to check on her after he had called her on the phone and she hadn't picked up. When she hadn't answered her door either, he had assumed that she was in the shower, but he knew her well enough to know that it didn't take her this long to get ready for church, not to mention that she wasn't the type to get ready for anything two hours early.

The overhead light was on in the living room, a light that had definitely been turned off when he had left her apartment the night before, and still the pounding on her front door wasn't yielding the desired results. Pulling his cell phone out of his pocket, he dialed her number again. Relief pulsed through him when she answered with a casual hello.

"Where are you?" Quinn demanded, not stopping to consider how abrupt his tone might sound.

"I'm at the beach," Taylor said slowly. "Where are you?"

"Standing outside your apartment."

"It's not time for church already, is it?"

"No." Quinn shook his head and started for the stairs. "What are you doing at the beach? You shouldn't be out by yourself."

"Yes, Daddy." Taylor said, and Quinn could visualize the smirk that was surely on her face.

"Where on the beach are you?"

"Quinn, I'm fine," Taylor told him. "I just needed some fresh air and some time to relax. I'll be back in plenty of time to get ready for church."

"Of that I have little doubt," Quinn muttered and then hung up his phone. He broke into an easy jog, his cell phone still in his hand. A couple minutes later he spotted her sitting on the sand, the ends of her red hair blowing in the breeze. Instinctively, he looked around and surveyed the area.

Three surfers were standing on the beach, their boards in hand as though they were getting ready to leave. A young father was walking along the water's edge a short distance away with two little girls scampering along behind him holding plastic buckets and looking for seashells. The shops along the boardwalk had yet to open, with the exception of a surf shop a block away, but it didn't look like it was doing any business at the moment.

Quinn walked toward Taylor, slowing as he approached. The tension he had noticed in her shoulders the night before was now visibly absent, her legs crossed in front of her as she stared out at the water. Then he realized that her hand was moving, and his focus shifted to the pad of paper she held in her lap. He stopped angling toward her, amazed at the way she moved the hunk of charcoal over the paper in seemingly random motions and managed to capture the feeling of the moment.

He realized now that it wasn't the water she was watching but rather the surfers. The sketch revealed all three men, their surfboards standing vertically in the sand as they stood casually and chatted. One had stripped his wetsuit down to his waist, and Taylor had captured the water gleaming off of his back as clearly as the stripe down the center of his board. Quinn stared at her hand moving until she finally slowed her strokes and then used the edge of her thumb to lighten one of the lines.

"This is how you relax, huh?" Quinn asked, finally taking those last few steps so he was standing beside her.

Startled, Taylor turned and looked up at him, lifting a hand to shade her eyes. She took a breath as though trying to steady her nerves and then managed a smile. "Hi." She looked around the beach and then stared back up at him. "Are you checking up on me?"

Quinn shrugged and then sat down on the sand beside her. "It's a nice day out. I thought I'd come see what you were up to."

"Really?" Taylor looked at him quizzically.

"I also wanted to make sure you weren't hanging out on the beach by your sister's place all alone when there are possibly people after you," Quinn admitted. "You can't blame me for worrying after the week you've had."

Taylor gave him a timid smile. "You're sweet to worry."

"Sweet?" Quinn grimaced. "Please don't say that around any of the guys."

Her smile widened. "Afraid I'll ruin your bad boy image?"

Quinn flashed her a grin now. "It's not an image."

"Right." Taylor chuckled. She closed her sketchbook and then looked over at him. "All of the bad boys I know spend their Sunday mornings checking up on their neighbors before going to church."

Quinn wiggled his eyebrows. "Maybe I'm undercover."

"Oh, I'm sure that's it." Taylor slid her supplies back into her bag and then stood up. She hesitated briefly before offering a hand to Quinn. "Are you going to walk me home?"

"Maybe." Quinn took her hand and let her help pull him to a stand. He then took a step toward the road keeping her hand in his. His eyes scanned the area, and again he didn't see anything suspicious. Maybe Taylor's move was exactly what was needed to keep her safe.

"I meant to ask you, how are you getting to work tomorrow if you don't have a car?" Taylor asked.

"Tristan will pick me up on his way in."

Taylor nodded absently and fell silent.

"Why?"

"I was just wondering." Taylor's shoulders lifted. "I need to figure out how I'm getting to the train station tomorrow, but I think I'll probably just take my mom's van and leave it in the parking lot."

"Where are you going tomorrow?" Quinn asked.

"New York." Taylor's eyebrows drew together as she looked at him. "I told you my agent wants me to go up there to help identify the damaged paintings."

"I didn't know you were planning to go tomorrow," Quinn told her, suddenly apprehensive. "What time is your train?"

"I haven't gotten my ticket yet, but I thought I'd take the one that leaves at nine-thirty."

"Can you push it off for a day?" Quinn asked. "We have a training exercise tomorrow I can't get out of, but after that I should be able to take a few days off so I can go with you."

"You're going to come with me to New York?" Taylor looked at him, and Quinn saw the surprise in her eyes.

"Is that okay?" Quinn stared back at her, an unexpected streak of insecurity pulsing through him. "I mean, is there a reason you don't want me to come? Some boyfriend up there I don't know about?"

"Hardly. I just didn't expect you to take off work and everything just because of a fire." She stopped walking and tightened her grip on his hand so he would stop too. Her emotions were raw. "Do you know why all of this stuff has been happening to me?"

"No, but I'm not going to rest easy until we find out," Quinn promised. He slipped his arms around her, hoping to reassure her. Her hands came around his waist, and Quinn noticed the way Taylor clung tightly to him as though he were her lifeline. He could almost feel her expectations crashing over him, but he couldn't manage to pull himself free. For once, he wasn't sure he wanted to. Instead, he stared down at her, wondering how he was supposed to handle the rush of emotions Taylor kept pulling out of him.

Insecurity filled Taylor's voice. "Are you sure you can get leave to come with me?"

"I'll work something out," he promised, more than a little surprised at the way Taylor's needs had become such a priority in his life. He gave her a reassuring smile as he tugged on her hand to start her down the street once more. "Besides, after what happened in Paris, I don't want you staying anywhere alone."

Taylor stopped walking again and looked at him warily. "You can't honestly expect me to share a hotel room with you."

Again, Quinn nudged her into motion. "We'll get a suite. His and hers rooms."

Taylor managed a smile. "Has anyone ever told you that you're very overprotective?"

"I have three younger sisters," Quinn reminded her. "Of course they have."

18

"WHAT'S WITH THE NEW ARTWORK?" Jay asked when he walked into Quinn's and Tristan's office on Monday morning.

"We're redecorating," Quinn said simply.

"Oh, okay," Jay said, accepting the brief explanation. He held out a set of keys to Quinn. "Thanks for letting me use your car this weekend."

"No problem." Quinn took the keys and then considered for a moment. "Have you had a chance to call about your car yet?"

"Yeah, I called the service station, and they said they have to order the part. It should be in by Wednesday."

"In that case, why don't you hang onto these until then?" Quinn suggested. "I'm heading out of town tomorrow anyway, so I won't need it."

"Where to?" Jay asked as Brent walked through the door.

Brent's eyebrows lifted as his eyes met Quinn's. "Yeah. Where to?"

Quinn gave Brent an awkward grin. "Hi, Brent. I need to talk to you about taking some leave."

"So I heard. What's going on?" Then he waved at two of the paintings on the wall. "And where did these come from?"

Before Quinn could respond, Seth wandered into the office, looked at Quinn and Tristan, and asked, "Did you tell him yet?"

"Tell me what?" Brent looked over at Seth.

Seth closed the door and motioned to where Tristan was sitting at his desk. "We had an incident at Tristan's place this weekend."

"What kind of incident?" Brent asked.

"The kind that involved the coroner," Seth told him. He went on to explain what happened.

"I must be completely out of the loop here." Brent shifted his attention to Tristan. "Explain to me why Seth was putting up surveillance at your place."

Tristan explained the events since Taylor had arrived in Virginia Beach and their concerns that Taylor may have inadvertently painted something she wasn't supposed to see.

"This is crazy." Brent looked at Quinn. "Have we looked at these paintings?"

"The four that we hung up here are the ones that were in her car," Tristan told him. "Quinn thought they would be safer here than with Taylor."

Brent nodded in agreement. "Smart move. Even if someone thinks to look here, they'd never get past the guards at the front door without being noticed."

"Exactly," Quinn said. "And I don't want them in an empty apartment while Taylor and I are in New York."

"Which brings me back to my original question." Brent's eyebrows rose. "Why do you need to take leave?"

"Taylor has to go up to New York to identify which two paintings of hers were damaged. After what happened in Paris, I don't want her traveling alone."

Brent looked from Quinn to Tristan. Then he looked back at Quinn with a new understanding. "What are the chances that all of these incidents could be tied to our national security?"

"I don't know," Quinn answered impatiently.

In response, Brent gave Quinn a deliberate and meaningful stare.

It took several seconds for Quinn to catch on. Then he cocked his head to one side. "Actually," he said slowly, trying to gather his thoughts. "It could be very relevant to our national security. In fact, there's a sketch artist from NCIS who's coming over to meet with me this afternoon."

Tristan suppressed a smile. "If Taylor did paint something important enough for someone to try to steal, we owe it to her to find out what it was."

"And I'm sure NCIS would appreciate the help in finding a motive for this guy that broke into Tristan's place," Seth added.

Beside him, Jay looked at each of his teammates, the confusion obvious on his face. "Is this one of those times that I'm not supposed to ask any questions?"

The other four members of the Saint Squad all nodded in unison.

Seth put a hand on Jay's shoulder. "Don't worry, Jay. You'll learn how to read our minds eventually."

"But for now, go see if you can find Amy," Brent told him. "I need to see what's on the training schedule, but as of this afternoon, Quinn, you're on protection detail."

Jay had taken a step toward the door, but now he turned around to look at Brent. "What about the rest of us?"

"I think it may be time to hone up on some of our investigative skills," Brent told him cryptically as the door opened and Amy walked in.

"There you guys are." Amy looked at them impatiently. "You need to get going. You have a dive in less than two hours."

"We're coming," Brent told her. Then he turned to look at Quinn. "You realize you won't be able to fly for a couple of days since we're diving today."

Quinn nodded. "We're taking the train."

"In that case, let's go."

Amy looked at all of them, confused. "Who's taking the train?'

* * *

Taylor parked her mom's van in the parking lot of the train station in Williamsburg where Tristan and Riley would pick it up later in the day. Then she shifted to face Quinn. "Are you really sure you don't mind coming with me?"

"Why do you keep asking me that?"

"I don't know." She let out a sigh, grasping at some way to explain her insecurities. How could she ask if he was coming because he cared about her or if he was just doing a favor for Tristan? She was almost afraid to hope that his feelings for her might mirror what she felt for him. She could also admit, at least to herself, that she had once again begun visualizing a future that included Quinn in it. After what happened the last time she had let herself dream of such a future, she needed to know how Quinn felt.

Quinn's eyes narrowed. "Is this going to be one of those 'where does our relationship stand' kind of talks?"

A little surprised that he seemed to have picked up on her thoughts, she shrugged. "Maybe."

"Taylor, stop analyzing everything," Quinn insisted. "You matter to me, okay? I'm coming with you because I want to make sure that you're safe. It's as simple as that."

She stared at him for a long moment and knew that their history together was anything but simple. "There's something I need to know," Taylor said, forcing the words out before she could reconsider. "What happened at Tristan and Riley's wedding that made you not want to see me anymore?"

Quinn shifted in his seat to face her, his eyes unreadable. Then he let out a sigh. "I'm sorry, Taylor. It wasn't anything you did." He paused for a moment as though trying to choose his words carefully. "I guess it freaked me out when everyone kept talking about us getting married. I wasn't ready to deal with it, especially with us living on different continents. Does that make any sense?"

Taylor considered his words. Then slowly she nodded. "I guess so, but I'm not sure where I stand with you now."

Quinn's eyes met hers. "I'm worried about you."

"Is that all?" Taylor managed to ask.

"No, that's not all." Quinn shifted in his seat and reached out to run his fingers through her hair. Slowly, he leaned forward and kissed her gently.

As soon as his lips were on hers, Taylor felt her world spinning out of control. Slowly, her insecurities melted away and warmth seeped through her. Her survival instinct faded as Quinn changed the angle of the kiss, and she lost herself in the sensation. She wanted to protect herself from being hurt again, but she no longer knew how.

When Quinn pulled away, his eyes were dark, and he looked as overwhelmed as she felt. A shiver ran through her as he continued to play with her hair, and her reality came into focus. As scared as she was of being hurt again, it was already too late. She was already hopelessly in love with Quinn.

Quinn's voice was low when he spoke once more. "I really did miss you while you were gone. I'm here because I want to spend time with you now." Then a slow smile crossed his face. "Of course, I'm not sure that I'm likely to take you to another smoothie bar anytime soon."

The corners of Taylor's mouth curved up. "I thought Navy SEALs liked adventure."

"Some adventures are more embarrassing than others." Quinn pushed his door open. "Come on. Let's go get our tickets."

Together they gathered their bags, locked the van, and headed for the train station. After they bought their tickets, they joined the handful of others on the platform to wait for the train. Quinn led Taylor to a bench that was on the far end of the platform and then sat down with her so he could see everyone else who was there.

"You don't really think anyone could follow us, do you? No one even knows where I live," Taylor asked skeptically. "Or are you just being paranoid?"

"Overprotective, maybe. Emily used to call it my 'big brother syndrome,'" Quinn said. Then his eyes darkened as he turned to look at Taylor, his face suddenly unreadable.

Not quite sure what had caused his change of mood, she asked, "You have three younger sisters, right?"

"Yeah," Quinn said, the tension apparently easing out of him. "My family is constantly after me and Tristan to visit more often, but my sisters keep my folks pretty busy, especially now that Cassie is expecting a baby."

"Will this be their first grandchild?"

Quinn smiled now and nodded. "My mom is thrilled. She's been waiting for her first grandbaby for a long time."

"How long has your sister been married?"

"About two years."

"That's not too long of a wait then."

Quinn's smile dimmed, and he nodded absently. Taylor studied him for a moment, sensing that there was a deeper meaning to his words, a meaning she couldn't understand.

A look of relief crossed his face when the sound of a train rumbling toward them vibrated through the air. Quinn stood up, but Taylor remained seated and simply stared at him. She had always appreciated the way Quinn was so readable. Even though he didn't typically say a whole lot, he was straightforward in his words and actions. Before today, Taylor had always felt that Quinn was exactly who he appeared to be.

She knew him to be a dedicated Navy SEAL, someone with a strong testimony of the gospel of Jesus Christ and a man who was still enjoying the single life because that was the way he wanted to live. Never before had she ever felt like there was anything he wasn't willing to talk about. Now she wasn't so sure, and she found herself suddenly unsettled.

As the train came into view and Quinn picked up their bags, Taylor realized that she didn't know him nearly as well as she thought she did. She also realized as she stood up beside him that she didn't just want to know more. She needed to know everything. Now she could only wonder if there would ever be a time when he would trust her enough to share whatever secrets he was keeping.

19

QUINN RETRIEVED THEIR SUITCASES FROM the trunk of the cab as he listened to the typical sounds of Manhattan. A constant flow of people moved past them on the sidewalk, horns honked, and sirens sounded in the distance. Exhaust fumes and the lingering scent of hot dogs from a nearby vender assaulted his senses.

Taylor stepped up onto the sidewalk near the uniformed doorman at the entrance to their hotel. One hand gripped the strap of the leather bag slung over her shoulder, and her other hand rested on the laptop case that hung from her other shoulder. Her eyes shifted from side to side as she watched everyone who passed by.

She seemed different now than she had when they had first boarded the train nearly eight hours earlier, but Quinn couldn't quite put his finger on why. He supposed part of it was her obvious ease and comfort in the city. While he had hauled their suitcases out of the train station, she had effortlessly hailed a taxi and rattled off the address of their destination from memory.

During the cab ride, she had been oddly quiet, but he sensed that she was absorbing every sight and sound of the city, soaking it all in as if she couldn't get enough of it. Quinn stepped up onto the sidewalk beside her, and the doorman immediately pulled the door open for them.

"Have you stayed here before?" Quinn asked her as he followed her through the brightly lit lobby toward the registration desk.

"No." Taylor shook her head. "I didn't think it would be a good idea to stay at the same place as last time." She lowered her voice. "Just in case someone really is following me. And I hope you don't mind, but I put the reservation under your name."

"That's fine," Quinn said, a bit surprised that Taylor had thought to take such precautions.

Taylor smiled at the desk clerk. "Hi, we have a reservation. The name is Lambert."

"Yes, Ms. Lambert." She began punching keys on the keyboard even as Quinn felt his stomach clench at the clerk's assumption that he and Taylor shared the same last name.

The clerk retrieved some paperwork from a file and set it in front of Taylor. "Please sign here."

Taylor glanced over at Quinn. In unspoken understanding, he reached for the paperwork and signed in the proper place.

A moment later, they had their keys and moved to the elevator. As soon as they were inside, Taylor said, "This is so weird."

"What?"

"Sharing the same hotel room."

"It's a hotel suite," Quinn said, even though he understood her meaning perfectly. "But I know what you mean. At least it's me who's going to be in the next room instead of some hired security guard you don't know."

Taylor's eyebrows lifted. "Yeah, but I wouldn't be dating some random security guard."

"I would hope not." Quinn grinned. Then, with his hands still gripping their suitcases, he leaned forward and kissed her. "And I promise not to take advantage of the situation."

Humor sparked in her eyes. "Much."

Quinn just laughed. "I can tell you really trust me."

"If I didn't trust you, you wouldn't be here," Taylor reminded him as the elevator doors slid open. "Come on. Let's drop off our luggage. Then we can go grab something to eat."

Quinn followed her down the hall, passing a dozen or so rooms before they reached theirs. He noticed the entrance to the stairwell halfway between their destination and the elevator. Then he turned and made sure they weren't being followed as Taylor slid the keycard into the lock and pushed the door open. She took three steps before turning back to look at him.

"Wow," Quinn said, looking around the living area. A rectangular dining table was set off to the side, and the living room was as large as the one in his apartment in Virginia, only this one had better furnishings. He put down their luggage and flipped the security lock behind him. "Dare I even ask how much this place is costing?"

"I'm not sure," Taylor admitted.

Quinn's eyebrows lifted. "You rented a hotel room without knowing the price?"

"Not exactly." Taylor shifted her laptop bag and set it down on the table. "Evan Bridgeton, the owner of the gallery, is taking care of the bill. He insisted on paying for it since the only reason we're here is because of the fire."

"Did he make the reservation?" Quinn asked skeptically.

Taylor shook her head. "No. He pretty much told me to get a reservation wherever I wanted and to send him the bill."

"He must be pretty impressed with your artistic abilities to give you a blank check like that," Quinn told her.

"Evan is the one who is pushing for me to have my own showing next year." Taylor smiled at him. "For a while after I signed with Felicia, I was talking to him more than I was to her."

"I guess in your line of business, it's good to have admirers." Quinn carried their suitcases down the hallway that led to the bedrooms, surprised to see that there were two bathrooms as well. "Which room do you want?"

"It doesn't matter." Taylor picked up the hotel's information packet on the table and began flipping through it as Quinn deposited his suitcase in one room and put Taylor's suitcase in the other. He then did a security check of the room, pleased to see that the windows were sealed shut.

Once he was satisfied that the bedrooms were secure, he headed back into the living room. Taylor glanced up at him and asked, "Where do you want to eat? I'm starving."

"I hate to say it, but it might be better to order in. I'm not sure I want to take the chance of someone seeing you, especially on our first night here."

"Quinn, do you know how many people live in the city?" Taylor looked at him like he was crazy. "What are the chances that anyone would even notice me?"

"About the same as someone chasing you from Paris to New York to Virginia to mess with your paintings."

Taylor stared at him. Then she let out a sigh. "Okay, point taken."

"I'm sure a hotel of this size has a decent room service menu," Quinn told her.

"What about this place?" Taylor pointed to an ad in the hotel restaurant guide. "There's a noodle shop right next door." She turned the page. "Or there's a Mexican food place close by."

"Do they deliver?"

"The noodle shop does." Taylor grinned up at him. "I could go for some lo mein."

"Sounds good," Quinn agreed. He proceeded to check out the living area, again finding nothing of concern. Finally, he picked up the remote and flipped on the television.

Taylor's eyebrows lifted. "Are you going to tell me what you want, or do you want me to just pick something for you?"

"Pick two things you like, and we can share." He sat down on the couch and changed the channels until he got to the evening news. Watching the news was a daily ritual Quinn had started shortly after joining the navy. He liked to say that he was just checking out the scores for whatever sport was in season, but he knew part of the ritual was a way for him to find assurance that he was going to be able to go to bed at night and not get a middle-of-the-night wake-up call telling him to report for duty.

Logically, he knew that he would hear of any real crisis long before the local newscasters, but he still found time to watch the news whenever he was in one place long enough to turn on the TV.

With the restaurant guide still in her hand, Taylor crossed to sit on the couch beside him. She picked up the hotel phone on the end table and called in their order. After she hung up, she leaned back beside him.

"Tired?" Quinn asked, stretching his arm out casually, his hand resting on her shoulder.

"Yeah." Taylor nodded, shifting a little so that her head was resting against him. "How about you?"

"A little." Quinn muted the television as it switched to a commercial. "After our dinner is delivered, we'll set up a few security precautions. That should help both of us sleep a lot better tonight."

"What kind of security precautions?"

"Just a few tricks I've picked up over the years," Quinn told her. "Just don't try to leave the suite without telling me first."

Taylor's eyebrows rose. "I get the feeling I don't even want to know what you're planning."

"Probably not." Quinn pulled her a little closer and leaned back more comfortably on the couch. He couldn't remember the last time he and Taylor had simply spent time together without actually doing something, and already he could imagine many more nights just like this one. "This is nice."

"Mmmm hmmm," Taylor agreed as the muscles in her shoulders relaxed. She sat there in silence for several minutes and then added, "You know, this is the first time since I've been back in the US that I don't feel like I'm constantly looking over my shoulder."

"I can understand that," Quinn nodded. "Things have been crazy since you got back."

"I know." Taylor lapsed into silence for a moment. "Do you think this will all be over soon?"

"Don't worry." Quinn rubbed a hand over her shoulder. "I'll keep you safe."

Taylor shifted so she could look up at him. "Thanks."

Quinn stared down at her, struck with the fact that this was what he missed the most in his life, these simple moments of friendship and companionship. His stomach lurched as he considered the other emotion he had been craving, one that he had avoided for so long. He ran a finger along her cheek, suddenly overwhelmed by his feelings.

How had he not realized that he was falling in love with Taylor? Slowly, he lowered his lips to hers for a lingering kiss. "You're welcome."

20

"Good morning," Taylor said sleepily when she walked out of her room at seven o'clock on Wednesday morning. Quinn was sitting at the table with her laptop, a notepad and pen by his right elbow and a plate of food by his left. He was dressed casually in jeans and a plain navy blue T-shirt. His feet were bare, and his hair still looked damp from his shower.

Quinn looked up at her and smiled. "Morning. Did you sleep okay?"

Taylor raked her fingers through her hair in an effort to smooth out the worst of the tangles. "I think that's the best I've slept since Paris."

"Glad to hear it." Quinn motioned to the plate beside him that was heaped with muffins, bagels, and pastries. "Did you want something to eat?"

"Yeah, thanks." Taylor selected a cream-filled Danish and sat down beside him. "How long have you been up?"

"About an hour." He tilted his head toward the computer screen. "I wanted to take another look at your paintings. I keep hoping something will jump out at me to explain what's going on."

"What do you think you're going to find?" Taylor asked. "I painted landscapes mostly. What would anyone want with them?"

Quinn pulled up a photo of one of her paintings. "What about this one? Do you know who these people are?"

"I'm sure I have their names in my files somewhere, but I won't get those until my belongings arrive from Italy."

"You have their names?"

"Of course." Taylor's eyebrows drew together. "You don't really think I would paint someone without their permission, do you?"

"Actually, yeah."

Taylor shook her head. "I ask anyone who can be recognized to sign a release form before I ever paint them."

"Even for your street scenes?"

"Kind of." Taylor's shoulders lifted. "If someone stops to talk to me, sometimes I'll ask if I can put them in the painting. Otherwise, I don't paint the faces of the people in the scene, and I fill them in later with people who have signed release forms. A lot of artists work that way."

"That pretty much blows our theory that you might have painted someone who didn't want to be seen." Quinn rubbed a finger along his chin. "But there is this ship here."

"What about it?"

"It's flying the Libyan flag."

"And . . ."

"And it's possible that it was transporting something it wasn't supposed to." Quinn leaned back in his chair. "If it was supposed to be carrying freight and it's riding that high in the water, someone might want to get to this painting before it's put on display."

"But how would anyone even know about it, much less who painted it and where it might be?" Taylor shook her head. "It's a nice theory, Quinn, but I think it has to be more personal than that. Whoever keeps doing all of this must know me. How else would they be able to track me to Virginia Beach? I didn't even fly there. I drove."

"Information like that isn't as hard to track down as you think," Quinn said cryptically. "You said yourself that you felt like someone was following you when you were in New York. If you were followed to the car dealership, it would have been simple to figure out that you had bought a car, maybe tag it with a tracking device before you headed down to Virginia."

Taylor's eyes narrowed. "Is that why you checked underneath my car after it was broken into?"

"That was one of the reasons," Quinn admitted. Then he motioned to the computer screen and promptly changed the subject. "We need to make a list of anyone you can think of who might have seen your paintings."

"You're kidding, right?"

"No, I'm not." Quinn shook his head. "Whoever has been following you obviously had to have seen your paintings, or we wouldn't have a problem."

"Quinn, it isn't that easy. I had people following me around all over when I was in Europe." Taylor ran her fingers through her hair, pulling it back away from her face. "Sometimes everyone would leave me alone, and other times I drew a pretty good crowd, especially after the article on me came out. I have no idea who those people were. I couldn't even tell you if they were locals or tourists."

"What article?"

"It was kind of a who's who in the art world. I was featured as one of the promising new artists in Europe right before the new artists showing in Paris."

"Wow. That must have given your sales a boost."

"Yeah," Taylor nodded. "I signed with my agent two days later."

Quinn sighed and seemed to reconsider his request. "Let's start by focusing on the people you do know. Your agent, people with the gallery, anyone who might have attended your showing in Paris."

"This may take a while."

"I know." He glanced at his watch. "Is there a certain time we're supposed to be meeting your agent?"

"Nine o'clock."

"Maybe you'd better get ready, and we'll work on this later," Quinn told her. "We're going to need to make a couple of stops on our way."

"We are?"

"Preventative measures."

* * *

Quinn ushered Taylor out onto the street from the subway station, keeping one hand on her back as he guided her through the last of the rush-hour crowds. He then turned toward her agent's office that was located three blocks away.

"Don't you think this is overkill?" Taylor asked him, motioning to the knit cap on her head that was currently hiding all of her hair. "First you make me wear this thing, and then we had to take three different subway trains to make sure we weren't being followed. Couldn't we have just taken a taxi?"

"Taxis log their fares," Quinn told her. "And if someone is looking to reacquire you, your agent's office is a logical place to do it."

Taylor stopped walking and was immediately bumped into by the impatient pedestrian behind her. "You think someone's waiting for me there?"

"Come on," Quinn took her hand and led her forward. "This time of day it's going to be easy to blend into the crowd. Just keep walking like you're late for an appointment."

"We *are* late for an appointment," Taylor reminded him, glancing down at her watch to see that it was already ten minutes after nine.

"Good, then it should be easy," Quinn told her. He kept his eyes in motion, subtly scanning the street ahead for anyone who might be loitering near Felicia's office building. As they neared their destination, Quinn realized that there were too many possibilities for him to even make a list.

Several people were standing outside of the building with cell phones to their ears. A limo was parked across the street, the tinted windows making it impossible to see if anyone was inside other than the driver. Utility workers were setting up a barricade in the road near a manhole a half a block down, and a saxophone player sat on the corner playing some weeping jazz as a few people passing by dropped coins and bills into his open case.

Quinn dug a few coins out of his own pocket and dropped them into the man's case as they passed and then led Taylor inside the building lobby.

"Can I take this hat off now?"

"Not yet." Quinn shook his head. "Wait until we get upstairs."

Taylor let out a sigh and led the way to the elevators. A few minutes later, they walked into the plush offices of Ferrier Illusions. Quinn had taken some time to research the agency that morning before Taylor had gotten up. He could admit now that he had been surprised to find out that it was one of the premier art agencies in Manhattan. When Taylor had announced that she had an agent, he hadn't realized that she had signed with an *agent*.

He followed Taylor to the circular reception desk.

"Hi, Suzanne. I'm here to see Felicia," Taylor told the receptionist. "I'm sorry we're running a little late."

"She's on a call right now, but as soon as she gets off, I'll let her know you're here." Suzanne smiled at Taylor and motioned to the couch in the waiting area. "Please take a seat."

"Thanks." Taylor sat down, but Quinn surprised her when he remained standing.

"Can you tell me where your restroom is?"

"Down that hall to the right."

"Thanks." Quinn leaned down and spoke quietly to Taylor. "I'll be right back."

Taylor's eyebrows drew together, surprised that he was leaving her alone even for a couple of minutes. "Okay."

Quinn returned a few minutes later just as Suzanne picked up the phone.

"Felicia, I have Taylor Palmetta here to see you." Suzanne paused for a moment and then nodded. "Okay, I'll send her right back."

She hung up the phone and spoke to Taylor. "You remember where her office is?"

"I do. Thanks." Taylor took a step toward a hallway to the right of the reception desk and then glanced back as though making sure Quinn was following her. "Can I take off the hat now?"

Quinn grinned at her. "Yeah."

"Thank you." Taylor pulled off the hat, causing her hair to spill out wildly. With a quick shake of her head, she ran her fingers through her hair, raking it into near submission. She then stuffed the hat into her bag as she turned a corner and led the way into a large office where a sophisticated woman was sitting behind a desk that Quinn guessed was an original Chippendale.

The woman appeared to be about forty, her blond hair perfectly colored and styled. Her clothes were designer, her nails freshly manicured, and Quinn guessed that she probably spent several days a week working out at the gym.

The moment she looked up and saw them, her features softened into a surprisingly warm smile. She stood up and crossed to them. "Taylor! I'm so glad you could make it in." She gave Taylor a friendly hug. Then she glanced over at Quinn.

"This is Quinn Lambert. He's my . . ." Taylor trailed off as though not quite sure how to explain his presence.

"I'm the overprotective boyfriend," Quinn finished for her and offered his hand.

Felicia smiled and placed her well-manicured hand in his. "Nice to meet you, Quinn. Please, come in and sit down."

"I assume you still haven't found the pictures," Taylor said as Felicia settled back into her seat behind her desk.

"I'm afraid not." Felicia shook her head, her voice sympathetic. "After the fire at the warehouse, the gallery had all of your paintings shipped to their showroom since the security is much tighter there."

"Where is the showroom?" Quinn asked.

"Just a couple of blocks away," Felicia told him, and then her eyes shifted to focus on Taylor. "We're hoping you'll be able to look at the remaining paintings and figure out which ones were lost."

"Exactly how many paintings are there?" Quinn asked.

"Forty-seven, not including the eight we've already sold," Felicia told him, almost apologetically. "I know it's not going to be easy figuring out which two are missing."

"Actually, if you can tell me which ones were already sold, I should be able to," Taylor told her. "I brought copies of the photos I took before all of the paintings were shipped."

"That's great." Felicia's eyes brightened.

"Has anyone figured out what started the fire?" Quinn asked.

She shook her head. "Not that I know of."

Quinn considered for a moment. "Is there any way you can arrange for me to see a copy of the surveillance tapes? I'd like to send them to a friend of mine to have them analyzed."

Felicia gave Quinn a quizzical look.

Taylor leaned forward. "Quinn is worried that the fire might have something to do with what happened in Paris."

"You aren't a private investigator, are you?"

"No, ma'am. Nothing like that."

When Quinn didn't offer any further explanation, Taylor explained for him. "Quinn is a Navy SEAL."

A combination of disbelief and awe crossed her face. "Really?"

Quinn nodded, ignoring her reaction. "I also need to visit the warehouse."

"I can give you the name and number of the inspector who is handling the case," Felicia offered, pulling a business card out of her desk. She scribbled the information on a piece of paper and handed it across her desk to Quinn. "The gallery manager should be able to arrange for you to visit the warehouse."

"That would be great. Thanks."

A knock at the door caused all of them to turn as a man walked in. He was well dressed, his dark hair peppered with gray. "I'm sorry to interrupt, but I heard Taylor Palmetta was here."

"Gregorio, I'm glad you dropped by." Felicia stood up and moved to shake his hand. Then she turned to Taylor. "You remember Gregorio Amici from the showing in Paris, don't you?"

"Of course." Taylor stood as well and shook the hand he offered her. "It's good to see you again."

"You too. I have to admit, I'm becoming quite the patron of your work." He smiled charmingly at her.

"That's good to hear." Taylor's smile widened.

"I don't think I've met your friend."

"I'm sorry." Taylor shifted her focus to Quinn. "This is Quinn Lambert."

"Good to meet you," Quinn said as he took his turn shaking Gregorio's hand.

"Are you an art enthusiast, Mr. Lambert?" Gregorio asked.

"It depends on who the artist is."

He let out a polite laugh. "Yes, I understand what you mean. I'm hoping Taylor will paint a few more pieces for me to hang in my gallery before the holiday season." Gregorio turned to Felicia. "But I do want to see her other pieces before you sell any more. They've been very popular with my patrons."

As soon as he left the room, Taylor asked, "Did you want us to go over to the gallery showroom now?"

Felicia nodded. "That's a good idea. I have a driver who can take you over there. Then I thought we could meet for lunch. We have a few things we need to discuss about your upcoming showing."

Taylor's eyes lit with excitement. "Have you locked in a date yet?"

"January 26," Felicia told her. "I know that's not a lot of time for you to add to your collection, but when the date opened up, the gallery owner said he wanted you to be the one to fill it."

"Seriously?" Now disbelief crossed Taylor's face.

"Seriously." Felicia smiled encouragingly. "Our biggest struggle right now is making sure we have enough paintings for your showing. I sold three more last week."

Quinn looked at her, confused. "I thought you said that only eight of Taylor's paintings have been sold."

Felicia shook her head. "No. That's how many have already been delivered. The others are still at the gallery."

Quinn scratched his head. "I know I'm pretty dense when it comes to the art world, but how do people even know about Taylor's work? She's only been back in the country for a few weeks."

"Most of the pieces we've sold were from the Paris showing in May," Felicia told him. "Taylor had ten pieces on display. Anything that didn't sell immediately was put into a catalogue that was available through all of the art brokerage houses that had someone in attendance. We've been getting calls consistently on Taylor's pieces since the catalogue was printed last month. Those calls resulted in the sale of some of her newer pieces."

"I guess that makes sense," Quinn said. "But I would have thought that a catalogue would have been printed right after the showing. Why wait three months?"

"This was a new artist showing, one in which all of the pieces on display are by unrepresented talent," Felicia explained. "We wait for three months to do the catalogue so that agents like me can have time to sign the talent we're interested in and the artists have representation to take care of the business end of things before they get bombarded with buyers."

"Do all artists find agents this way?"

"A lot of the good ones do." Felicia nodded.

"One of the catches with the Paris showing is that you don't get into their catalogue unless you have an agent before it goes to print," Taylor added.

"So if you hadn't found an agent, no one would see your paintings?"

"That's right." Taylor nodded.

Felicia reached for her phone. "I'll have our driver meet you out front."

Quinn looked at her skeptically. "How will we know which car is for us?"

"Taylor knows which one it is," Felicia told him before turning her attention to the assistant on the other end of the phone. After issuing her request, she hung up the phone and stood. "I'll plan on seeing you for lunch. Quinn, will you be joining us?"

Quinn nodded. "Like I said, I'm overprotective."

Felicia smiled knowingly. "I think Taylor can use a bit of overprotection right now."

"I'm glad you agree." Quinn grinned. Then he motioned to Taylor. "Hat."

"Quinn." Taylor's voice came out in a whine.

"Come on. Put it on."

With a sigh, Taylor pulled the hat out of her bag, twisted the length of her hair up into a makeshift bun, and then covered it up with the knit cap once more. "Happy?"

"Ecstatic." Quinn nodded. Then he turned to Felicia to see her smothering a grin. "See you later."

They made it several steps into the hall before they heard Felicia's laughter ring out behind them.

21

"ANYTHING NEW?" TRISTAN ASKED THE minute Steinert walked through his office door.

"Not a whole lot." He shook his head. "We're still trying to identify the guy Quinn saw from the composite sketch he helped us with. So far we haven't had any hits."

"What about the other incidents?"

"No fingerprints or anything to go on from Palmetta's car when it was broken into. Only one witness who might have been able to identify the guy, but all we got was that he was dark haired and average build."

"Quinn said he saw the guy run off, but he wasn't close enough to see anything but his back," Tristan added.

"There is one thing about all of this that puzzles me," Steinert commented. "If someone is trying to keep some of Palmetta's paintings from being seen, why are they trying to steal them? Seems to me that it would be easier to destroy them. A fire, car bomb. Even acid."

"Maybe they are trying to destroy them. After all, she lost two in that warehouse fire in New Jersey," Tristan reminded him.

"That's true. What worries me is how close together these different incidents took place. It makes me think that whoever is behind it is getting desperate. Usually, that's when criminals stop worrying about getting caught. Instead, the focus shifts to accomplishing their objectives," Steinert told him.

"You said that the dead guy from my place looked like a local hire. It sounds like someone doesn't want to be connected to the crime but they're willing to pay a lot of money to get the job done."

Steinert nodded in agreement. "My team traced the wire transfer back to Nicholas Orton's account. Unfortunately, it led to a numbered account in Switzerland."

"Which means the money could belong to anyone."

"Not exactly." His mouth curved into the beginnings of a smile. "We do know that a significant number of deposits to this particular account have been made in cash. That means we're probably dealing with someone in western Europe."

"We kind of figured that," Tristan said. "I made a list of everywhere Taylor painted while she was in Europe. She definitely made her rounds."

"I'd like a copy of that list. Any information at this point would be helpful."

"No problem," Tristan agreed. "I'll print it out right now."

"Any word yet from the Palmetta girl since she left for New York?"

"I spoke with Quinn early this morning," Tristan told him. "They were heading over to the gallery to try to identify the damaged paintings, but Quinn is having the security tapes sent to us from the night of the fire. He's also hoping to go over and see the warehouse himself, but I don't know how he's going to manage that with Taylor."

"Tell him to stay focused on keeping the girl safe," Steinert said. "I'll get someone to go check out the warehouse."

Tristan nodded. "We appreciate any help you can give us."

* * *

"What are you thinking about?" Taylor asked as she scribbled down an inventory number on the back of one of her photos. "You look so serious."

"I was just wondering. Were all of these paintings in the warehouse when the fire started?" Quinn asked as he finished putting away one of the paintings Taylor had already catalogued.

"As far as I know. Why?"

"None of them look damaged. I would have thought that they would have had some water damage or at least have been covered in soot."

"That is odd." Taylor shrugged her shoulders. "I guess I'm lucky that I only lost two."

"I guess so." Quinn's voice hummed with suspicion. He retrieved another painting and put it in front of Taylor for her to identify. He looked around the storage room where her artwork was currently being housed, realizing for the first time what a daunting task identifying everything was going to be. "You realize that it is going to take at least two days to get through all of this, don't you?"

"I do now." Taylor nodded. "I don't know what I was expecting, but I didn't think we were going to have to spend so much time moving things around just so we could look at each painting."

The faint ringing of a cell phone sounded in the room. Taylor reached for her bag and fished her phone out of it. "Hello?" Taylor glanced up at Quinn as she nodded and spoke into the phone once more. "Okay, thanks for letting me know."

"Who was that?" Quinn asked.

"The car dealership. My car is ready."

"I don't know that I want you driving your car until we figure out who is behind all of these problems, especially after we went through the trouble of moving you to someplace new," Quinn told her. "If you park your car in the apartment parking lot, you might as well be announcing where you live."

"I know." Taylor nodded. "I was thinking that I may just have to leave the car at the dealership for now. I don't know what else to do."

Quinn considered for a moment. "I think I might have an idea. Do you have the keys with you here, or did you leave them at home?"

"The dealership has one of the keys, and the other one is in my apartment. Why?"

"Just wondering." Quinn glanced at his watch. "It's almost time for lunch. Let's get this one identified, and then we can take a break."

* * *

Vanessa Johnson pulled out her attendance sheets for the past three weeks. Rarely did she have anyone not show up for her class, especially since a waiting list had been in place since the moment it had been created. After spending more than a year deep undercover for the CIA, Vanessa had abandoned the life of a spy and now used her expertise to teach those men and women who were hoping to someday work as undercover agents or as handlers for one or more of those agents.

The classes were small, only one slot for each division in the Directorate of Operations. Yet, for each of the last three classes, she had faced an empty chair in her classroom. She hadn't put it together at first, but now she noted the office that had registered her newest absentee. She flipped the page and checked the missing attendant from the previous week and the one before that. As she suspected, they were all from the same office.

With her students currently on their lunch break, Vanessa picked up the secure phone on her desk. She flipped open her phone directory and scanned the numbers in front of her until she found the training officer for the

European division. Punching in the numbers, she waited while the phone rang twice before a woman answered. "Training office. Can I help you?"

"I hope so. This is Vanessa Johnson."

"Vanessa Johnson?" she repeated. "We have quite a few people here that are anxious to take your class."

"That's what I was calling about," Vanessa told her. "The last three participants from your division haven't shown up."

"What?" she asked, sounding sincerely surprised. "I don't understand. The branch chiefs are supposed to let me know if someone can't make it so we can send an alternate. Hold on a second and let me see which branches we're dealing with here."

Vanessa waited, listening to the rustle of papers through the phone.

"Here it is," she said. Then the silence stretched out for several long seconds. "All three of them were the same branch."

"Which one?"

"Western Europe."

Vanessa grabbed a pen out of her desk drawer. "Can you give me that branch chief's number?"

"Oh, you don't have to call him. I'll take care of this and make sure it doesn't happen again."

"Actually, the reason I need to talk to him doesn't have anything to do with my class. I have some information I need to pass along."

"Oh," she said, apparently caught off guard. "Are you sure there isn't a message I can pass along?"

"No, thanks. I just need his name and number."

"All right," she said hesitantly. Then she rattled off a man's first name and a secure telephone number.

"Thank you for your help. I really appreciate it," Vanessa said and then pressed her finger on the receiver to hang up the phone. Reading the branch chief's number, she dialed the phone once more.

This time it only took one ring for someone to answer the phone, and impatience vibrated through the line. "Graham."

"Hi, this is Vanessa Johnson," she began. "I'm hoping you can help me with some information."

"I'm sorry, but this isn't a good time right now," he said, clearly preparing to dismiss her. "Can you call back sometime next week?"

"I don't think so." Vanessa's voice was firm. "I noticed that the personnel in your branch have missed my class for the past few weeks."

"You're calling because my people were absent?" Incredulity and impatience filled his voice.

"No, I'm calling because I may have information related to why they've been absent."

"I'm listening."

"I don't know if this has anything to do with your problems up there at headquarters or not, but we've had a string of incidents with a woman here who recently returned from Europe," Vanessa told him. "I'm starting to think that you might be able to shed some light on why."

"What kind of incidents?"

"Basically, we're dealing with a bunch of petty crimes, but all of them circle back to the paintings this woman created while living in Europe over the past year," Vanessa began. "Since arriving home, her car has been broken in to, two of her paintings were destroyed in a warehouse fire in New Jersey, and someone broke into her sister's place. She also returned to her hotel room in Paris a few weeks ago to find a lot of blood on the floor."

"Do we know who was in her room?" Graham asked, his impatience replaced by interest.

"She doesn't have a clue."

"And you said two of her paintings were destroyed?"

"That's right."

"After they cleared customs?"

"Yes, I believe so," Vanessa informed him. "I need to know what you're dealing with on your end if we're going to piece this all together."

"One of our contacts in Paris hasn't checked in for almost a month. The last time we heard from him, he said he had uncovered some new technology, something that would be disastrous if it was smuggled into the United States."

"What can you tell me about it?"

"Not much, at least not on the phone," Graham told her. "We've spent the past four weeks searching for any sign of our agent, but he's dropped off the face of the earth. We're hoping that he just hasn't been able to get word out or that he was forced to go into hiding, but at this point, we can't be sure of anything."

"I know it's a long shot that all of this is related, but I'd appreciate it if you'd keep me in the loop," Vanessa told him and then gave her name again along with her phone number.

"Vanessa?" Graham said her name as though he were trying to piece together a puzzle. "Wait a minute. You're the one who was undercover in Ramir's organization last year, aren't you? The one who married the Navy SEAL?"

Vanessa hesitated, automatically ready to shield the truth from everyone. Then she reminded herself that this man also had a top-secret security clearance and that her undercover work was no longer considered "need to know." After a brief pause, Vanessa said, "That's right."

"Your name actually came up the other day as someone who might be able to help us out," Graham told her.

"What can I do?"

"Is there any way you can come up to Langley? I think we need to meet."

"My class doesn't wrap up until tomorrow afternoon, but I should be able to drive up and meet with you sometime Friday if you want."

"That would be great," Graham said, some of the anxiety melting out of his voice. "And if you could bring this artist friend of yours, too, I'd appreciate it."

"She's in New York right now, but I'll see if she can meet me there."

"Please do," he said. "I'm starting to worry that we may not have much more time to uncover the truth."

"In that case, I'll see you on Friday morning."

"Thanks."

22

"THANKS FOR DINNER," TAYLOR SAID as she and Quinn walked hand in hand from the subway station toward the hotel. "I thought for sure you'd insist on eating in our room again."

"I didn't want to go straight back to our hotel from the gallery anyway," Quinn admitted.

"Well, the food was great, so thank you."

"You're welcome." Quinn smiled over at her. He glanced behind them, and instantly his demeanor changed. His pace was still steady, but his eyes darkened and seemed to have a new awareness. He tightened his grip on her hand as they approached their hotel. He lowered his voice and said, "Keep walking."

"Okay." Taylor's shoulders tightened.

Instead of going inside, he continued past their hotel and then walked toward the shopping plaza next door.

Then in a normal voice he said, "You should be able to find a new sweatshirt in here. I still can't believe you forgot to pack one."

Taylor looked up at him, confused for a moment. Then she realized she needed to play along, even though she desperately wanted to turn around and see if someone was following them. "I thought I brought one."

Quinn gave her hand an encouraging squeeze and led her inside the plaza. Then he quickly turned into the first store they reached, a women's clothing store.

Before Taylor could say anything, Quinn pulled her to the side of the door where they weren't visible from anyone entering the plaza but where Quinn could see everyone passing by.

"What's going on?" Taylor whispered.

"There was a guy walking behind us that I noticed on the subway. I just want to make sure he isn't following us."

"Now what?" Taylor asked.

"We wait a few minutes." Still keeping his eyes on the door, Quinn reached down and took one of the sweatshirts off of the rack. Then he pointed to the dressing room a short distance away. "Why don't you go try this one on?"

Taylor lowered her voice to a whisper and leaned closer to him. "Because it isn't my size."

"Then pick one that is," Quinn whispered back. "And go into the dressing room over there."

"This one's cute," Taylor said, plucking one at random that was her size.

"Go ahead and try it on," Quinn suggested mildly, his eyes still trained on the door. "I'll wait here."

"Okay." Taylor weaved her way to the back wall where the dressing rooms were located. She ducked inside one, latched the door, and leaned back against it. Surely Quinn was just overreacting. Or was he?

Nerves danced in her stomach as she glanced down at her watch and wondered how long she should wait before walking back out to find him. What would she do if there really was someone following her? Was Quinn still in the store, or had he gone out searching for the man he was concerned about? After several endless minutes, Taylor finally cracked the door open and poked her head out to see Quinn still standing guard. He glanced over at her and gave her a subtle nod to join him. Leaving the sweatshirt in the dressing room, she walked over to him, her eyes questioning.

"Let's go."

"Did you see him again?"

Quinn shook his head, but he took Taylor's hand and led her away from the entrance, instead walking farther into the shopping plaza.

"Where are we going?"

"Just because I didn't see him again doesn't mean he isn't waiting outside," Quinn told her. "There's another exit that leads to the back entrance of our hotel. We'll go in that way."

Emotionally numb, Taylor nodded and walked beside him. By the time Quinn used his hotel keycard to enter through the side entrance, her stomach was sick with worry, her nerves warring inside of her. Even her breath was becoming ragged as she looked around anxiously.

"Relax," Quinn told her. He led her into the stairwell and up one flight of stairs. When they reached the landing for the second floor, he pushed the door open and walked out into the upstairs lobby. "Come on. We can take the elevator from here."

Taylor took a deep breath and felt her body tremble.

Quinn led her into the empty elevator, his eyes narrowing as he took a good look at her. "Hey, come here." He gathered her close, the strength of his arms wrapping around her. "I'm sorry. I didn't mean to scare you, but we can't be too careful."

Taylor took a steadying breath, but it did little to calm her unsettled emotions. She felt Quinn edge backwards, and then he used one of his fingers to tilt her chin up so that he could see her face.

"Are you okay?"

Taylor nodded, blinking back the sudden urge to cry. She felt her control slipping, overwhelmed that every time she started to feel safe something happened to remind her that someone was still looking for her.

Quinn pulled her close once more, his hand trailing down her back to rest at her waist. Her own hands tightened around his neck, and she could feel the tension there as though he were as scared of what was happening as she was. She let herself draw comfort from him as the elevator continued upward, and slowly her trembling subsided.

"Come on." Quinn took her hand when the elevator doors opened, looking down the hallway in both directions before pulling her out of the elevator and starting toward their room. He then studied their door, noting that the Do Not Disturb sign was still in place, as was the barely detectable thread fastened to the bottom of the door to alert him if anyone had entered while they were gone.

After Quinn swiped his keycard, he led Taylor inside and engaged the security lock. He then began checking all of the windows.

"What are you doing?" Taylor asked, setting her bag down on the table. "I thought you were sure the door hadn't been opened."

"The door isn't the only way in," Quinn told her, moving into the bedrooms to complete his security sweep.

"The windows are sealed, and we don't have a balcony," she called after him. "I don't think anyone could get into this room without going through the front door."

Quinn emerged from the bedroom and walked toward her. He stopped a foot in front of her and waited for her to look into his eyes. His voice was low when he spoke. "I could."

"Could what?"

"I could get into this room without using the front door."

Taylor stared at him, not sure if she should really believe him. She knew Navy SEALs were highly trained, but surely even they wouldn't be able to enter a hotel room on the fourteenth floor without being detected. She crossed her arms and took a step back so she could see him more clearly. "Really?"

"Yes, really," Quinn said. His tone was so matter-of-fact that Taylor found herself believing him. "From the roof, it's actually not that complicated."

"Great."

"For a SEAL."

"Then I hope whoever has been following me isn't a SEAL."

"Me too."

* * *

Quinn pressed speed dial on his cell phone and sat down on the couch in the living area. He had waited for almost an hour after Taylor went to bed to make the call so he wouldn't have to worry about her overhearing anything that might upset her further.

The phone rang four times before Tristan answered groggily.

"Sorry to call so late, but I wanted to see if you guys had made any progress today," Quinn said.

"Not much," Tristan said, a little more alert now. "We know that the guy who fell from my balcony was a local hire and that whoever hired him has a Swiss bank account."

"Which basically tells us what we already knew," Quinn finished for him. "Whoever we're dealing with is from Europe."

"Yeah. Also, I wanted to let you know not to worry about going to the warehouse. Steinert sent someone over there to check it out, and we looked over the surveillance tapes."

"Did you find anything?"

"Nothing. The cameras shorted out before anyone ever came into view," Tristan told him. "I'm starting to think that whoever did the warehouse job was a pro."

"Unlike the guy who went into your place."

"Exactly," Tristan agreed. "The good news is that Vanessa may have stumbled onto something. She said one of her contacts wants to meet with her at Langley on Friday. She was hoping Taylor could be there too."

"We might be able to finish up here tomorrow. If so, we can take a train down and stay with my folks tomorrow night," Quinn told him. "I'd like to get Taylor out of the city as soon as possible."

"Is everything okay?"

"I think so." Quinn ran a hand over his face, pushing aside his fatigue as well as his worry. "There are just so many possibilities. It's hard to tell if we're being followed or if I'm being paranoid."

"Well, I appreciate you going up there with her. After what happened at my place, Riley is going to be a nervous wreck when we go back to stay at our condo."

"You told Riley what happened?" Quinn asked, concerned.

"Yeah, but she hasn't said anything to Taylor," Tristan told him. "She was so worried about how stressed Taylor is that she suggested not telling her about it."

"By the way, I have an idea of how we might flush the guy out that's been following Taylor in Virginia Beach."

"How's that?"

"The dealership called. Her car is ready," Quinn said pointedly. "Might be interesting to see what would happen if it were picked up and left in a parking lot somewhere."

"With a little surveillance going on outside?"

"Exactly."

"You know, Jay could use a little more practice on surveillance," Tristan said with humor in his voice. "I'll talk to Brent in the morning and see what I can do."

"Sounds good."

"And let me know if you run into any problems making it down to meet with Vanessa."

"It shouldn't be a problem, but I think that if we're going to end up in northern Virginia on Friday, I might stay there for the weekend," Quinn said now, considering. "It would do Taylor some good to be someplace where no one would expect her to go."

"That's not a bad idea," Tristan agreed. He hesitated a moment and then added, "You should give Mom a call and let her know you and Taylor are coming. That will totally make her week."

Quinn smiled to himself. "You're probably right. If you come up too, it will turn into a family reunion."

"We might be able to swing that," Tristan agreed. "I'll see if Riley wants to drive up on Friday night. Then if you want, you and Taylor can drive home with us on Sunday."

"That sounds like fun," Quinn agreed, already looking forward to seeing his family. "But this time I get to harass Wendy's new boyfriend."

"She has a new boyfriend?"

"She always has a new boyfriend." Quinn grinned. "And you had that last guy so scared of me by the time I met him that I didn't get to have any fun."

"Fine." Tristan chuckled. "But I get to help."

"Deal."

23

VERNON RIESENOUR STUDIED THE WORKSHEETS and diagrams on the table in front of him and considered what would happen if the men who were financing his efforts gained access to the technical specs of his invention. Of course, he no longer needed the details of how to construct the ingenious device. Everything he needed was stored in his head, making these plans useless to him. Concerned that his invention would be used for purposes other than his own, he had deliberately only made one prototype, a handheld device comprised of eight easily assembled pieces.

The main electronic component was high tech, a miniaturized version of a computer motherboard. An adapter connected the main component to three cords. Fitting into those cords were the power source, the magnetic card that could feed into any credit card or ATM slot, and the flash drive that contained all of his ingenious programming. With all eight pieces intact, that programming could change the world in a matter of seconds.

Vernon understood that his supporters had given him financial backing as a way to advance their political agenda. Vernon didn't care about their secondary objectives. He only cared that the Americans would take notice, that they would feel the pain of having their world come crumbling down around them the way his had so many months before.

He glanced over at his suitcases by the door, hating that recent events were forcing him to flee the home he had shared with his family. One suitcase held his basic necessities, the clothing and personal items he would need until he could return home. The other contained his memories, various photos and other reminders of what had been stolen from him.

A heavy sigh escaped him, and Vernon gathered the papers in front of him. With his worksheets in his hand, he stood and crossed to the fireplace in his living room. He picked up the matches off of the mantel and struck one to life. Then he held the flame to the corner of the papers he held and lowered them into the fireplace. He stared at the flames without seeing them, his entire focus already on what would come next.

* * *

The gallery manager, Evan Bridgeton, looked at the two photos on the work table in front of him. One of the paintings was of the cliffs in Ireland, and the other was of a sidewalk café in Paris. "These are the paintings that were stolen."

"Stolen?" Quinn immediately straightened. "I thought they were destroyed in a fire."

Evan shook his head. "That's what we thought too, but the arson investigator and the police believe that a small fire was set to mask the theft."

Quinn's mind quickly readjusted to this new information. "How many paintings do you believe were stolen?"

"Only these two."

"Wait a minute." Taylor spoke now, her eyes wide. "You're telling me that someone broke into a warehouse filled with valuable artwork and didn't steal anything but my paintings?"

"That's right."

"How many other paintings were there in the warehouse?" she asked.

"Thousands," Evan told her. "We've never seen anything like this before."

"Why would someone go to so much trouble to steal my paintings?" Taylor asked. "And why these two? They don't have anything in common."

Quinn laid a hand on her shoulder. "Except that they were painted by you."

Taylor sighed. "Yes, except for that."

Evan picked up the two photos. "Can I keep these? The police will want copies."

"That's fine."

"Thank you for coming in to help us sort this out. Thefts at our gallery are rare, so we take these matters very seriously." Evan reached out and shook Taylor's hand. "Felicia or I will be in touch as soon as we learn anything from the police."

"Thanks," Taylor said before turning to Quinn. "I still can't believe this."

"Don't think about all of this now." Quinn glanced at his watch. "Come on. We should have just enough time to make our train."

"I thought we weren't leaving until tomorrow."

"Change of plans." Quinn led her outside and then lifted his hand when he got to the curb. As soon as they were safely inside a taxi, he gave the driver the address of their hotel.

She looked at him, confused. "I thought you didn't want to go straight back to the hotel."

"It shouldn't matter now," Quinn told her, but still he shifted to look at the cars behind them.

"Okay," Taylor said skeptically. "I'm trusting you."

Quinn's eyes came back to land on her. Then he reached for her hand and gave it a reassuring squeeze. "Always a wise decision."

* * *

He was bringing Taylor home to meet his parents. How was it that he had never thought of this trip in quite that way before? Quinn looked over at Taylor who was still blissfully unaware that they were taking the train to Alexandria instead of Williamsburg.

The train rolled into the DC station, and Taylor shifted, her eyes remaining closed as she continued to doze beside him. Quinn knew that she was exhausted, and he suspected that their trip to New York had only made it worse. After spending two nights in the same hotel suite with her, he knew that she was staying up late at night as though afraid to go to sleep. She was also prone to getting up at least once or twice during the early morning hours to make sure nothing had changed since she had gone to bed.

The fact that she had claimed that her time in New York was the best she had slept since Paris made him wonder exactly how much she had been sleeping while in Virginia. Maybe spending a couple of nights at his parents' house would give her the chance to find some peace for a few days and some time to unwind. Of course, that was assuming that she could handle the inevitable questions and speculation from his family.

Until Quinn had purchased their tickets in New York, it hadn't dawned on him that this would be the first time he'd brought a woman to his parents' home since Emily. Now he wondered how Taylor would feel about the underlying meaning his family would read into this momentous event. At least his mother and sisters would recognize his visit with Taylor as momentous. His dad would probably just look at him in his quiet way, offer his unspoken understanding and support, and then welcome Taylor into their home.

As the train rumbled out of the DC station, Quinn pulled out his cell phone and sent his mom a text message to tell her that his train was on time. He had considered surprising her completely, but he didn't think she would appreciate being caught unprepared for company. Not that Quinn had ever seen it happen, but he knew his mother. She loved to fuss over him, and she wouldn't be happy if he denied her the opportunity.

Plus, from a purely selfish perspective, Quinn knew that by announcing his arrival, he was guaranteed to get some of his favorite meals over the next few days. He couldn't remember the last time he had eaten a good pot roast.

As the train neared the station, Quinn put his hand on Taylor's shoulder and shook her lightly. When she didn't stir, he spoke softly. "Taylor. Wake up."

She cracked one eye open. "Are we there already?"

"Yeah," Quinn said as the train slowed and then gradually came to a stop. "This is our stop."

Taylor shifted to sit up straighter, rolling her shoulders back to stretch. "I'm sorry. I didn't mean to sleep the whole way."

"That's okay. You needed it." Quinn stood up and retrieved their luggage from the overhead bin. He led the way down the aisle and off of the train. As he expected, his mother was standing on the platform waiting for him.

"Quinn!"

"Hi, Mom." Quinn glanced back at Taylor long enough to see the confused look on her face. Then his mother had his face in her hands and was pulling him toward her to kiss his cheek.

"Oh, it's so good to have you home." Eileen Lambert beamed at her son. Then her gaze shifted to the woman who had stepped beside him.

"Mom, this is the friend I was telling you about," Quinn said and then looked at Taylor with a mischievous smile. "Taylor Palmetta, this is my mom, Eileen Lambert."

Eileen reached for Taylor's hand, grasping it with both of her own. "It's so nice to meet you. I have heard so much about you from my boys and Riley."

"It's nice to meet you too." Taylor smiled at her and then sent a chastising look at Quinn before turning her attention back to Eileen. "Riley speaks highly of you. And, of course, I already know that you must be a saint to have survived Quinn and Tristan as teenagers."

"They definitely kept life interesting." Eileen laughed. She motioned toward the stairs leading away from the platform. "Let's get you home. I'm parked over this way."

Quinn nudged Taylor forward and fell into step behind his mother. He leaned over and spoke quietly in Taylor's ear. "By the way, we're stopping in northern Virginia for a few days."

Her eyebrows lifted. "Oh really?"

"Do you mind?" Quinn asked, suddenly wondering if surprising her was such a good idea after all.

"It depends."

"On what?"

"Is there any chance we can go eat at Red Hot & Blue?"

"How did you know there was a Red Hot & Blue up here?"

"One of my favorite art stores is down the street from there." Taylor grinned at him. "And we have to go right by Arlington every time we go to the temple."

Quinn laughed. "I suppose we can find time to eat out."

"Then I'm sure we'll get along just fine this weekend."

"That's all it takes, huh?" Quinn asked now. "Some good food and all is right in your world?"

"Pretty much," Taylor nodded. "That and being somewhere that no one is following me."

"Yeah, I thought that my parents' house might have some advantages in that area of your life too."

Taylor reached for his hand and gave it a squeeze. "Thanks."

Quinn winked at her. "Anytime."

24

"You invited the whole family over?" Quinn asked his mother as Taylor stood at the kitchen counter slicing a tomato for the hamburgers he and his father were preparing to grill.

"Of course I invited everyone." Eileen nodded. "When was the last time you saw your sisters?"

"Debbie came down for Labor Day weekend."

"And she spent most of her time on the beach while you were working." Eileen picked up a plate of raw hamburger patties and passed them to Quinn. "Make sure to tell your dad that Taylor wants hers well done."

"Yes, ma'am." Quinn took the plate from her, glanced over at Taylor and then headed outside onto the deck where his father was heating up the grill.

"Quinn said all of your daughters live nearby?" Taylor asked once Quinn closed the door behind him.

Eileen stirred some mayonnaise into a bowl of potato salad and nodded. "We try to get together at least once every month or so, but any time Quinn or Tristan comes to town, it always turns into a family reunion."

"I imagine they don't get the chance to come home very often."

"Some years are better than others." She looked out the window at her husband and Quinn, a smile lighting her face. "My husband sure loves it when the boys are home. You can imagine how outnumbered he is the rest of the time."

"Oh yeah," Taylor laughed. "My dad's been feeling that way for a while now. My brother is just finishing his mission in Brazil, and I think out of everyone, Dad is the most anxious to get him home."

"Quinn was telling me that you've been living in Europe."

Taylor nodded, a quick thrill whipping through her at the thought of Quinn telling his mother about her. She let her eyes wander to the two men outside. The scene was so all-American, the bond between the two men almost tangible. She looked over at Eileen, suddenly feeling a bit hesitant. "Do you think they'd mind if I sketched them?"

"I don't see why they would."

"I'll be right back." Taylor hurried into the living room and grabbed her bag, pulling her sketchbook and a pencil out as she came back into the kitchen. Dropping her bag on one of the kitchen chairs, she did a quick pencil sketch of Quinn's father, complete with the spatula in one hand. The love and joy on his face was visible as he glanced over at his son. Quinn was leaning against the deck railing, his hands tucked into the pocket of his hooded sweatshirt and one foot crossed in front of the other. He was home in every sense of the word.

Taylor lost all track of time and of what Eileen was doing in the kitchen as she let her focus center on Quinn and his father. She finished one sketch and was considering starting a second when Quinn pushed away from the railing and headed for the door. Not sure how Quinn would feel about being her model of the moment, she closed her sketchbook and dropped it and her pencil into her bag as the back door slid open.

"Hey, Mom. Dad says he needs a clean plate to put the burgers on."

Eileen handed him the platter that was already on the counter. "After you give that to your dad, I need you to get some napkins from downstairs."

Quinn gave the plate to his dad and then motioned to Taylor. "Come on; I'll show you Dad's man cave."

"Man cave?" Taylor asked curiously.

"Yeah." Quinn opened a door off of the hallway and started down the stairs. "It's where he goes to hide from all of the girls."

"I'm surprised my dad never thought to do something like that." Taylor laughed. She followed him into the basement where a big screen television was set up along with three recliners. "Are these other chairs for you and Tristan?"

"When we're home." Quinn grinned at her. "But we might make room for one more while you're here."

"Oh really?"

"Yeah, really." Quinn reached for her hand and leaned down to kiss her.

In that moment, Taylor let herself believe that she was the center of his world. She could see her future, rich with adventure, family, and love. At the center of it all was Quinn. When he pulled back, Taylor smiled up at him. "Is that why you wanted me to come down here?"

Quinn grinned back at her. "I have a feeling we're not going to get a lot of alone time this weekend, especially once my sisters get here."

"In that case—" Taylor's eyes sparked with mischief as she pulled him closer for another kiss.

Quinn held her close for a moment and then stared down at her. "You know, I like the way you think."

Taylor laughed. "You'd better get those napkins before your mom comes down to get them herself."

"She would too." Quinn crossed the wide room and opened a door on the far side. A moment later he reemerged holding a package of napkins. "Let's go see if the terrible trio has shown up yet."

"Terrible trio?"

"Three girls sharing a single bathroom upstairs. Believe me, I'm lucky to have escaped with my sanity."

"That must have been years ago."

"And I'm still trying to recover." Quinn led her back upstairs where the kitchen was now crowded with people.

"Look who's returned," one of them said as she hugged Quinn. "It's the prodigal son."

"Yeah, yeah." Quinn smirked at her. Then he motioned to Taylor. "Taylor, this is my brother-in-law, Steve, and these are my sisters." Quinn pointed at each as he rattled off their names. "Cassie, Debbie, and Wendy."

"Nice to meet all of you," Taylor said as she replayed the three names in her mind. Cassie, Debbie, and Wendy. Her thoughts quickly jumped to the conversation they'd had about his brotherly protectiveness. But just now, he didn't name an Emily. She looked over at Quinn, her curiosity piqued. Who was Emily then? An old girlfriend maybe? Or a friend of the family? The way Quinn had mentioned her so casually at the train station a few days ago, she had just assumed Emily was one of his sisters.

Wendy took a step forward. "Quinn said that you've been living in Europe. That must have been incredible."

"It was." Taylor smiled at her.

"Did you visit Paris?" she asked. "I've always wanted to go there."

"I did," Taylor said, but before she could expand on her answer, Quinn nudged her toward the table.

"Come on. Let's eat while it's hot." He pulled a chair out for Taylor. "If we wait to eat until after Wendy is done grilling you about Paris, we'll all starve to death."

"Very funny." Wendy rolled her eyes and then lowered her voice and spoke as though her comment were only intended for Taylor. "He always gets grumpy when he's hungry."

"That would mean he's always grumpy," Debbie chimed in.

Quinn just shook his head and sent his father a pitying look. "How do you handle them all on your own, Dad? We're completely outnumbered."

"I don't know why they pick on you, son," David Lambert said as he approached the table. "They're always nice to me."

"Figures," Quinn muttered.

"Come on. Everyone sit down." Eileen carried the bowl of potato salad from the kitchen and set it down on the table.

Quinn waited for all of the women to sit down before he claimed the chair beside Taylor. The moment everyone was seated and the blessing on the food was said, Wendy started in on Taylor about Paris again.

"Was the Eiffel Tower incredible?" Wendy asked. "You must have gone there."

"I did," Taylor nodded. "I actually did a couple of paintings that had the Eiffel Tower in them."

"Oh, I would love to see them."

"Maybe we'll take you with us to New York in January for Taylor's showing," Quinn said, as though it were already a given that he would accompany Taylor to the event.

Taylor instantly smiled, unable to deny the pleasure that surged through her as Quinn spoke of a future that included her.

"That would be so cool!" Wendy's eyes widened with excitement.

"Maybe we'll all go up," David said now. "I'm sure Tristan and Riley will be there."

"They'd better." Taylor grinned and then turned to look at Quinn. "I just hope the navy cooperates and doesn't send Quinn and Tristan somewhere that week."

"We might consider putting in for a few days of leave."

"Wow." Cassie's eyebrows lifted, and she gave Quinn a speculative look. "He never does that for us."

"I'll put in for leave when junior arrives," Quinn said, pretending to be offended. "Or at least when you bless him."

"Or her."

Taylor just smiled as the bantering around the table shifted from one topic to another. The Lambert family was a lot like hers. She could understand why

Tristan had chosen them to be his own and why Riley enjoyed her visits with them so much.

As Quinn started interrogating his youngest sister about her latest love interest, Taylor leaned back in her chair and, for the first time in weeks, felt like she was really home.

25

JAY LEANED AGAINST A THICK branch as he perched fifteen feet off of the ground in a mature oak tree. The leaves had already turned a deep golden brown, but thankfully only a few of those leaves had fallen. So far he had been able to conceal himself nicely in the fall foliage. He let out an impatient sigh and shifted the communications headset he wore. "Why didn't we let NCIS handle this stakeout?"

"Because you can use the practice," Seth told him from his position on the roof of a two-story house across the street from where Taylor's SUV was currently parked. The two houses were both rentals, both currently vacant. Tristan and Brent had stood watch for the first half of the night and Seth and Jay had come to relieve them shortly before midnight.

"You always say that," Jay grumbled.

"And it's always true," Seth countered. "Do you see anything?"

"Nothing yet." Jay shifted his binoculars, and his eyes swept over the parking lot again. "We've been at this for hours. I'm starting to think that this guy already gave up on finding Taylor."

"Either that or he knows that she isn't in town."

Jay opened his mouth to agree when he heard footsteps in the fallen leaves below. Silently he shifted, searching the darkness for any movement. Several seconds ticked by before he saw it, the black-clad figure skulking through the shadows and heading for Taylor's car. Then he skirted around the vehicle and continued toward the back gate.

"Got something," Jay said, his voice barely louder than a whisper. He pulled a small remote from a pocket on his combat vest, holding it in his left hand even as he retrieved the gun from his shoulder holster.

"I see it," Seth responded. "I'm calling it in. Get ready."

Jay held his position, hoping that the locked gate would buy them a little extra time. Sure enough, he heard the rattle of the lock against the metal latch, and then the person below stayed in the shadows of the fence and headed for the dark front door. Jay lowered himself steadily as he watched and waited. The moment the intruder reached for the doorknob, Jay pressed the button on the remote, and the whole yard illuminated with floodlights.

"Hold it right there!" Jay yelled out as he jumped the last few feet to the ground.

The figure spun around, a gun already in his hand.

"Gun!" Seth shouted the warning through the communications headset.

Jay saw the pistol, felt the weight of his own, and pulled the trigger, his shot echoing with another ringing through the night. Then suddenly the man at the front door dropped lifelessly onto the concrete porch.

* * *

"That's him," Tristan said. "That's the guy Quinn and I chased in front of my building."

Steinert nodded to the coroner, who then set about transporting the body. "I'll see what we can do to get an ID on this guy, but it would have been nice to be able to question him."

"Sorry, but you know as well as anyone that pointing a gun at a SEAL usually doesn't end well," Tristan told him.

"We're going to impound the car too," Steinert told him. "We'll have the lab check it out for tracking devices."

Tristan nodded in agreement. "Quinn took a look when it was broken in to, but he didn't see anything."

"That doesn't mean there wasn't one there. There are dozens of places one could be hidden that wouldn't be easy to find."

"Yeah, I know." Tristan glanced over at Seth and Jay who were talking to one of Steinert's men. "Let us know what you find."

Steinert nodded. "And tell your sister-in-law she might want to lay low for a while longer."

"I will," Tristan told him, already dreading the moment when he would have to break the news to Quinn.

* * *

"This is what your asset was working on?" Vanessa stared down at the photograph in front of her, trying to make sense of the jumble of cords and tubes that Graham seemed so concerned about. "What is it?"

"It's a gate crasher," he told her. At Vanessa's blank look, he expounded. "If connected to the right computer, we think this thing could take down anything from banking records to Wall Street."

Vanessa's eyebrows lifted. "Like some kind of computer virus?"

"Not exactly." Graham leaned on the corner of the work table. "A computer virus has to get through whatever firewalls and security encryptions that are in place to protect our computers. Even if one gets through, they can usually be contained by disconnecting the infected computers from the system."

"And this thing?"

"Cracks through all of the firewalls and security systems. Apparently it rewrites the operating software in a way that our tech people believe could bypass all protocols." He hesitated before adding, "Including those on our government systems."

"And this is what your missing agent was working on?"

Graham nodded. "Our intelligence indicates that this gate crasher is on its way to the US from western Europe, but we don't know if it's already here or not."

"What would this have to do with Taylor Palmetta and her paintings?"

"We aren't sure," Graham admitted. "But her passport shows that she was in Paris around the same time our asset disappeared. We're hoping she saw something, or even better, painted something that will give us a clue as to what happened to him."

"I'll call and see how early Quinn can bring her in." Vanessa glanced at her watch to see that it was almost 7:30 in the morning. "With any luck, they can be here by 9:00."

"Good. We need to get a handle on this as soon as possible."

* * *

"Why didn't you tell me last night that we had an early appointment today?" Taylor asked, trying to tame her damp hair with her fingers.

"I didn't know what time our appointment was until an hour ago," Quinn told her as he led her toward the front door. "Besides, I didn't expect you to sleep in so late."

"Seven o'clock isn't exactly late," Taylor insisted. Then she shivered involuntarily in the cool morning air and stuffed her hands in the pockets of her jacket. "It's freezing out here."

"It's not that bad." Quinn shook his head and pulled the passenger door open for her.

"Yeah, if you're a polar bear," Taylor said grumpily. She climbed into the car, again running her fingers through her hair.

Quinn slid behind the wheel, started the car, and immediately turned on the heater. "Will you feel better if I tell you that we're going to Red Hot & Blue for lunch?"

Taylor shifted her eyes to look at him, her eyebrows lifting speculatively. "Maybe."

Quinn suppressed a grin and put the car in gear.

"Where is this meeting we have to go to?" Taylor asked. "And who even knows we're in town?"

"Vanessa said she needed to talk to us," Quinn told her. "We're meeting her at Langley."

"Langley?" Taylor shifted in her seat and stared at him. "As in CIA headquarters?"

"Yes, that Langley."

"Why would someone want me to go to CIA headquarters?" Taylor asked. "Or is this something for you and you're still afraid to leave me alone?"

Quinn shook his head and glanced at her. "It's you they want to talk to."

"Why?"

"We'll find out when we get there." Quinn turned onto the George Washington Parkway and headed out of Arlington toward Langley. He normally loved this drive with its thick trees on one side of the parkway and the Potomac River peacefully flowing by on the other. He spotted a couple of crew teams out practicing on the water, but other than that, the river was quiet.

Taylor sat silently staring out at the river for several minutes before speaking again. "Do you think Vanessa knows who's following me?"

Quinn shook his head. "I think she's hoping you can tell her."

"Obviously I don't know."

Quinn considered for a minute. "Think of all of these things that have happened as a big puzzle. We have some of the pieces, like the fact that your paintings appear to be at the heart of the problem, but we know we're still missing a lot of the other pieces."

"Okay." Taylor lifted her hands and then let them drop back into her lap. "How do we find the other pieces?"

"I think that's what Vanessa is hoping you can help her with," Quinn told her. "You know what you painted and when. You know who you talked to, who you were friends with, where you stayed. All of this information might lead us to find answers to the bigger questions: who and why."

"I guess that makes sense," Taylor said as Quinn turned off of the parkway onto Route 123. She was quiet again before asking, "How long are you planning on us staying with your parents?"

"Until Sunday." Quinn's eyebrows lifted. "Your sister and Tristan are supposed to get here sometime tonight."

Surprise lit her eyes. "Riley and Tristan are coming?"

Quinn nodded. Then he motioned to her bag as he turned into the main CIA headquarters entrance. "You're going to need to show your ID."

Taylor pulled out her wallet as Quinn slowed the car to a stop at the security station and an armed guard approached the car.

"Can I help you?"

Quinn dug his wallet out of his pocket and showed the guard his military ID. "We're here for a meeting with Vanessa Johnson."

The guard took Quinn's ID and checked it against a clipboard he held. He then motioned to Taylor. "I'll need your ID too, miss."

Taylor passed it to Quinn, who then handed it to the guard.

Again the guard checked his clipboard. "Wait here for a moment please."

Quinn nodded, watching as the guard picked up a phone presumably to verify that they were still cleared to enter the facility. A moment later he returned and handed them a map and a temporary parking pass.

"Have you been here before?"

Quinn shook his head.

"Okay, you'll follow this map to the west parking lot." He pointed to the left and then tapped the map to show them where the west lot was located. "It's a bit of a walk to the front entrance of the original building, so the easiest way to get there is to wait at one of the shuttle stops. A bus will come by and take you to the main entrance." He handed Quinn and Taylor their IDs back. "The guards inside will direct you from there."

"Okay, thanks." Quinn nodded to him and then waited for the security gate in front of him to lift.

As they drove past the security station, Taylor took a steadying breath. "I didn't realize it was so complicated to get in here."

"This is probably one of the most secure locations in the world," Quinn said as he followed an access road around the new building until he reached the parking lot. He pulled out the map, realizing that the main entrance was probably at least a half mile away. "Did you want to take the shuttle, or do you want to walk?"

"Let's take the shuttle," Taylor suggested. "I don't want to find out what will happen if we get lost."

"Good point," Quinn agreed. They locked up the car and walked over to the sign that looked like a typical bus stop on a public street. Of course, this wasn't a public street. A minute later an average-looking bus came into sight and then rolled to a stop beside them.

Quinn put his foot on the first step and started forward. He showed the bus driver the paper the guard had given him, and then he led Taylor to the front seat where the driver had indicated. A couple of minutes later, the bus pulled under the overhang in front of the original headquarters building.

The bus driver turned to look at them. "Go right through those doors. If your escort isn't inside waiting for you, the guards should be able to help you out."

"Thanks." Quinn ushered Taylor off the bus and then started up the steps to the wall of glass doors. He pulled one of the doors open, waiting for Taylor to enter before following her inside.

He took one look at the number of armed guards inside and the security screening system and found himself nodding his approval. He doubted even his squad would be able to make it inside undetected. Then he heard his name being called.

"Quinn. Over here." Vanessa crossed the lobby to where they stood just inside the doors. "Hi, Taylor."

"Hi," Taylor managed, her eyes wide.

"Come on. Let's get you through security."

Quinn took Taylor's hand in his, gave it a reassuring squeeze, and then tugged her along as they followed Vanessa. With Vanessa's help, they quickly navigated their way through the rest of the check-in procedure. Everything went smoothly right up until Quinn tried to walk through the security checkpoint.

Sirens screeched, lights flashed, and guards drew their guns.

Beside Quinn, Vanessa shook her head and muttered, "Well, there went my credibility."

Quinn's eyes met hers, and suddenly he realized what had caused the problem. Slowly, he lifted his arms and shook his head, not sure if he should be embarrassed or amused.

A young officer in his early twenties approached Quinn first. "Sir, please step back from the security gate."

Quinn took a step back, slowly turning to face him. "I'm sorry."

Vanessa held up her hand and stepped forward. "It's my fault. I didn't ask him to surrender his weapons." She approached Quinn, lifting the back of his shirt to reveal the handgun he always kept holstered there. Turning it butt out, she handed it over to the officer. "Where's the other one?"

Quinn nodded to his left ankle, standing still while Vanessa leaned down to relieve him of his second weapon. She handed this one over too and then turned to the guard behind her. "You can turn off the alarms now."

The older man stared at her for a moment and then nodded, hitting a button to disengage the lights and sirens.

The younger man now stepped forward. "Please come over here, sir."

Quinn did what he was asked, glancing over at Taylor who still had a panicked look on her face. As Vanessa began explaining to the guards that Quinn was cleared to carry weapons on military bases and hadn't realized he would be asked to surrender them while at CIA headquarters, Quinn gave Taylor an apologetic smile. If nothing else, he had little doubt that they wouldn't be followed in here.

26

"I heard there was some excitement downstairs," Graham said as he approached Vanessa and offered a hand.

"I'm afraid so," Vanessa grimaced. "The good news is that our building is secure and our SPOs shouldn't need to do any more training drills this month."

"SPOs?" Quinn asked.

"Guards," Vanessa told him, motioning for him to come into the conference room along with Taylor. "Taylor Palmetta and Quinn Lambert, this is Graham. He's the one who asked to meet with you."

"Come in and sit down," Graham said. As soon as they were seated at the conference table, he motioned to Taylor. "You're the artist."

"That's right," Taylor nodded.

"Good." He pulled out a notepad and pen. "Let's see if we can help each other."

* * *

Taylor's head was spinning by the time Vanessa escorted her and Quinn out of the building. Graham had asked for information she had never considered as possibly being important. Over the past several hours, they had reconstructed every place she had been the last few months, who she had met, what she had shipped back to the United States as well as when and where her paintings had been transported.

To her surprise, Graham had a copy of her passport records, which helped jog her memory on what dates she had traveled between countries. Quinn had brought copies of the photos of her missing paintings, although Graham seemed more concerned with her other paintings, paintings that someone might still be after. Graham also told them he would track down the shipment of Taylor's personal belongings so they could access the release forms that had been signed by the various people she had painted.

The only thing that Taylor now had to locate were her shipping records, which Vanessa promised to fax to Graham as soon as they all returned to Virginia Beach.

"You look overwhelmed," Vanessa said as they approached the security station.

"I am." Taylor shook her head, still unnerved by what had happened with Quinn earlier. "This isn't exactly a normal day for me."

"Your life hasn't been normal lately," Vanessa pointed out. She led them through security and then took their visitor badges and turned them in.

Retrieving Quinn's weapons took a little more time and a lot more explanation, with the guards finally returning the weapons to Vanessa, who promised not to give them back to Quinn until after he left the compound.

After they walked outside, Quinn turned to Vanessa. "I'm really sorry about the weapons. I never even thought about it."

"I know." Vanessa grinned at him. "But, of course, you realize that I have to tell Seth about this, and he's going to tease you mercilessly."

Quinn grimaced. "Well, it won't be as bad as when Jay accidentally shot Seth."

"Jay shot Seth?" Taylor asked, her eyes wide.

Quinn nodded. "With a tranquilizer dart."

"Poor Jay." Vanessa laughed. "He still feels bad about that."

"Yeah, but at least his blunder wasn't in front of twenty armed guards."

"I'm just glad your instincts didn't kick in to fight back."

"I only do that with the bad guys."

"When you know who the bad guys are," Taylor added.

"Graham has been working on some ideas of how to filter through all of this information and identify who's causing the problem. Give him a few days, and I think we'll have a much better picture of what you stumbled into."

"I hope so." Taylor followed Vanessa as she started walking in the opposite direction of where they had parked. "Where are we going? I think we're parked over that way."

"Yeah, in the west lot." Vanessa nodded. "I'll give you a ride over there. I'm parked over here."

Quinn turned to look at Taylor. "I'm trying to decide which is scarier, trying to find our way back to our car by ourselves or driving with Vanessa."

"If you want your weapons back, you're stuck with me," Vanessa told him, not the least bit offended. "Besides, the cops on the compound here are stricter than any others I've ever seen. The last thing I need is another speeding ticket."

"Another?"

"I got one here my second week working." Vanessa nodded. "You would have thought that someone would have warned me."

Quinn chuckled as he opened the door for Taylor and then climbed into the backseat. A minute later, they were pulling out of the parking lot next to the front of the CIA headquarters building, and Vanessa turned to the right, taking them the opposite way from where they had come.

"We'll take you on the scenic route," Vanessa told them before they could ask why she had turned in the opposite direction.

Taylor looked at the side of the headquarters building, at the grassy area and the mature trees that created a peaceful setting in what was certainly a very stressful place. She wished she could stand right there on the edge of the grass and just stare for a few hours, ideally with her paints and a canvas to keep her company.

Taylor motioned to the picturesque setting. "Is there any way I could get a picture of that building?"

"I could probably get you one. Why?"

"I just think it would make a really cool painting, with all of the leaves turning in the background," Taylor told her. "And I doubt the CIA is going to let me set up an easel here in the middle of their compound."

"Not likely," Vanessa agreed with a smile. "But I know one of the agency photographers. I'll ask him if he'll snap a photo for you and get it cleared."

"That would be great."

"We're in that section over there," Quinn interrupted, pointing to where he had parked.

"I never realized how big this place is," Taylor commented as Vanessa turned where Quinn indicated and drove slowly until they reached their car. "It's a lot more intimidating in person."

"Especially when your first time here is with Quinn while he's armed."

"So are you going to give me my weapons back now?"

"I'll follow you out. I can't give them to you until then."

"Vanessa, it's not like I'm going to shoot anyone."

"I know, but this isn't the kind of place where we want to bend any rules," Vanessa insisted. "Where are you going next?"

"Actually, I promised to take Taylor to Red Hot & Blue for lunch. Do you want to join us?"

She smiled. "I could take a lunch break."

"In that case, we'll meet you over there," Quinn said. "Unless you want to drive with us."

"I'll meet you there," Vanessa told him. "It's easier than dealing with the security trying to get back in."

Quinn let out a short laugh. "Isn't that the truth."

* * *

"Would you mind if we stopped by an art store on our way back?" Taylor asked as they walked toward their car in Rosslyn. "The place I was telling you about should have the size of canvases I like."

"I thought one canvas was pretty much the same as another," Quinn said.

Taylor shook her head. "There are a couple of sizes that aren't easy to find, and I'm getting anxious to start painting again."

"Just point me in the right direction." Quinn unlocked the car and opened her door.

Taylor shifted in her seat to try to get her bearings. As soon as Quinn started the car, she said, "Turn left on Wilson Boulevard."

"Okay." Quinn weaved his way through the traffic and followed her directions until he came to a specialty art supply store.

"It shouldn't take me long to get what I need."

Quinn climbed out of the car and looked at her over the top as she got out on the other side. "I'll believe that when I see it."

Taylor blinked at him in mock surprise. "Don't you trust me?"

He reached for the door, his eyebrows raised. "In an art store? Not a chance."

"I always knew you were smart." Taylor grinned at him. She walked into the store, her eyes brightening the moment she saw the racks of paints and stacks of canvases.

"Can I help you?" the tall, thin man behind the counter asked.

Taylor turned to look at him, the grin still on her face. "Absolutely."

The store clerk immediately returned her smile. "Do you need help picking out supplies, or do you know your way around?"

Taylor shot an amused look at Quinn before looking back at the clerk. "I want to do a little browsing, but I have a list that you can help me with." She dug a piece of paper out of her bag and handed it to him.

"Let's see what we have here." He read down the handwritten list, nodding to himself until he reached the bottom. "I should be able to help you with most of this, but I'm not sure if we have all of the canvases that you want." He tapped a finger on the list. "These were discontinued quite a while ago."

Taylor leaned closer and then shook her head in frustration. "If I had realized how hard those would be to get, I would have stocked up while I was in Paris."

"I'm surprised you found a place that carries them," the clerk told her. "A lot of people who want the custom sizes are starting to make their own."

"I'd rather spend my time painting than pulling splinters out of my fingers trying to make my own canvases," Taylor said.

"I might have one or two canvases back in the storage room that are similar in size," the clerk told her. "Let me go check for you and see. I assume you want professional quality."

"Yeah, thanks." Taylor gravitated toward a display of paints, considering what colors she might want to pick up while she was here. Within a minute, she had three in her hand and was contemplating buying a new palette.

"Do you already know what you want to paint next?" Quinn asked her.

"I have a few ideas," Taylor nodded. "What I really want to do is camp out on Virginia Beach for a few weeks and do some work there, but I've been too paranoid to sit outside for that long, especially using an easel."

"If Vanessa comes through with that photo of CIA headquarters you'll have a project you can work on."

"Yeah." Taylor continued to select supplies.

"I still can't believe how many paintings you did last year."

"It's not that surprising when you consider that I was in an art program that forced me to come up with at least one a week. Besides, I usually work on more than one at a time."

"Really?"

She nodded. "I can only paint for so long without the changing light messing me up, so I typically have one I work on in the morning and a different one for the afternoons."

Quinn's eyebrows lifted as she moved from the paints to look at charcoal. "Why do I get the feeling that you could spend all day in here and never get bored?"

Taylor glanced over her shoulder and grinned. "Because you're very perceptive."

When the clerk reemerged from the back room holding two canvases, Taylor carried her selections to the counter. After she finished paying, Quinn picked up the canvases and led the way out to the car.

"Were you afraid you would never get me out of there?" Taylor asked.

"I was starting to wonder." Quinn unlocked the car and put the canvases in the backseat. "Are you ready to go back now?"

Taylor nodded just as Quinn's phone rang.

Quinn pulled his phone from his pocket, glancing at the caller ID long enough to see that the number wasn't identified. He pressed the talk button. "Lambert."

"Quinn, we've got a problem." Vanessa's voice came over the line, tension vibrating through it.

"What?"

"I can't say over the phone. I need you to get back in here," Vanessa told him. "I'll meet you at the front gate."

Quinn looked at Taylor, saw the concerned look on her face, and then immediately took another look around them to make sure they were really alone. "We'll be right there."

27

TAYLOR LOOKED AT THE PHOTOS in front of her, trying to remember if she had ever seen these men before. Her heart was still racing and had been ever since Quinn had answered his phone. At first she had thought he was being called out on assignment, but when he said they were going back to CIA headquarters, her concerns had expanded beyond just worrying about Quinn's safety and the fear of being left alone.

Vanessa had met them at the front gate, and they had been rushed through the security checkpoints. This time, however, Vanessa had led Taylor to a conference room where two women were waiting for her with a stack of photos. After dropping her off, Vanessa had taken Quinn with her to meet with someone else.

"This one looks familiar." Taylor pointed to a photo of a bald man who appeared to be in his fifties. She leaned closer and nodded as she tapped a finger on an arc-shaped scar that was visible on the man's chin. "I remember wondering how he got that scar."

"Can you remember where you saw him?"

Taylor closed her eyes, trying to bring him into focus in the right setting. Her mind flipped through several scenarios, and then finally she opened her eyes and nodded slowly. "I'm pretty sure it was in Paris." She picked up the photo and studied it more closely. "Yeah, I remember now. I saw him when I was painting a sidewalk café."

"When?"

"It would have been about a month ago. That was one of the last places I went before coming back home," Taylor told her. "Graham has all of the dates of where I was and when."

The woman picked up a paper from the file in front of her. "Here it is. You were in Paris from August 20 to September 6." She looked up at

Taylor with intensity. "Can you remember how close to the end of your trip it was?"

Taylor thought a moment longer. "Yeah. It was the painting I finished the day my hotel room was broken into. It's the last one I did before I left."

The woman looked at Taylor and then turned to look at the other woman in the room. A silent message passed between them, but Taylor didn't understand the meaning. All she knew was that the tension had increased tenfold.

"Do you remember if he was with anyone?"

Taylor let out a frustrated sigh. "I saw thousands of people in cafés and walking along the street while I was in Europe."

"But you remember him." The older woman pointed to the photo she had identified. "Why?"

"I don't know." Taylor thought back, trying to figure out why he had stood out in her mind. She closed her eyes, replaying that day. "It had been raining. I remember I had to set up farther away from the street than I normally would because I was worried the cars would splash water up on my canvas."

"And the man in the picture. When did you first notice him?"

"That morning when I first set up." Taylor looked over at her, the image beginning to clear in her head. "That's right. I remember seeing him first thing in the morning, maybe five minutes after I set up my easel. He had sat down at one of the tables outside, but almost everyone else was eating inside. Then I think he left, but I saw him again around lunchtime. He walked over and asked to look at what I was painting. I had the canvas so far back that no one could walk behind me."

"Was that it?" she asked. "Was he alone?"

"He was alone when I first saw him that morning and when he talked to me," Taylor nodded. "A little while later he met someone for lunch."

"Man or woman?"

"Man, forty-ish, probably Italian. He was wearing Armani, expensive shoes and watch . . ." Taylor trailed off. "And the painting I was working on was one that was stolen from New Jersey."

"Are you sure?"

"I'm positive," Taylor nodded. "Quinn and I just finished identifying the missing paintings yesterday."

"Thank you for your help," the woman said now, her tension increasing yet again.

Taylor pointed at the photo. "Who is he? And what does all of this have to do with me?"

The woman ignored Taylor's question. Instead, she said, "Please stay here with Ellen. Your friends should be done in a few minutes."

"Okay," Taylor said, sinking back down into the padded conference chair. As the woman left the room, Taylor could only wonder what in the world she could have said to cause so much tension.

* * *

"We found our asset this morning," Graham said the minute Quinn walked through the door with Vanessa.

"Where?"

"His body was found in an abandoned farmhouse an hour outside of Paris."

"He's dead?" Quinn's jaw clenched.

"I'm afraid so." He dragged a hand over his face, but Quinn couldn't tell if it was in frustration or if he was attempting to hide his reaction to the news.

"What happened?"

"He was shot execution style. Single bullet to the head." Graham took a deep breath as though settling his emotions. "I'm sure in your line of work you realize that this raises the stakes for your friend. If whoever killed our asset is the same person following Taylor Palmetta around, we're dealing with a lot more than just some petty crimes."

Quinn's stomach twisted uncomfortably. "What was the last intel you got from your asset?"

"That's need to know."

"And I need to know." Quinn's voice was low but firm. "Taylor and I have given you everything we know, but it's me and my family who are the ones sitting around wondering when someone's going to come at Taylor next."

"Graham, you need to read him in," Vanessa said, compassion in her voice. "And we need him and the rest of his squad involved. They may be our best shot at finding out who did this."

Graham was silent for several seconds, and then he took another shaky breath. "We may already know who did this."

Quinn straightened. "Who?"

"Vernon Riesenour, a computer scientist living in Marseille. His wife was Iraqi. She and their two sons were killed in a skirmish when one of our patrols was ambushed," Graham told him.

"And you think he's looking for payback against the US?"

Graham nodded. "The last time we heard from our asset, he was concerned about the possibility of an attack on the financial systems in the United States."

"How?"

"Did you hear about the incident in London last month?" Graham asked.

Quinn shook his head.

"Three banks, all located on the same street, had mysterious computer crashes," he told him. "All three had their ATMs crash completely. When they went to look at the machines, the surveillance cameras were blank, all of the money was gone, and the banks' computer systems were compromised."

"The surveillance cameras were blank?"

"These two photos are all we have to go on. This one is from a secondary surveillance camera at one of the banks." Graham pulled out a photo and passed it to Quinn. "We believed this system had to be plugged into one of the banking computers, but from what we know now, whoever uses it could access it anywhere, even through an ATM machine."

"Which means we have no defense against it unless we keep the device from making it into the country." Quinn shook his head. "What about the other photo?"

"It was uncovered yesterday in Paris. Apparently our asset had hidden it in an encrypted file on his computer. He must have been killed before he got the chance to send it."

"But what makes you think this thing is going to be used in the US instead of Europe? Why go to all of the trouble to smuggle it into the US?"

"We now think the robberies in London were just a test run," Graham told him. "There's been chatter about extremists in Abolstan planning an attack on the US. We think this may be it."

"You think Riesenour has teamed up with Abolstani extremists?" Vanessa's eyebrows lifted. "If they hit one of the major banking centers, they would not only manage to walk away with several hundred thousand dollars in a relatively short period of time, but by crippling the financial systems, we could end up with anything from confusion to absolute chaos."

Just imagine what would happen if millions of people suddenly couldn't access their money or use a debit or credit card."

"This would make the LA riots look like a peace treaty." Graham nodded. "Not only that, but in the encrypted file we uncovered today, our asset noted the possibility of a doomsday sequence in the gate crasher's programming."

"What kind of doomsday sequence?"

"Basically, whoever is using it could plug into various financial and military computers, but nothing would happen until a designated time. When that time arrives, the systems would crash simultaneously."

"That would be devastating," Vanessa managed.

"Do we know how it's being smuggled into the US?" Quinn asked, focusing on the practical.

"That's what we're still trying to find out," Graham said. "We also haven't managed to uncover any kind of money trail."

"If he's out for revenge, you aren't going to find one," Vanessa said.

"He doesn't have the resources to pull this off by himself." Graham shook his head. "We're sure that someone provided him with the money and resources he needed to develop this technology on his own. But as we already told you, if he succeeds, he could seriously cripple the entire financial industry in this country and send us backward a hundred years. We could literally be thrust back into a bartering system overnight. And the ramifications of a breach in our military systems would be disastrous."

"Why haven't you taken this guy out?" Quinn asked impatiently.

"Our intel suggests that the components have already been shipped. We need to know how and where, and we need to find out who is behind this before we go after him."

Quinn looked at him skeptically. "Does customs even know to look for this stuff?"

"Not specifically, but since 9/11, customs uses x-ray screening a lot more than it used to. Small items aren't any easier to get through than larger items now." Graham hesitated a moment as though considering how much information to divulge. Then he let out a sigh and added, "Also, some of this equipment may have originated from some sources that have electronic markers that would be easy to detect."

"What kind of markers?"

"Riesenour used to work for a contractor who provided electronic equipment for the French government. The photos we have indicate that some of the high-end computer components may have been used."

Vanessa looked at him with new understanding. "And those computer components are marked electronically to ensure they can't slip out of their country undetected."

Quinn looked from Vanessa to Graham. "I don't understand."

"They're tagged electronically because they are extremely valuable and . . ."

"And potentially dangerous," Quinn finished for her.

The office door opened, and one of the women who had been with Taylor walked in. "Taylor Palmetta just identified Cress. She may have been the last person to see him alive."

"What?"

She nodded. "Not only that, she said that she remembered him having lunch with an Italian man, around forty years old. She also said that one of her paintings that was stolen in New Jersey was the same painting she was creating the day she saw Cress."

"Are you sure?" Quinn asked.

Vanessa looked at him. "Do you think she might have accidentally painted Riesenour?"

Quinn shook his head. "That wouldn't make sense. She always has people sign waivers before she paints them."

"On a street scene, she couldn't get waivers from everyone."

"She said that she does," Quinn told her. "Besides, what about the second painting?"

"It could have been stolen just to throw us off," Graham suggested.

"Pull up the picture of the missing paintings," Quinn told Graham. "See if there's anything that this Riesenour guy had to worry about."

Graham sifted through a stack of papers on his desk and picked up a page-sized printout of Taylor's stolen paintings. "You're right. Her paintings don't show anyone's face. She has them all blurred."

"Then why was it stolen?"

"I have absolutely no idea."

"Do you know where Riesenour is now?" Quinn asked. "Maybe it's time we bring him in for questioning."

"It isn't that simple," Graham told him. "Even if we manage to locate him, he isn't going to come to the United States willingly."

Quinn's eyebrows lifted. "I wasn't exactly planning on asking his permission."

"Questioning Riesenour might be the best chance we have to head off this attack," Vanessa said. "That needs to be one of our top priorities."

"I'll talk to the chief of station in Paris and see if he can shake some information loose. In the meantime, we need to find out if Riesenour has figured out how to get this equipment past customs," Graham said.

Vanessa nodded and looked at Quinn. "And obviously your main priority is to keep Taylor safe."

28

Dawn was just breaking when Taylor walked into the Lamberts' kitchen on Saturday morning. She still wasn't sure exactly why she and Quinn had been called back to the CIA the day before, but she was certain that Quinn and Vanessa knew a whole lot more than they were telling her. And being left in the dark was driving her crazy.

The tension she had sensed at CIA headquarters had followed them back to Quinn's childhood home. Tristan and Riley had already arrived from Virginia Beach, but instead of the casual welcome Taylor would have expected, Tristan had immediately pulled Quinn aside for a private conversation. Even Riley seemed to know more than she was telling.

All evening the tension had hung in the air. Gone was the light-hearted ribbing she was accustomed to when she was around Tristan and Riley.

Taylor half expected to see either Quinn or Tristan in the kitchen when she walked in, but to her surprise, it was dark and empty. She continued through the kitchen and walked to the back door where she could see the beginnings of the sunrise. She considered a minute, wondering if she dared go out onto the deck by herself. She peeked outside, looking around to see if anyone could be hiding in the shadows, but there was nothing but the fenced yard and the trees beyond it.

"You're just being paranoid," Taylor whispered to herself, hoping that her words were true. Certainly she would be safe in Quinn's backyard. Still trying to convince herself of that fact, she went back upstairs to retrieve her bag and a hoodie from her room.

Five minutes later she was settled on the deck, completely engrossed in the view of the sun rising over the woods behind the Lamberts' townhouse, her sketchbook on her lap and one of her new graphite sticks in her hand. When the back door slid open an hour later, she barely even noticed.

"What are you doing out here?" Quinn asked, successfully startling her back to reality.

Taylor dropped the pad onto her lap and lifted a hand to her now rapidly beating heart. "Are you trying to give me a heart attack?"

"Are you trying to give me one?" Quinn countered, clearly annoyed. "Taylor, you can't just walk outside by yourself like this. I've been looking for you for the past ten minutes."

A little ripple of fear worked through her, and Taylor tried to fight it. "I guess you should have looked here first."

Quinn shook his head. "If you had your cell phone with you, I would have known where to look."

Taylor's eyes met his. She wanted him to insist that she was safe here, even though she could see in his expression that he wasn't sure. "If no one knows that I'm here, I should be perfectly safe in your backyard."

The muscle in Quinn's jaw jumped, and he stared down at her with a combination of irritation and concern. "I have no idea who knows what about your current location, but I do know that I can't protect you if I don't know where you are."

"Exactly when did you become my protector?" Taylor demanded, her fear and frustration seeping into her words. "I appreciate everything you've done for me, but it's getting really old turning into everyone's charity case."

"What are you talking about?"

"Don't patronize me." Taylor let out a frustrated sigh. "Everyone's so worried about my safety, but none of you will tell me anything about why this is all happening."

Quinn started to open his mouth, but she held her hand up. "And don't tell me you don't know anything."

"I know that you need to trust me and that you shouldn't go anywhere alone."

"I kind of figured that already." Taylor bit back on the threatening well of emotions. "Any idea when that part of my life might change?"

Quinn shook his head, and his tone softened. "Why don't you come inside and have some breakfast?"

"No thanks," Taylor said, her annoyance overriding logic as well as the demands of her stomach. She shifted in her chair so that once again she was staring out at the sunrise. She thought that Quinn would go back inside and leave her alone, but instead, he lowered himself into the chair beside her.

"What did they tell you when we went back to CIA headquarters yesterday?"

Taylor's shoulders lifted, and she turned again to look at him. "Nothing. They just put a bunch of pictures in front of me and asked if I recognized any of the people in them."

"Did you recognize any of them?"

"A bald guy that I saw in Paris." Taylor's eyes met his. "Who is he?"

"I don't know," Quinn said. He saw the frustration light in Taylor's eyes, and he held up a hand and said, "Really, I don't know, but he was working for the CIA."

"Was?"

Quinn's jaw tensed. "What else did you tell them?"

"He was around most of the day when I was working on one of the paintings that was stolen. At one point, he even came over and looked at it," Taylor told him. "Then he met with some guy at the café, and that's the last I remember seeing him."

"Did you recognize the other guy in any of the pictures they showed you?"

"No, but that doesn't mean he wasn't in one of them," Taylor said. "The only thing I really remember about him is that he dressed really well. Most of the people I saw on the street that day weren't wearing Armani suits. I guess that's why he stood out a bit in my mind."

"Can you draw a picture of what he looked like?"

"Quinn, I'm not sure I can remember what he looked like."

"Just try," Quinn pressed. "Try to sketch what you saw that day when the bald guy was eating lunch. Put in any of the details you can remember."

"Okay," Taylor sighed. "I'll try."

"Good." Quinn shifted closer to her as she flipped to a blank page in her sketchbook. "Start with the bald guy."

Taylor began sketching, first the table at the café where the two men had sat together and then the CIA agent. When she tried to create the second figure, she wasn't able to do much beyond the general shape and size of him and the clothes he wore. "I'm sorry, but I just don't remember much more than that. It was more than a month ago."

"That's okay." Quinn leaned forward. "Forget about him for a minute and tell me what else you saw. Fill in the rest of the scene."

"All right." Taylor's hand started moving again, another table, a waiter, water dripping from the awning.

"That's good. What about cars? Were there any parked in front of the café?"

"It's a no parking zone." Taylor shook her head. "Except for a few minutes there was some kind of utility van." She sketched in the outline of the van, narrow by American standards, with two men sitting in the front seats. "That's generally what it looked like, and it had some kind of logo on the side."

"Is this where it was parked?"

"Actually, it was more in front of where the two men were sitting."

"Were you there when the van left?"

Taylor nodded.

"Were the two men still there?"

She thought for a minute and then shook her head. "No, now that you mention it, I don't think they were. And I don't remember seeing them leave, but then again, I wasn't really watching them that closely either."

"The van wasn't in your painting, was it?"

Again she shook her head. "No, I was nearly done with the painting by then. I didn't put any vehicles in it except for a few blurring past on the road."

"I need to go call Vanessa. Are you sure you won't come back inside?"

"Let me finish this one sketch, and then I'll come in, okay?"

"Okay, but don't be long," Quinn insisted. "It makes me nervous when you're out here alone."

"You aren't planning on keeping me locked up inside all day, are you?"

"Not necessarily." Quinn shrugged a shoulder.

"Good, because I was hoping you'd take me into DC. I'd love to do some work around the monuments." She looked up at him, her eyes pleading. "I really need to spend some time outside, or I think I might go crazy."

"I have a better idea," he told her. "How about a picnic lunch across the river from DC? The view is great, and we won't have to deal with the crowds."

"There are places up here where we won't have crowds?"

"Sure, if you know where to look," Quinn told her. "Hurry up and finish your sketch. We can go out early if you want."

"I'd like that."

* * *

Quinn was just hanging up with Vanessa when Tristan knocked on his bedroom door and pushed it open.

"Is everything all right?" Tristan asked.

"I was just updating Vanessa." Quinn leaned back against the windowsill, thinking how small this room seemed now and wondering how he and Tristan had managed to share it successfully during their teenage years. "Taylor saw a white utility van in front of that café in Paris. I think it was the vehicle used by Cress's killer to get him away from there."

"Taylor saw him leave?"

"No, but she doesn't remember them being there after the van left," Quinn told him. "I think Vanessa was right. Taylor saw things that were important, but she doesn't know what they were."

"That still doesn't explain why anyone would go after her or her paintings."

"I know." Quinn rubbed at his forehead.

"Quinn, I know you're worried," Tristan told him. "We all are."

"I just don't know how much longer I can do this. It's like Emily all over again."

"You don't have to do this. We can keep Taylor with us or set up a safe house for her somewhere."

Quinn shook his head. "You know I can't walk away."

Tristan's stare intensified. "You've fallen in love with her, haven't you?"

Quinn's eyes shot up to Tristan's. He should have known Tristan would recognize his feelings even though he hadn't yet been able to voice the words to Taylor—had barely been able to acknowledge them himself. Quinn took on an impatient and pleading tone. "Can we not do this right now? We have to neutralize Riesenour before he finds Taylor."

"We will," Tristan said with certainty. "But in the meantime, you and Taylor need to talk."

"We talk all the time."

"About Emily?"

"There's nothing to say about Emily," Quinn insisted, even though he knew his words weren't true. Since that day at the train station, he had been wondering how to bring up Emily again, how he could explain to Taylor that Emily's death had left a hole in his heart that had only recently begun to heal. He couldn't even be sure when the healing process had started, but he was starting to think that it had coincided with Taylor's arrival in Virginia.

"There's a lot to say," Tristan countered. "And you know it."

Before Quinn could say anything else, Tristan walked out of the room. A second later Quinn heard him greet Taylor in the hallway.

Quinn pushed away from the window and crossed to the door just as Taylor reached it. Her hair was down, curling madly over her shoulders, and her cheeks were rosy from being outside in the cool morning air.

"Are you ready to go?"

"Yeah. I just need to grab a couple of things downstairs." Quinn reached for her hand before she could move back out in the hall. Then without a word, he leaned forward and kissed her softly.

He tried to push aside his fears and let himself live in the moment, but all he could think of was what would happen if this was the last time he ever got this opportunity. What would he do if tomorrow he woke up and Taylor was no longer here? The doubts lingered, but as he pulled her closer, snaking his free hand around her waist, he was faced with the simple reality. Taylor was alive, and he knew he had to do everything in his power to keep her that way.

29

"THIS IS PERFECT." TAYLOR APPROACHED a wooden bench overlooking the Potomac River. Underneath the clear blue sky, she could see the Jefferson and Lincoln Memorials with the Washington Memorial spearing up into the sky behind them. From the quiet of Roosevelt Island, she could pretend that the busy weekend traffic didn't exist on the nearby George Washington Parkway.

She had already stopped twice to sketch scenes along the way, starting with the footbridge leading from Rosslyn onto the island. When she had tried to stop a third time, Quinn had gently nudged her along, promising that she could stop again on the way home. Now she could see why he wanted her to keep going. This view could keep her busy for weeks if she had the right supplies.

Her sketchbook already in her hand, she lowered herself onto the bench and retrieved a hunk of charcoal from her bag.

"Is this quiet enough for you?" Quinn lowered the backpack he held onto the bench and sat beside her.

Taylor nodded, her hand already pressing charcoal to paper. "I'm surprised it isn't more crowded."

"It will be as the day goes on. Besides, most people park on the other side of the island." Quinn began rifling through his backpack and fished out two water bottles. "Here."

"Thanks." Taylor set her charcoal down long enough to take it from him, but she put it down on the bench unopened and went back to sketching.

"I never realized how focused you get when you're drawing." Quinn opened his water bottle and took a drink.

"Mmm hmm," Taylor responded, barely registering his words. The reflection of the Jefferson Memorial in the water and sunlight streaking across the white columns of the Lincoln were fascinating. Her fingers could barely keep up with what she wanted to do.

She finished one sketch and flipped the page, completely forgetting that Quinn was even beside her. Time ceased to have meaning as she considered the images she wanted to paint. Coming back to this spot with her supplies would be the ideal situation, but she hoped she could recreate the feeling using her sketches. She wrote a few notes in the margin of one, referring to the colors and techniques she would use.

More than two hours passed before she finally set down the charcoal and flexed her hand to work out the cramps developing there.

"You're amazing," Quinn said, finally breaking through her concentration.

Taylor looked over at him, suddenly feeling guilty that she had been completely ignoring him. "I'm sorry. I should have told you to bring a book or something," she apologized. "I tend to get tunnel vision when I'm working."

The corner of Quinn's mouth lifted into the beginnings of a smile. "I noticed." He reached over and tapped a finger on her sketchbook. "But I think watching you is more interesting that reading a book."

"I doubt that." Taylor shook her head and pushed her hair back behind her shoulders. "You must be bored."

"Don't worry about me." Quinn opened his backpack wider. "Are you ready for a break? I brought some food."

"That sounds good." Taylor shifted closer to look in his bag. "What did you bring me?"

"Nothing too fancy." Quinn handed her a sandwich and then pulled a bag of chips out of his backpack along with a plastic bag filled with cookies.

"Are those the cookies your Mom made yesterday? I thought they were for some ward party."

Quinn shot her an innocent look. "I only swiped a few."

"That's what Tristan said this morning when your mom caught him eating one." Taylor gave him a disapproving look as she unwrapped her sandwich.

"Which means Tristan will get blamed for taking these too," Quinn told her with a grin. "I didn't get caught."

"Your poor mother must have had quite a time raising you." Taylor shook her head. "I don't know how she managed to stay sane."

"She has a good sense of humor."

Taylor laughed. "She would have to with you and Tristan."

Quinn shrugged and settled back on the bench as he ate his lunch. He stared out at the monuments for a few minutes and then asked, "You're going to paint this, aren't you?"

"Yeah, I am," Taylor agreed easily. "This view is so different from what most people see when they look at DC. It's so peaceful and you can feel the history of it all."

"My dad has always been big into history. He used to take us into the city at least a couple of times a month to see something."

"My folks were like that too." Taylor thought back to her own childhood and the way her dad always wanted to go out and see something whenever he was home. "I can't count how many times I've been to Jamestown and Williamsburg."

Footsteps rustled in the fallen leaves, and Quinn shifted to look at the young family walking toward them. He watched them as they passed by and then began packing up all of his and Taylor's trash and motioned to the trail. "We should probably get going."

"Okay." Taylor slid her sketchbook into her bag and stood up. She fell into step beside him, her mind drifting back to that morning when she had gone upstairs to find him. She had heard the tail end of his conversation with Tristan. His mention of Emily had left a burning inside of her to know more, to know why Emily was so important that Tristan felt Quinn needed to tell Taylor about her.

They walked away from the river for a few minutes in silence until, finally, Taylor knew she wouldn't be able to wait any longer to find some answers. She glanced over at him, took a deep breath, and forced out the question. "Who's Emily?"

Quinn's head whipped around, a surprised expression on his face. "What?"

"You heard me," Taylor said gently. "Who is Emily?"

Quinn stared at her, and Taylor could sense the storm of emotions rushing through him. For a moment it was as though he couldn't speak, and Taylor regretted letting her curiosity get the best of her. Then finally Quinn spoke. "Who told you about Emily?"

Taylor took a step closer to him and laid a hand gently on his arm. "You did."

"You overheard me talking to Tristan this morning?"

"I heard Tristan mention her, but I've been wondering about her since I found out that Emily wasn't one of your sisters," Taylor told him. "You mentioned her at the train station in Williamsburg."

Quinn looked away, staring out at the trees for a long moment.

"Quinn, talk to me," Taylor pleaded. "Why did Tristan say you needed to tell me about her?"

"Because she's dead," Quinn forced the words out.

Taylor absorbed the shock of his words, felt the pain and helplessness vibrating from him. Tension settled over them as understanding pulsed through her. "You were in love with her."

Quinn nodded.

Taylor felt her heart squeeze in her chest. She took several steadying breaths before she managed to ask, "What happened?"

"Non-Hodgkin's lymphoma." Quinn said the words as though there were a bad taste in his mouth. "She got sick, and in less than a year, she was gone."

"I'm so sorry."

"Everybody was sorry." Quinn's shoulder jerked up. "But that didn't change the reality."

"No, I suppose it didn't." Taylor stood there for a moment, not sure what to say or do.

Quinn took a deep breath as though trying to clear his head. Then he took a step down the path and motioned back toward the park exit. "Come on. We need to get back."

Without a word, Taylor stepped beside him feeling like her own reality had shattered. Was this why Quinn had backed away from her before? Had the pain of losing Emily made him unwilling to open his heart completely to anyone else?

She had been prepared to find out that Emily was an old girlfriend, maybe one who had broken his heart, perhaps someone who had run off with someone else. Never had she dreamed that the other woman was literally a ghost from his past.

* * *

Quinn didn't know whether to be furious or relieved. Taylor hadn't said a word since they'd started back to the parking garage in Rosslyn where Quinn had parked the car.

She hadn't acted the way he had thought she would. Somehow, Quinn had conjured up the image of Taylor being jealous or annoyed that he hadn't told her about Emily or that she would press for more information.

How long they had been together, how they met. Something. Yet, Taylor continued to walk silently beside him as though realizing he wasn't quite ready to volunteer any more information.

He opened the car door for her and studied her for a moment as she gave him a timid smile and slipped into her seat. As he walked around to the driver's side, he debated with himself. He thought back to Tristan's casual comment that morning, his observation that Quinn had fallen in love with Taylor.

Quinn glanced over at Taylor, not quite ready to share that fact with her. He slid the key into the ignition but didn't start the car. Instead, he shifted to face Taylor. "I'm sorry if I was short with you back there. It's just not something that's easy to talk about."

Taylor forced a smile. "I should be apologizing to you for prying. I can't imagine how hard that must have been for you."

Quinn stared at her, taken aback by the sincerity on her face. Then he reached for the keys and started the car. Taylor was the first person he had ever dated who knew anything about Emily, and now he was faced with whether he was prepared for Taylor to know everything. He put the car in gear, pulled out of the parking garage, and, after a brief internal debate, turned away from home and headed for King Street.

30

"Where are we going?" Taylor shifted in her seat and tried to get her bearings as Quinn turned onto King Street in Alexandria.

"There's something I need to show you." He kept his eyes on the road as they passed by centuries-old houses. Finally, he turned into a narrow driveway.

Taylor looked at him as they passed through a gate, and she saw the old-style tombstones.

Quinn kept his eyes on the narrow paved road, navigating it as though he had done so often. He circled around the center section of the cemetery and then turned down another driveway that weaved through some mature trees and down a hill. Finally, he pulled into another section of the cemetery, parking beside a tree that appeared to have been planted within the past few years.

Quinn got out of the car and circled to her side to open the door. He reached for her hand, his eyes somber and sincere. "Will you come with me?"

"Okay." Taylor let him help her out of the car. She walked beside him, looking down at grave markers as they passed. Some were bronze markers that were flat on the ground, and others were traditional tombstones. As Taylor looked at the death dates, she realized that this was a newer section of the cemetery.

Quinn slowed, and Taylor's eyes shifted to the next name. And her breath caught in her chest. The bronze marker was simple, the name engraved in delicate script letters: *Emily Lambert*.

Taylor's eyes immediately filled, and she fought back the urge to cry. Emily wasn't just an old girlfriend Quinn had fallen in love with. She was a woman he had loved so much that he had married her.

She looked up at Quinn, speechless.

A gentle breeze whispered through the surrounding trees, and for a moment, neither of them said anything. Then Quinn looked down at the grave marker and let out a sigh. "We'd only been dating a few months when she found out she was sick," Quinn told her, his voice surprisingly calm. "At first the doctors thought she would be able to beat it. Then she started treatment and was struggling a bit. I remember hearing her parents say something about how she needed to be positive and try to look forward in her life."

"And you married her."

"I married her." Quinn nodded. "I loved her. She loved me. I wanted to be with her for as long as we had."

"How long?"

"Almost nine months." Quinn leaned down and ran a finger over the dates at the bottom of the marker.

Taylor read the dates and then read the death date again. "I came to Virginia on the anniversary of her death."

Quinn stood up once more and nodded. "Yeah. I came up to visit Emily early that morning, and then you were at Tristan's that night."

"No wonder you weren't acting like yourself," Taylor said, more to herself than to Quinn. She looked back at the grave marker, her eyes focusing on the eternity symbol beneath Emily's name. "Can you tell me what she was like?"

"She was fun and caring." Quinn looked down at the symbol, the interlocking rings. "When I was with her, I felt whole."

"Quinn, I'm so sorry."

"I know." He stepped closer to her, taking her hand in his. "I wasn't trying to keep this from you. It's just really private. Even the guys in the squad don't know about my wife."

Taylor nodded, a lump forming in her throat. She swallowed hard, not sure what to think of the gesture Quinn had just made by sharing this part of his past with her. Her eyes were moist as she looked up at him. "Thanks for sharing this with me."

Quinn looked down at Emily's grave and then his eyes met Taylor's. Taking a step forward, he reached for her hand and leaned down to kiss her. The kiss was brief and surprisingly reassuring. "She would have really liked you."

Taylor managed a small smile. "I'm sure I would have liked her too." She looked down at the marker and then took a step toward the car. "Why don't I give you a few minutes alone? I'll meet you at the car."

"You don't have to do that," Quinn started to protest.

"Yes, I do." Taylor managed a smile, one that held a quiet understanding. Then with a last look at the grave marker, she turned and left Quinn alone with his thoughts.

* * *

"Vanessa, what are you doing here?" Tristan asked when he answered the door.

"I wanted to talk to Taylor. Is she here?" Vanessa asked.

"No, she's out somewhere with Quinn." He motioned her inside and waited for her to walk through the door so he could close it before he asked, "Is everything okay?"

"I'm not sure," Vanessa said, her voice unusually tense. "I've been going over all of the information Taylor gave us. I have a crazy theory, but I need to ask her a few questions."

"Come on in and sit down. They should be back any minute." Tristan guided her into the living room. "Tell me what you're thinking."

"Who else is in the house?"

"My mom and Riley went out shopping, so it's just me and Dad, but I think he's outside doing yard work," Tristan told her. "Not that it would matter anyway. He spent his whole career in intelligence."

Vanessa nodded and sat down in one of the living room chairs as Tristan lowered himself into the other one. "Did you know that Quinn called me this morning?"

"Yeah, he said something about Taylor seeing a van the day your asset disappeared," Tristan told her. "We were wondering if that's why someone's been after her. To figure out what she saw."

"I don't think so. In fact, I think the reason she saw our asset is because he was following her."

"What?"

"Just hear me out." Vanessa shifted forward in her seat. "We know that someone is trying to smuggle the components of this gate crasher into the US, right?"

"Yeah," Tristan nodded. "But I have no idea if they would be able to get all of the pieces through customs."

"That's what I was thinking too." Vanessa nodded. "Our bad guys can't risk bringing most of the components on an airplane because they would never make it past the x-ray machines."

"Same thing with customs. Between the x-ray screening and random checks and testing, there's no way to be sure they could slip all of the pieces past security."

"Unless they couldn't be x-rayed."

"You lost me."

"Artwork goes through a different kind of screening. If they found a way to hide the components inside a painting, it might be possible to slip each piece through customs one at a time."

"You think Taylor's paintings were being used to smuggle the pieces of this gate crasher into the US?" Tristan shook his head. "That's pretty far out there."

"I know, but one thing Taylor mentioned has really been bothering me."

"What's that?"

"She said that our asset came over and looked at her painting. He even talked to her."

"Yeah. So?"

"So he's been trained to stay out of sight. He never should have engaged anyone on the street, especially someone who might be able to identify him later," Vanessa told him. "That's Undercover 101 and definitely not a mistake a long-term asset would be likely to make."

"So you think he suspected Taylor's artwork was being used."

Vanessa nodded. "I think he approached her to see if he could figure out how."

"Or maybe he knew how," Tristan countered. "And he approached her to see if she was involved."

"It's possible," Vanessa agreed. "My guess is that someone found a way to hide the various pieces inside the framework of the canvases. Somehow they passed the canvases off to Taylor, knowing they'd get sent to the US eventually, where they can pick them up somewhere. They might have even planned to buy the paintings to reacquire their smuggled goods."

"I guess it's possible. She would make the perfect cover," Tristan said with a shake of his head. "She's talented enough that she wasn't going to buy a canvas and not use it, and they must have realized that she was shipping her artwork home at regular intervals."

"Exactly." Vanessa nodded. "Whoever is behind this probably scouted her out at the showing in Paris."

"But what would they have done if she hadn't been picked up by an agent?"

"I don't think they started feeding canvases to her until after she signed with Felicia."

"How would they know?"

"Anyone who attended the showing could have figured that part out," Vanessa said as the garage door sounded. A moment later Quinn and Taylor walked in.

They both came in and exchanged greetings with Vanessa and Tristan. Tristan looked at Taylor suspiciously when she didn't greet him with her normal cheerful voice. One glance at Quinn told him why.

Quinn took Taylor's hand and led her to the couch and then looked at Vanessa. "So what's going on?"

"I'm hoping Taylor can clear a few things up for me."

Taylor sighed. "I've already told you everything I know."

"I know this is frustrating, but I think we're starting to see the big picture." Vanessa leaned forward. "The day you painted that street café in Paris, was that before or after someone broke into your hotel room?"

"It was the same day," Taylor told her. "The break-in happened a few hours after I saw the man in the picture."

"And was that painting in your hotel room when the break-in occurred?"

Taylor shook her head. "No, I still had it with me."

"That's what I thought." Vanessa nodded. "I think it was our asset who broke into your room, probably looking for that painting. In fact, it was probably him who was killed there."

Taylor's face paled. "But why?"

Rather than answer her question, Vanessa asked another. "In all of that information you gave us at CIA headquarters, you mentioned that you normally bought your canvases in Italy. Is there anyplace else that you bought them?"

"Yeah, a place outside of Paris." Taylor nodded. "There's an odd size that I like that I couldn't find anywhere else."

"How did you find out about the store near Paris?"

"I don't know." Taylor's eyebrows drew together. "I think someone at the Paris showing must have told me about it."

"It's important, Taylor," Vanessa said gently. "Do you remember who?"

"I talked to so many people during that trip." Taylor sighed.

"This is just a guess, but it was probably someone you talked to after you signed with your agent."

Quinn interrupted, keying in on something else Taylor had said. "You said you liked painting on odd-sized canvases. When did you first start using them?"

"Felicia suggested it." Awareness lit her eyes. "She said there was a gallery in New York that was always looking for this particular size but that it wasn't easy to find. She told me I could get a few quick sales if I created some for her."

"Is she the one who told you where to get the canvases?"

"No, it was someone else," Taylor told them. "One of the gallery buyers."

"Which one?"

"I can't remember off of the top of my head, but I'm pretty sure he's the one who bought the first painting I did of that size," Taylor said. "Felicia would have a record of who it was, but I think it was either Raoul Ballen or Gregorio Amici."

"And that painting you did of the Paris café, was it on one of those odd-sized canvases?"

Taylor nodded. She shifted to look at Quinn. "And so was the other one that was stolen."

"You might be right," Tristan said to Vanessa. "All of the pieces support your theory."

"What theory?" Quinn asked.

Vanessa looked from Quinn to Taylor and then back at Quinn again. "This is all hypothetical, but you need to realize that it's still considered classified. The only reason I'm willing to share this with you is that you're all so deeply involved." She shifted her attention to Taylor again. "Taylor, you can't say anything about this to anyone."

"I understand." Taylor nodded. "But I need to know who I'm hiding from."

Vanessa nodded. Then slowly she explained how Taylor fit together with the many other pieces of the puzzle.

31

"I'm still not sure I understand all of this," Taylor said, her mind struggling to keep up with all of the technical jargon. "Exactly what are they supposed to be smuggling in my paintings?"

"The information I was given yesterday shows that we're dealing with several different pieces of equipment, some as small as a flash drive or a credit card, and others long and thin like pieces of computer cable," Vanessa told her. "If I'm right and they're smuggling them within the framing of your paintings, our guess is that it would take anywhere from six to ten canvases to transport all of the pieces."

Taylor tried to absorb the information, overwhelmed by the realization that her art was being used as a delivery method. "When would they get this stuff inside my canvases?"

"My guess is that they were already inside when you purchased the canvases," Vanessa told her. "They were probably reserved for you, and you just didn't realize it."

"What we need to determine is how many of your paintings could already be in their possession," Quinn told her. "We know that they have at least the two that were stolen."

Vanessa nodded. "And Taylor said that the gallery owner already purchased at least one of her paintings."

"But why did they steal those other two? Why didn't they just buy them like the first one?" Tristan asked.

"They didn't get the chance," Taylor spoke up. "A few of my paintings never made it into open listings. Evan Bridgeton saw the photos of several of my paintings before they were ever shipped stateside. He decided he wanted to do a private showing with me, so I started sending all of my paintings to his gallery instead of to my agent."

"How many paintings did you do on that canvas size?"

"I don't know, eight or ten," Taylor told them. "I remember they gave me a deal that if I bought a certain number, they'd give me two free. When my household effects catch up with me, I'll be able to tell you exactly how many because I can look it up on my receipts."

"When are those supposed to arrive?"

Vanessa answered for her. "The CIA is diverting the shipment. It should be here within the next couple of days."

Taylor pulled her cell phone out of her pocket. "I can try calling Felicia. She should have a detailed inventory of everything she's sold."

"Including the sizes?"

"Probably."

"Call her," Vanessa agreed. "Just don't tell her why we need the information."

"Actually, we should already have most of that info," Quinn interrupted. He looked at Taylor sheepishly. "I got copies of your sales records when we were at your agent's office."

"How did you do that?" Taylor asked. "And *why* did you do that?"

"I thought we might need the info eventually." Quinn shrugged. "As for how, you probably don't want to know."

"Great," Taylor muttered. "Now I've got you guys spying on my agent."

"He was gathering useful information," Tristan corrected.

"That's right." Quinn nodded, virtuously grabbing the lifeline Tristan had thrown him. "I was gathering useful information."

A little smile appeared on Taylor's face before she managed to fight it. "Well, let's see what you've got."

"Be right back." Quinn left the room and returned a moment later with a paper in his hand, along with the photos of Taylor's paintings. Then he motioned to the dining room. "Let's take this in there so we can spread these out on the table."

Everyone stood and followed him into the dining room where he was already spreading out the photographs of the paintings that had been sold. Quinn looked up at Taylor. "Can you remember which were on the odd-sized canvases?"

Taylor stared down at the photos and then reached down and moved several aside. "These were all sold at the showing in Paris, so I know I bought those supplies in Italy." She then pulled one toward her. "This one is the first one I did on one of those canvases."

Quinn looked down at the sheet he held and made a note in the margin. Then he pushed a photo toward her. "What about this one?"

She recognized it as one of those she had painted in Paris right before coming home. "Yeah, that's one too."

"And this one?" Quinn asked.

"No, that one was a standard size."

One by one, Quinn pushed the photos toward her, slowly helping her sort through them. When she had finally identified the last one, she looked up at him. "How many are there?"

"Seven," Quinn told her, his face uncharacteristically hard. "The same buyer purchased all of them." Quinn shifted his attention to Taylor. "It was Gregorio Amici."

"Gregorio?" Taylor's eyes widened. "Are you sure?"

Quinn nodded, and he motioned to her bag. "I want you to call Felicia. See if she knew that Gregorio was coming by the day we were at her office."

"It's Saturday."

"She gave you her cell phone number. Use it," Quinn insisted.

"Okay." Taylor grabbed her cell phone and made the call. When Felicia answered on the fourth ring, Taylor found herself apologizing. "Felicia, I'm so sorry to bother you on the weekend, but I need to ask you a quick question."

"No problem, Taylor. What is it?"

"Did you know Gregorio was coming by the day that I was at your office?"

"No, he just dropped in. Why? Is there a problem?"

"I was just wondering. I thought it was odd that he happened to be there when we were."

"It was pretty strange. Up until a few months ago, he never used to come into our offices at all. We always went to see him," Felicia told her.

Taylor felt her stomach sink. "Thanks, Felicia. I hope you enjoy the rest of your weekend."

"You too."

Ignoring the mystified tone of Felicia's voice, Taylor hung up the phone and looked at the inquisitive faces staring at her. "She said he didn't have an appointment that day. She also said that up until a few months ago, he never used to come into her office at all."

"And you said he might have been the one who told you where to buy those canvases?" Vanessa asked.

Taylor nodded.

"It sounds like we have enough on Gregorio Amici to have him brought in for questioning," Vanessa said. "I'll get the ball rolling to have him picked up."

"You realize that if the two stolen paintings were the ones they were missing, they could have all of the pieces in their possession," Tristan stated.

"I don't think so." Vanessa shook her head.

"Why not?" Quinn asked.

"Because the paintings were stolen before we caught that guy in Tristan's condo. They're still looking for one, and they don't know where it is."

Taylor looked at Vanessa wide-eyed. "What happened at Tristan's condo?" She noticed Tristan and Quinn guiltily exchange knowing looks. "What didn't you tell me?"

"There was some trouble the night we stayed at your parents' place," Tristan told her.

"We didn't want to worry you," Quinn added.

Taylor shook her head, fighting back annoyance and fear. "What happened?"

"It was similar to what happened with your car," Quinn said, choosing his words carefully. "It looks like the guy was trying to look through your paintings, probably trying to find out if you had the one they were missing."

"Did he say why he was there? Or who sent him?" Taylor asked. Then she noticed the way both men glanced at the floor before looking over at Vanessa. Taylor shifted her attention to look at Vanessa. "He's dead?"

Vanessa nodded.

Taylor brought a hand up to cover her mouth. Quinn stepped closer and slipped his arms around her. Despite her frustration, Taylor let him pull her into a comforting embrace.

"It's going to be okay," he whispered softly into her ear. Then, still keeping an arm around her waist, he pulled away and looked at Vanessa. "What do we do now that we know there's a missing piece still out there?"

"I think your weekend is about to be cut short." Vanessa gave Quinn an apologetic look. "Graham is pushing to let your squad go in and get Riesenour."

"A snatch and grab in Paris?" Tristan asked.

"He's not in Paris," Vanessa said. "Our latest intel shows he's in Abolstan."

"Great," Quinn muttered.

Taylor looked at Vanessa with confusion. "I thought we pulled our troops out of Abolstan."

Vanessa looked at Taylor as though just realizing she was still there. "I'm going to have to take Taylor back into headquarters for a debriefing."

"You can take her in and talk to her, but after that, we need to move Taylor into a safe house," Quinn said.

Vanessa looked over at him apologetically. "As much as I agree with you that Taylor needs to hide someplace safe, I doubt we'll be able to get a safe house approved."

"Why not?" Quinn asked, his eyes darkening. "She's already had someone come after her at least twice that we know of."

"Someone's come after her paintings twice," Vanessa corrected. "Taylor isn't a key witness to any crime, and no one has actually threatened her."

"Bureaucracy at work," Tristan muttered.

"I'm more than happy to hide out somewhere, but I really do need to have my art supplies with me," Taylor said, her mind still reeling from the reality of why her art had been selling so quickly. Even as her confidence wavered, she stood a little straighter and added, "I have a show to get ready for, and it's time I get back to work. Besides, I need to do something to keep my mind off of all of this."

"As crazy as it sounds, the safest place for you is probably at your new apartment," Vanessa commented. "The security system hasn't gone off once since you've been out of town, and Seth's dropped by a couple of times and said there hasn't been any suspicious activity there."

"Are you sure?" Taylor asked skeptically. "You said someone broke into Riley and Tristan's place, and that's only a couple of blocks away."

"Yeah, but whoever has been looking for your painting now knows that you aren't staying there anymore. Besides, the security system at your apartment is probably better than anywhere else you'd consider staying."

"Riley is going to stay at your parents' house for another week or so," Tristan said. "It sounds like this thing may be coming to a head soon, so hopefully it won't be long before I'm comfortable taking her back home."

"Did you want to stay with Riley instead?" Quinn asked.

Taylor shook her head. "If you really think my apartment is safe, I'd rather stay there since that's where all of my supplies are."

"I need to get back to headquarters." Vanessa stood. "Taylor, I really need you to come with me. You've been privy to information that is highly classified. The agency is going to need to talk to you about what you know and what you are allowed to do with that information."

Vanessa turned to Quinn. "I can bring Taylor back after her debriefings."

Taylor looked from Vanessa to Quinn, wishing she could ask him to come with her. As much as she wanted her life to get back to normal, having Quinn with her made her feel safe.

"Go with Vanessa," Quinn told her gently. "As soon as you get back, we'll get ready to head back to Virginia Beach."

Taylor nodded. "Okay."

"I'll talk to you later." Quinn leaned down for a brief kiss.

Taylor expected to see some kind of reaction from Vanessa and Tristan after Quinn kissed her in front of them, but surprisingly, they seemed unaffected, as though they expected Quinn to kiss her good-bye.

Quinn turned to Vanessa. "I don't have to tell you not to take her anywhere else."

"I'll keep her safe," Vanessa promised. She nodded at Quinn and Tristan and then escorted Taylor out the door.

32

"ABOLSTAN," QUINN SAID THE MINUTE Vanessa closed the door behind her and Taylor. He sank down onto one of the dining room chairs and shook his head. After taking Taylor to Emily's gravesite, his emotions were raw, emotions he wasn't ready to deal with right now. Instead, he focused his energy on the immediate threat of keeping Taylor safe.

"Riesenour sure picked his safe haven well." Tristan sat down across from him. "If it weren't for the fact that we've already infiltrated those borders a couple of times, the powers that be would never consider sending anyone in. I have a feeling Vanessa's right. Our weekend is about to be cut short."

Quinn nodded. "Yeah. Lucky us."

"What's eating at you?" Tristan leaned back in his chair. "Normally you don't care where we go or when."

"Normally my girlfriend isn't responsible for smuggling equipment into the country that could potentially wipe out our nation's financial system, not to mention the riots and chaos that would come afterward."

Tristan stared across the table at him for several seconds. "Yeah, that's a pretty good excuse. Almost believable."

Quinn forced himself to look Tristan in the eye. "What are you talking about?"

"Tell me what's going on with Taylor," Tristan insisted.

Quinn tensed and prepared to redirect the conversation, but before he could respond, Tristan held up a hand. "And I don't mean all of this stuff that involves smuggling. What's going on with *you* and Taylor?"

Quinn rubbed a hand over his face before looking back at Tristan. "I still can't believe I did it. I took her with me to visit Emily."

Tristan's eyes widened. "Wow. I didn't expect that."

"Why not? Just this morning you were bugging me to tell her about Emily."

"Yeah, but this is huge. You don't even like *me* to go with you to visit Emily." Tristan shook his head. "I knew you were in love with Taylor, but I guess I didn't realize things were moving along so fast. I guess you'll be planning a wedding before too much longer."

Quinn's eyes narrowed. "I never said I was getting married."

"Sure you did. I just missed all of the signs. I also never realized that you fell for her before she even left for Europe last year," Tristan said as Quinn shook his head in denial. "Think about it. How many dates did you go on while Taylor was in Europe?"

"Am I supposed to be counting?"

"It's kind of hard not to when you can count them all on one hand and still have fingers to spare," Tristan told him.

"Just drop it, okay?"

"What's your problem?" Tristan pressed. "Riley kept me pretty up to date with Taylor's life while she was gone. She didn't date any more than you did."

Quinn let himself consider Tristan's words despite the fear that shot through him. He did love Taylor, but what would he do if something happened to her? Surviving the loss of Emily was still something he struggled with daily. He couldn't imagine losing Taylor too. He thought of how she had acted when she saw Emily's name, when she realized that the woman lying in the cold, hard ground was his wife.

He lifted his eyes to meet Tristan's. "I didn't expect her to act this way."

"Act what way?"

"I thought Taylor would be mad that I never told her I'd been married before."

"Was she?"

"No." Quinn shook his head. "She saw Emily's name, and she looked at me like she was about to cry, not because she looked mad or anything. It was almost like she just found out one of her friends had died." Quinn shrugged his shoulders. "I don't know. Maybe she just felt sorry for me."

"Of course Taylor felt sorry for you. She just found out that your wife is dead," Tristan said, pointing out the obvious.

"My wife that she didn't know existed until this morning."

"What do you want me to say?" Tristan asked now. "Taylor's a great girl. I think she's as in love with you as you are with her. The question is, when are you going to do something about it?"

"There's nothing to do about it. I'm not looking to replace Emily," Quinn told him, even as he wondered what it would be like to be married again.

"Taylor isn't the kind of girl who would try to replace Emily," Tristan countered. "But maybe it's time you start thinking about building a future for yourself that includes more than just the navy."

Quinn pushed away from the table before Tristan could continue with the familiar lecture. "Don't start on me about what Emily would want. I don't need that right now."

"I don't need to tell you what Emily would want." Tristan stood up, his face serious. "You already know. You're just afraid to admit it."

Quinn clenched his fists, an irritating feeling of vulnerability seeping through him. Before he could respond, the door opened, and his dad walked in.

"Hey there," David Lambert greeted them. "What are you two up to today?"

Tristan looked at him apologetically. "I'm afraid we're going to have to take off for Virginia Beach this afternoon."

David looked from Tristan to Quinn and then back again. "Did you get a call?"

"Not yet, but it'll be coming soon."

David nodded thoughtfully. "Well, I'm sorry you can't stay longer, but it was great having you here while it lasted." He turned his attention to Quinn. "And I'm glad you brought Taylor to meet us. She's everything we hoped she'd be."

Quinn felt his heart squeeze in his chest, not prepared for the understanding and expectation in his father's voice. He managed to nod at him, and then he glanced over at Tristan. "I need to get some air."

Tristan nodded in unspoken understanding. "I'll call you if Taylor gets back before you do."

Quinn nodded and quickly left the room.

* * *

"What have you got for me?" Brent asked Seth as he walked into Seth's office with Amy following behind him.

Seth held out a file and waited for Brent to take it before he spoke. "The only thing we're sure about is that Riesenour is the brains behind this gate crasher system. The CIA believes that if he can get all of the pieces into the country and get it assembled, our financial system could be thrown back about a hundred years. If he can gain access, our military systems could also be jeopardized."

Brent's eyes narrowed as he glanced through the file. "And he's hiding in Abolstan?"

"I'm afraid so." Seth nodded.

"Where?" Amy asked, moving closer to her husband so she could read the file with him.

"Not far from Khalar," Seth said. "Vanessa and her buddies over at CIA think that the best way to figure out who's planning this attack is to do a snatch and grab. They're hoping he'll give them the info they need to stop this before it happens."

"Great," Brent muttered. "He's hiding far enough inland that it won't be easy to get in and out undetected."

"Getting in won't be a problem. We could do a HAHO jump," Seth suggested, referring to a high altitude, high opening parachute jump that would allow them to insert behind enemy lines without their ride being detected.

"That would get us in but not out." Brent shook his head. "I think we're going to have to go in on a helo. If we come in over the coast north of Khalar, we should be able to get in undetected."

"Could one of you explain to me what all of this has to do with Taylor?" Amy asked.

"They think the pieces of this equipment are being smuggled into the country inside her paintings."

"Inside her paintings?"

Seth nodded and pointed to the painting on the wall across from him. "I already checked out the ones hanging here at the office and didn't find anything, but Vanessa said there's a certain size canvas that they think has a hidden compartment in the framing."

"That's pretty risky, trying to smuggle something through like that, especially using an artist who isn't involved," Brent said.

"Vanessa said she talked to one of her contacts over at customs to see how plausible her theory is. According to him, paintings that were created by American citizens are treated pretty much like anything else a citizen would send home. Paintings purchased overseas would be treated like imports and would go through a more intensive screening," Seth explained.

"I guess that makes sense," Amy conceded.

"Unfortunately, this is all theory. Right now our priority is going into Abolstan to retrieve Riesenour," Seth told them. "CIA has a couple more leads on who might be involved here in the US, and they'll probably turn that over to the FBI before long if they haven't already."

"Is Taylor going into protective custody?"

"Vanessa said she tried to get it approved, but they turned her down. Apparently there's no imminent threat against her life."

"Do you think she's in danger?" Brent asked bluntly.

"If Vanessa's right, yeah, I do." Seth nodded. "Quinn said he thought they were followed to their hotel in New York. He couldn't be sure, but I could tell he was worried. Not to mention the guy that Vanessa and I found in Tristan's place. They're after something, and they think Taylor has it."

"But you said you already checked out the paintings here."

"Yeah," Seth nodded. "And the CIA had some of their guys check out all of Taylor's paintings in New York to see if there was anything hidden in the framings. They were all clean."

"Is there anyplace else she might have some paintings stashed away?"

"Not that I know of." Seth shook his head. "But her household shipment hasn't arrived yet. Taylor said she had a couple of blank canvases that she shipped home, but she doesn't remember what sizes they are."

"When does her stuff get here?"

"Sometime this week," Seth told him. "She had it all shipped to Tristan and Riley's condo."

"That must be where it is," Brent said and then looked down at Amy. "Can you see if you can track down that shipment?"

Before Amy could respond, Seth interrupted. "I think the CIA is already diverting it, but I'm not sure."

"I'll go make some calls," Amy told them.

"Good." Brent dropped the file back on Seth's desk. "We'll get started on a mission plan."

33

TAYLOR'S STOMACH WAS IN KNOTS, and she was starting to wonder if she should just pack up and take off for someplace new, someplace where no one would know her. Then she looked over at Quinn and tried to decide if she could handle the price of walking away.

Quinn had been oddly quiet on the ride home from his parents' house. Then again, he hadn't said a whole lot since she had pushed him about Emily.

Taylor still couldn't believe that she hadn't known Quinn had been married before. Surely Riley must have known about Emily after spending so much time with Quinn's family. But never had she mentioned anything about the woman Quinn had loved and lost.

Taylor wasn't sure whether to be mad at her sister for not warning her or if she should be proud of her for protecting Quinn's privacy so diligently. In a way, she supposed she should be mad at Quinn for not telling her sooner, but after seeing the expression on his face when he had looked down at his wife's grave, she thought she could understand. At least a little bit.

Quinn's pain had been visible when he had been standing there. Had she not known better, she would have sworn that he had lost his wife recently rather than years earlier.

As Tristan pulled into the parking lot of her apartment complex, Quinn motioned for her to stay in the car. "Wait here. Let me check everything out before you come up."

Taylor didn't have the energy to argue. Instead, she simply nodded and watched Quinn get out of the car and head upstairs, while Tristan climbed out and stood guard over her and Riley.

Riley shifted around in the passenger seat. "Are you okay?"

Taylor shook her head. "Not really."

"You know you can come stay at Mom and Dad's with me and Tristan."

"No, I want to settle in. I need to paint." Taylor dragged her fingers through her hair and shook her head. "And I need to figure out how I feel about the fact that Quinn is a widower and no one ever told me."

"I'm sorry," Riley said, her voice quiet. "I didn't find out until a few months ago, and that was only because Cassie said something in front of me without thinking. Tristan made me promise never to talk about it to anyone, not even you. He said that Quinn is really private about that part of his life."

"I understand," Taylor managed to say as she shook her head in frustration. "I just feel like I've been hit by a truck."

"I'm sorry," Riley repeated. "Is there anything I can do?"

Taylor shook her head. "I think I just need to spend some quality time alone with some paint and canvas. Maybe that will help me sort through everything that's going on."

"Let me know if you need me to bring you food." Riley managed a smile. "I know how you are once you get started."

"I will." Taylor picked up her bag when she saw Quinn heading back down the stairs.

Tristan opened the car door for her. "It looks like it's all clear."

"Thanks." Taylor stepped out and moved to retrieve her suitcase from the trunk.

Quinn got there first. "I've got it."

"You two watch your backs," Tristan told them as Quinn slammed the trunk closed.

"You too." Quinn nodded at him. "Pick me up when the call comes, okay?"

"I will." Tristan nodded.

Quinn started for the stairs with Taylor following behind him. "When what call comes?"

Quinn didn't answer, continuing forward as though he hadn't heard her. He stopped and unlocked his door, pushing it open just enough to set his suitcase inside and reset his alarm. Then he locked it back up and continued to Taylor's apartment.

Taylor opened her door and heard Quinn follow her inside as she moved to the security keypad and disengaged the alarm. Then she turned to face him. "What call?"

"We'll be going on assignment soon, the one Vanessa was talking about earlier," Quinn told her after he closed her door and set down her suitcase. "I haven't gotten my car back from Jay yet."

"Oh." Taylor felt her stomach drop another notch. She set her bag on the table and dropped down onto a chair.

Quinn sat in the seat across from her. "Spill it. Tell me what's bothering you."

"What's bothering me?" Taylor felt the volcano of her emotions squeeze at her. "What's *not* bothering me? I just found out that my art is being used to smuggle contraband into the country. How could I be so stupid not to realize I was being used?"

"You aren't stupid," Quinn interrupted. "It could've happened to anybody."

"But it's happening to me. On top of that, there's some terrorist plot that I don't understand, and now I'm being targeted in some kind of villainous manhunt." Taylor pushed away from the table. She pulled open the refrigerator, staring at it blankly for a moment, and then slammed it shut. She turned to face Quinn. "How many more secrets are you all keeping from me? No one told me that someone broke into Riley's condo."

"We didn't want to worry you about things that are out of your control," Quinn admitted sheepishly. "When that happened, we didn't have a clue what we were up against."

"You didn't want to worry me?" Taylor echoed. "Do you really think I'm so fragile that you have to hide everything from me? Do you have any idea how frustrating it is to be completely in the dark like this? It's almost as bad as finding out that my art is selling because of what you can't see instead of what you can. Talk about humiliating."

"Taylor, don't think of it that way."

"I thought that my paintings were selling because I was talented, but I was wrong. How could I have been so arrogant to think I was that good?" She shook her head. "I've been making money off of criminals."

"Not intentionally. Besides, that doesn't diminish the fact that you are talented. The theft at the warehouse never would have been necessary if Evan Bridgeton hadn't been so anxious to buy your work for his gallery."

"Yeah, but I feel so used."

"How many other US artists were featured at that showing in Paris?"

"Three. Why?"

"And how many signed with agents?"

"I think it was just me."

"These people were using you *because* you're talented. If you hadn't been successful, they never would have even noticed you. In fact, they probably noticed you when that article came out on you in Europe."

"Great." Sarcasm dripped from her voice. "That makes me feel *so* much better." She lowered herself onto the chair beside Quinn and forced herself to face him. "And on top of everything else, I now know that you were married and I had no idea. It's a lot to take in."

"I know," Quinn said with surprising patience. "All of this was probably a shock for you. I just haven't ever been able to talk about Emily. It's always been easier to let people make their own assumptions."

"I don't know how you can stand to *not* talk about her." Taylor shook her head. "You obviously really loved her. You must think about her all the time."

"I miss her every day," Quinn admitted. "And every day I try to set that aside and pretend my life is just like everyone else's. I can't afford to let myself get distracted when I'm working, and if the guys knew about Em, they wouldn't see me the same way."

"No, they'd realize that you're stronger than they think," Taylor said softly. "Every time I think about reading her name, seeing your last name on that grave marker, I wonder how you make it through each day."

Quinn stared at her for a long moment, appreciating her sensitivity and insight. Then he reached for her hand. "Knowing you has helped."

Taylor's lips curved slightly.

He reached out and brushed her hair back behind her ear. Then slowly he lowered his lips to meet hers. The kiss lingered, as though Quinn were savoring every moment. Then he pulled back, his eyes dark as he stared at her. "I didn't think I would ever love anyone again after Emily died." His hand tightened on hers. "I realize now that I was wrong."

Taylor opened her mouth, the words *I love you* ready to tumble out. Then Quinn's cell phone rang, and the moment passed too quickly. Quinn answered the phone, exchanged a few brief words, and then hung up.

"That was the call you were waiting for?" Taylor asked, her stomach now churning with a new fear.

"Yeah." Quinn nodded as he stood. "Tristan will be by to pick me up in a few minutes. I need to go grab my gear."

Taylor stood as well. Her fear of being left alone and her concern for Quinn combined into the simple fact that she didn't want him to leave. She also knew that she didn't have any choice. "Be safe."

"You too." Quinn said, his voice serious. "Promise me that you'll be careful while I'm gone."

"I will."

"And I want you to check in with Max if you have to go anywhere," Quinn told her. "Have him walk you up to your apartment before you go inside."

"Max's job is to manage the apartment, not babysit me."

"He's a friend, and he'll want to make sure you're safe," Quinn insisted. "Promise me."

"Okay, I promise." Taylor reached for his hand. "If you promise to come back safe."

"Deal." Quinn nodded. "And one more thing. Do you know how to handle a gun? I know your sister can shoot."

"Yeah. Dad taught us how to shoot years ago. Why?"

Quinn reached down and pulled a gun out of the holster strapped to his leg. "I want you to keep this with you then, especially while I'm gone."

Taylor's eyebrows drew together. "Do you really think that's necessary?"

"I'll feel better if I know you're ready for whatever might happen," Quinn told her. "If someone you don't know tries to come through that door, hit the panic button on the alarm and get behind something. The kitchen counter or the bed in your room. Take cover and use this if you have to."

Taylor took the weapon, hating the cold feel of the metal against her hand. "I hope I don't have to," she said as she set it aside and looked back up at him.

"So do I." Quinn leaned down and pressed his lips to hers. When he pulled back, he stared down at her as though he was battling a storm of emotions and was determined to beat it. Then his voice dropped to a whisper. "I love you."

Taylor smiled now, a ray of hope slicing through her. "I love you too."

34

It was like an itch he couldn't scratch. The nagging feeling that he had forgotten something, something important, simply wouldn't go away. Quinn tried to push it aside, tried to concentrate on the words that were being said in the premission briefing.

"Are we really risking our necks going in after a guy that probably won't talk anyway?" Tristan asked in the briefing room on board the *USS Theodore Roosevelt.*

"Grabbing Riesenour is only part of the mission," Brent told him. "While the rest of us go get him, Seth and Jay are going to seize his computer files and any other information they can find. We need financials, specs, everything."

"Looking for the money trail?" Seth asked.

"Exactly," Brent nodded. "We may not be able to get Riesenour to talk, but he's got the information we need somewhere."

"When do we leave?" Jay asked eagerly.

"Four hours," Brent told him. "Make sure all of your gear is squared away, and get some rest while you can. It's going to be a long night." Everyone stood up to leave, but Brent called out to Quinn. "Hey, Quinn. Can you wait a minute?"

"Yeah." Quinn's eyebrows drew together with curiosity.

Brent waited until the room emptied before he asked, "Is everything okay?"

"Why wouldn't it be?"

"I don't know. That's why I'm asking. You look preoccupied."

"Sorry, Brent. I just keep feeling like I'm missing something." Quinn grasped at a way to explain it. "Kind of like when intel forgets to tell us about the most important information."

"We've had that happen a few too many times." Brent nodded with understanding. "But if all goes well tonight, everything should finally fall into place for Taylor. With us going after Riesenour and the authorities looking for Amici, hopefully the threat will be neutralized once and for all."

"Amici," Quinn repeated, a sudden feeling of dread churning in his stomach. His eyes widened. "Have they picked him up yet?"

"I don't know. Why?"

"He met me in New York when we were meeting with Taylor's agent." Quinn ran a hand over his face.

"He did?" Brent's eyes widened.

Quinn's words became rushed. "Taylor lives in the apartment next door to me. If he manages to track me down . . ."

"It would lead him right to Taylor," Brent finished for him. "I'll call Amy and have her check with Steinert to see if Amici's been picked up."

"And can you have him make sure Taylor's okay?" Quinn asked.

"Yeah. I'll have him send someone over to check on her."

"Thanks." Quinn took a deep breath and prayed that Taylor would stay safe.

Brent nodded. "Are you going to be okay on this mission?"

"I'll do my job."

Brent stared at him for a long moment and then he nodded. "I'll let you know if I hear anything."

* * *

"We had an agreement," Yusef Ben Marid said, his voice eerily calm.

Vernon Riesenour swallowed hard as he stared at the dark-haired, dark-skinned man in front of him. His voice wavered slightly as he spoke. "I told you, we had a minor delay. My associates assure me that everything will be resolved within the next day or two."

"Surely you know what happens when people double-cross us," Yusef said calmly.

"I'm not double-crossing you," Vernon insisted, suddenly grateful that he had taken so many security precautions to protect his invention from falling into the wrong hands. "I assure you, everything will proceed exactly as we planned. I just need a couple more days."

"A couple more days," Yusef repeated and slowly nodded his head.

* * *

Vanessa pulled into the parking lot at the security gate by the main entrance to the farm, the CIA's training facility. A guard was already standing beside the moving truck that was parked off to the side, and the driver was clearly not happy about something. He motioned to his clipboard, pointing irritably at it as the guard shook his head.

Vanessa crossed to where the guard was standing and asked, "Is this the truck?"

"Yes, ma'am," he said.

The driver turned to face her, his frustration now directed at Vanessa. "Are you the one responsible for diverting this shipment?"

"That's right."

"I don't know what's going on here. I've never had a shipment redirected two days before delivery. I'm going to need some kind of documentation, or headquarters is going to have my head."

"I'll take care of it," Vanessa told him. She handed the guard a stack of papers. "Ride in with him and have everything unloaded at that location. I'll meet you there."

The guard nodded and then picked up his radio to instruct another guard to open the gate. Thirty minutes later, the few pieces of furniture Taylor had shipped home along with some of her personal belongings were unloaded at the loading dock for the main facility, and the driver was finally on his way, along with the authorization he had been so anxious about.

"What have we got?" Larry Steinert asked as he climbed the steps and looked at the recently unloaded crates.

"I don't know yet." Vanessa looked over at him, her eyebrows lifting. "Did you have any trouble getting on base?"

"Not at all. I flashed my badge, gave them my gun, and everyone was happy," Steinert told her. "Except me since I had to give them my gun."

"Yeah, they're picky about that." Vanessa fought back a grin as she thought of Quinn's incident at CIA headquarters. "You ready to help me search all of this stuff?"

"You got it." He nodded. "Where do we start?"

Vanessa held up the manifest. She glanced over it and read off a number sequence. "8076-2 is supposed to contain art supplies."

"8074, 8069," Graham mumbled as he read off the numbers painted on the sides of the crates.

"Here it is." Vanessa put her hand on the top of a crate that came up past her waist. She grabbed a crowbar that was hanging on the wall and pried the top off.

"What have you got?" Steinert asked, moving closer.

Vanessa reached in and pulled out the first of a half dozen blank canvases. She motioned to one of the security guards. "We need all of these to go through x-ray. We're specifically looking for anything that might be hidden in the frame."

"Yes, ma'am."

"By the way, I got a call from my contact at NYPD," Steinert said.

"And?"

"They went to pick up Gregorio Amici, but he's disappeared," Steinert told her. "He hasn't been to work for the past three days, and it looks like he moved out of his apartment."

"Great." Vanessa shook her head. "Now what?"

"We haven't found any indications that he's left the country, but our best guess is that he'll try to drive into Canada and fly out of there," Steinert told her. "He's definitely on the run."

"How did he know that we're on to him?"

"I don't know. I've been wondering the same thing."

The security guard came back carrying the stack of canvases. "These have been x-rayed. They all came back clean."

"Are you sure?" Vanessa asked, surprised.

"We ran them through twice. There isn't anything here but wood and canvas."

"Which means Amici is probably out there searching for whatever piece they're still missing, and we have no idea where it is." Vanessa let out a frustrated sigh.

"But he thinks that Taylor does."

"That's what I'm afraid of."

* * *

Quinn felt himself plummeting toward the ground and concentrated on breathing normally through his mask that was providing him the oxygen he needed to survive at the high altitude. For the moment, he couldn't think about Taylor, about the danger she could be facing. Instead, he counted off the seconds and then reached for the rip cord.

His body jerked with the force of the parachute opening, and his concentration shifted to the ground below. He had been the first to jump out of the high-flying aircraft, so he couldn't see his other teammates to make sure their chutes had opened. Tonight that wasn't his job. Instead, he was tasked with making sure their landing zone was safe.

Now that he was descending more slowly, he was able to unfasten his weapon from his vest and prepare for the worst-case scenario. The satellite images of the area showed their landing zone was clear or at least that it had been seven hours ago when the last photos were taken.

Quinn watched for movement, his finger on the trigger of his weapon. The night sky was dark, and the desert sand stretched out beneath him. They were aiming for the edge of that sandy expanse, fully aware that it was in the treacherous mountains to the north where they would find the chance to achieve their objective.

The ground loomed closer until, finally, Quinn secured his weapon moments before his feet touched down. He stumbled forward, fighting for balance as he started pulling his parachute in toward him. Moments later the rest of his squad was on the ground with him.

Together they rolled their parachutes up and buried them in the sand to hide their presence. Then they began the hike into the rocky pass toward Riesenour's safe haven.

35

IT WAS TOO EASY. QUINN looked through his sniper scope from the top of the hill overlooking the house that Riesenour was supposed to be hiding in. There didn't appear to be any guards posted outside, nor was there any sign of an exterior alarm.

Quinn shook his head. Something didn't feel right.

He shifted to his infrared goggles and stared at the structure. Again, a feeling of uneasiness settled over him. Not a single heat spot.

"What have you got Quinn?" Brent asked.

"I'm in position, but it doesn't look like anyone's home. Are we sure about the location?"

"Intel said they had a positive sighting twelve hours ago."

"Suggest we call for confirmation," Quinn replied. "Were they tracking movement in the area?"

"Hold your position," Brent responded. "Seth, check for updates."

"Affirmative," Seth said in his deep Southern voice. The night became silent once more until finally Seth spoke again. "Intel spotted a dozen men here earlier, but my infrared isn't picking anything up."

"It feels like a trap to me," Quinn muttered.

"Even if Riesenour isn't here, what about the computer?" Jay asked now.

"Seth, see if you're close enough to get remote access."

"Negative. We're in a dead zone."

"Tristan, you're with me," Brent said. "We'll check out the building. The rest of you hang back until we give you the go-ahead."

"Roger that," Quinn said, even though he hated this part of the job. He wanted to get in there and see for himself why their equipment wasn't picking up any life inside. In his mind there were only three possibilities: No one was home, some kind of reflecting shielding had been set up to fool their equipment, or whoever was inside was no longer breathing. Quinn wasn't sure he really cared which scenario it was as long as he and his squad all made it home alive.

* * *

He loved her. It had been forty-eight hours since Quinn had said those words to her, and Taylor still couldn't quite wrap her mind around the concept. Deep down, she wanted to know if he loved her as much as he had loved Emily, but the fact that he could say those three little words to her had to be enough. At least for now.

Taylor dabbed at the paint on her palette, efficiently transferring the paint from brush to canvas. Through her open window, she could hear the rain beating down on the pavement below and was grateful for it. The clouds had rolled in early that morning, and the impending storm had given her a reason to stay indoors. As anxious as she was to go to the beach and do some work outside, she knew she wouldn't feel safe going out by herself.

Instead, Taylor had pulled out her sketches from her time in Arlington with Quinn and had immersed herself in her art. Already, the white columns of the Jefferson Memorial had taken shape, contrasting against the green of the grass and the blue of the Potomac River. A few more hours working on the background, and Taylor hoped she would be ready to set this one aside and start something new, perhaps the sunrise from the Lamberts' back porch.

She stepped back and considered how she wanted the light to play off of the Washington Monument in the background. The heavy tarp that was spread out on her living room floor rustled beneath her. She had laid it down to protect the floor and had draped another thinner tarp over her kitchen table, which she was currently using to hold her supplies.

She was going to have to invest in a work table before long, but the frugal side of her couldn't justify paying full price in a store when a yard sale find would do just as well. Maybe if Quinn's mission was successful, she would feel safe enough to go shop yard sales again. Of course, that was assuming that Quinn's mission had something to do with her missing paintings.

She had just started creating the Washington Monument in the background when she heard a knock at the door. She fought against her natural instinct to just yell, "Come in." Instead, she put down her paintbrush and palette and moved to look through the peephole. Her shoulders relaxed when she saw Riley standing outside.

Taylor pulled the door open, a smile crossing her face when she saw the grocery bags in her sister's hands. "You've come to save me from starvation?"

"Something like that," Riley nodded as she walked inside. "It's nothing fancy. Just a rotisserie chicken and some potato salad."

"That sounds great." Taylor motioned to the kitchen counter. "I'm afraid we're going to have to eat in there. The kitchen table is busy at the moment."

"So I see." Riley set the bags down on the kitchen counter and started unloading the food.

Taylor pulled some plates out of the cabinet and asked, "Have you heard anything?"

"From Tristan?" Riley looked over her shoulder at Taylor and shook her head. "Nothing yet. My guess is that we won't hear anything for another day or two."

"It's hard waiting to hear, isn't it?" Taylor asked.

"Yeah, it is." Riley turned to face her sister. "I keep thinking it will get easier, but I don't really think it ever does."

"Leave it to the two of us to fall for a couple of Navy SEALs," Taylor said, remembering all too well her sister's struggles of learning to live with Tristan's career. She couldn't say she shared her sister's phobia of being involved with a military man, but Quinn's obvious concern for her safety made her wish he hadn't been called out of town while she was feeling so vulnerable.

Riley pulled off a drumstick and put it on Taylor's plate. "Can I ask how things are going with Quinn?"

Taylor couldn't suppress the smile that bloomed on her face. "He said he loves me."

Riley squealed with excitement and rushed over to hug Taylor. "Taylor, I'm so happy for you. And for Quinn. You both deserve to find some happiness."

"Thanks." Taylor returned her sister's hug. "I just hope it won't be long before we can find out what it's like to spend time together without always looking over our shoulders."

Riley nodded in agreement as she leaned against the counter. "You do realize that Quinn's life doesn't often fall within the definition of normal."

"I know." Taylor stabbed her fork into a piece of potato salad and took a bite. "But I kind of like that about him. Most guys go nuts with the kind of hours I keep."

"Well, you never have been one to keep to a schedule." Riley laughed. "What did Dad used to call you? A nonconformist?"

"That was just because he never could tell if I was going to bed at four in the morning or waking up at four in the morning." Taylor grinned. "It used to drive him nuts when he'd get up at five to go for a run and find me out on the front porch with my easel set up, painting a tree or something."

"I think his favorite was when you painted the deer eating Mom's favorite flowers in the garden."

Taylor laughed. "Yeah. They weren't too happy that I didn't chase them off."

Through the open window, Max's voice carried from below. "Hey, man. You can't park there. Those spaces are for residents only."

"Sounds like someone got on your manager's bad side," Riley commented.

"I didn't think Max had a bad side." Taylor moved closer to the window by her front door. "But I'm pretty sure Quinn talked to him before he left yesterday."

"What about?"

"Quinn made me promise that I would check in with Max if I go out anywhere and have him check out my apartment when I come home."

"I know Max and Quinn are pretty good friends," Riley told her.

"I got that impression." Taylor nodded and looked outside. The rain had slowed to a drizzle, and Max was now standing in the middle of the parking lot, his T-shirt and board shorts contrasting against the visitor's designer suit.

"That guy looks like . . ." Taylor said, more to herself than to Riley. Then recognition dawned. Taylor shook her head, trying to make sense of why Gregorio Amici would be standing in her parking lot arguing with Max. Then all of Quinn's warnings came flooding through her mind. "It couldn't be." She backed away from the window and tried to stem the panic rising up inside her. "How did he find me? I was so careful in New York."

Alarmed, Riley stepped toward the window. "Who is it?"

"Gregorio Amici. He's a buyer for a gallery in New York."

"Isn't that a good thing?"

"Normally, but no one knows that I live here, not even my agent." Taylor reached out and pulled Riley away from the window. "Quinn thinks Gregorio may be one of the people behind all of this stuff that's been happening."

Riley's eyes widened, and she started for the door. "We've got to get out of here."

Taylor reached out to stop her and shook her head. "Not that way. He'll see us." Taylor rushed to the security panel and hit the panic button. Sirens sounded immediately. She turned and grabbed her bag off of the table, gripping the side of it to make sure the gun Quinn had given her was still inside. "Come on."

"What are you doing?" Riley asked, even as she rushed after Taylor toward the hallway and into her bedroom.

Taylor slammed the door closed and locked it. She then reached into her bag, fumbling around until she managed to pull the gun free. She held it out to Riley. "Here. You're a better shot than me."

Riley's eyes widened. "How can you be sure this guy is after you?"

Before Taylor could answer, they heard the crashing sound of a door being forced open.

Within seconds, the sound of gunfire filled the air followed by total silence.

36

Tristan gagged the moment he reached the door. The smell of death saturated the air. The pungent scent of blood and decay combined with the absolute stillness of the night. Tristan could only think that he was glad Quinn wasn't the one here right now. He could sense the tension in him, especially since they had yet to receive any kind of confirmation of whether Gregorio Amici had been apprehended yet.

As much as Tristan had hoped that someday Quinn and Taylor would recognize their obvious attachment to one another, he wished now that it hadn't happened quite so soon. He didn't even want to consider that Taylor might not survive the danger facing her. Their lives would be forever altered, both for him and Riley as well as for Quinn. And Tristan remembered all too well what it was like to see Quinn's life fall apart. He couldn't bear the thought of seeing it happen again.

Tristan looked through the window. The scene before him only punctuated the stark reality. The people they were dealing with were cold-blooded killers.

"What have you got?" Quinn's impatient voice came over his headset.

"The reason we aren't seeing any heat spots. They're all dead." Tristan adjusted his night-vision goggles, his stomach clutching as he viewed the carnage spread out before him. It appeared as though someone had come in with an automatic weapon and shot everyone in a matter of seconds.

"How many?" Quinn asked tersely.

"I can see four from where I'm standing," Brent answered.

"And I've got at least three more over here," Tristan said. He checked the doorway for any signs of tampering. Sure enough, he found a trip wire near the hinge of the door. "The door is booby-trapped."

"Can you disable it?" Brent asked.

Tristan followed the wire to the incinerator device hidden just inside the doorway. If tripped, the whole house would have gone up in flames, destroying whatever clues might still be inside. "It'll take me a couple of minutes."

He studied the wiring, separating each one as he determined their function. Then he saw it: a cell phone tucked behind the bomb. "We might have a problem. It's rigged for remote access."

Brent's voice immediately sounded. "Seth, set up a jamming signal."

"Roger that," Seth responded. A moment later he added, "Okay, Tristan. You're all set. No cell phone signals can penetrate the area within a two-mile radius."

"Okay, here we go." Tristan pulled his knife from its sheath and pulled one wire away from the others. His teeth clenched as he uttered a silent prayer, slipped the knife beneath the wire, and slit it in half. Slowly, he let out a breath and sent up another silent prayer, this one in gratitude. "The bomb's disarmed."

"Tristan, you grab the computer. I'll document the scene. Then we're out of here," Brent ordered. "Seth, call for our ride. I want to be clear of this place before whoever did this realizes that we were here."

Tristan checked the doorway again and then inspected the floor before stepping inside. He tried to block out the horror staring back at him, moving through the structure in search of any type of computer equipment. He discovered three more bodies before he came to the room that had clearly been set up as the office.

A desk was in the middle of the room, bare except for a layer of dust. Tristan began his search for a computer or any data storage devices. He didn't find anything, nor did he see any evidence that anyone had used the room recently. He considered the possibility that perhaps whoever had killed everyone in the house had taken everything from the office.

Then he looked at the desk again. The dust was visible, even in the darkness. Yet none of it had been disturbed. Nowhere could he see an outline of where a computer might have been or anything else for that matter. Convinced that this room had not been used by Riesenour, Tristan left the room and continued down the hall. He checked four different rooms before he found what looked like the master suite.

"Tristan, status," Brent said over the headset.

"Still looking."

"We don't have much time."

Tristan continued into the room, checking inside the night table and the dresser drawers. He rifled through the clothes, coming up with nothing. Then he looked under the bed, shining his flashlight into the dark space beneath it. Again, he didn't find anything. When he straightened and stepped back, he heard a board creak beneath his foot. Immediately, he froze, his heart pounding as he realized that he had might have found another booby trap the hard way.

Fighting against his fear, he angled his flashlight at the floor, and a wave of relief shot through him. The floorboard had shifted slightly, just enough to reveal a hidden compartment in the floor. Tristan reached down and pushed the board aside to reveal a metal lockbox.

His eyebrows lifted, and he leaned down to study the lock. After checking to make sure that the lockbox wasn't booby trapped like the front door had been, he went to work on the lock, quickly springing it open.

When he opened the metal box, he let out a sigh of satisfaction. "I found it," Tristan announced as he grabbed the sleek laptop out of the drawer.

"Let's go," Brent ordered.

Tristan found Brent waiting for him at the front door. To his surprise, Brent was undoing the work he had done on the bomb. "What are you doing?"

"Rewiring this." Brent twisted two ends of exposed wire together and then stood up and motioned for Tristan to follow him out into the night.

As soon as they were back into the safety of the surrounding rock formations, Brent said, "Okay, Seth. Stop the jamming signal, and let's see what happens."

"Jamming signal is off."

"Nothing," Brent said, glancing back at the structure below.

"There's no way to be sure when someone might try to blow that place. Or even why."

"We aren't going to wait to find out," Brent said. "Let's go catch our ride."

* * *

Taylor's scream pierced the air as another gunshot rang out. She sucked in a breath, her heart hammering rapidly in her chest. Beside her, Riley was still holding Quinn's gun, but she too had ducked down behind the bed in case any of those gunshots penetrated the bedroom door. Somewhere in the distance, Taylor could hear sirens, but she didn't register the sound or why they were coming closer.

"Taylor, calm down." Riley put a hand on her knee, and Taylor could feel her sister's hand tremble. "Who else was out there?"

"I don't know," Taylor managed as she squeezed her eyes shut, a constant litany of prayers running through her mind. "I only saw Max and Gregorio." She reached down and gripped her sister's hand. "What are we going to do?"

Riley glanced up at the window and then crawled over to peek outside. "Remember when Landon used to sneak outside when he was a teenager?"

Taylor looked at her sister, completely confused.

"Come on." Riley set Quinn's gun down beside Taylor. Then she quietly unlatched the window and slid it open. "We're getting out of here."

"We're on the second floor."

"Pretend this is a fire drill, and there's no other way out." Riley removed the screen, pulled it inside, and set it down on the floor.

Taylor's eyes widened. "You're serious."

"Yeah." Riley nodded as she picked up the gun and engaged the safety. "You go first."

"You're crazy."

"Okay, I'll go first." Riley handed Taylor the gun. "But you keep this. Tuck it into your waistband."

Taylor put the gun in the back of her waistband and watched with amazement and horror as her sister swung one foot out the window and then shifted to sit on the windowsill with both feet dangling out. She then used her hands to grip the bottom of the window, rolled onto her stomach, and pushed her body outside until she was dangling six feet above the ground.

Taylor moved to the window just in time to see her sister let go and drop to the concrete below.

"Come on." Riley straightened up, quickly glancing around to make sure the alley was still empty. Then she looked up at Taylor. "Your turn."

Taylor shook her head, but when something came crashing down in her living room, she quickly reconsidered and decided to follow her sister's example. She scooted herself through the window and let herself dangle above the ground below. Her fingers pressed into the metal tracking of the window, and she counted in her mind, *Three, two, one.* Then she dropped down, her body jarring the moment her feet hit the ground.

She started to turn just as she felt the gun being pulled from her waistband. Whirling around, she saw Riley with the gun in her hands, the weapon trained on the men who had just turned the corner into the alley?

Both men lifted their hands. The older of the two spoke sternly, "Put down your weapon. We're with NCIS."

"Keep your hands where I can see them," Riley said, a barely perceptible waver in her voice. Then she pointed at the older of the two. "Let me see your ID. Two fingers."

He moved slowly and deliberately, reaching into his inside pocket and pulling it out with two fingers as she had instructed. Then he tossed it at her feet.

Rather than lean down to pick it up, Riley kicked the ID toward Taylor. "Check it out."

Taylor stared down at the black leather case for a moment, not quite able to process what was happening. Then Riley spoke again. "Taylor, pick it up and look at it. Tell me what it says."

Nodding, Taylor leaned down and opened the ID. "It says, *Special Agent Larry Steinert. NCIS.*"

Riley's shoulders relaxed marginally. "Let me see."

Taylor held the ID up for her sister to see, and then Riley let out a sigh of relief and slowly lowered her weapon.

Steinert motioned to the younger man at his left. "Go coordinate with the local LEOs." He then motioned to the open window and turned his attention back to Riley and Taylor. "You two are lucky to be alive after that stunt you just pulled."

"Jumping out of a window seemed like a better alternative to being shot at," Riley said with a tremor in her voice.

"What are you doing here?" Taylor managed to ask.

"Looking for Taylor Palmetta. I gather that's one of you."

"I'm Taylor." Taylor nodded.

Steinert looked at Riley. "And you are?"

"Riley Crowther. I'm Taylor's sister."

Steinert nodded as though all of the pieces of a puzzle suddenly fell into place. "It was your husband's commanding officer who asked me to drop in and check on Miss Palmetta. He was concerned that someone might have learned of her location."

"You mean Gregorio?"

"You knew him?" Steinert's eyes sharpened. "The man outside your apartment?"

"Gregorio Amici." Taylor nodded. "He's an art buyer for a gallery in New York."

"I know this isn't easy, but would you be willing to identify him?" Steinert asked. "I want to make sure we're talking about the same person."

"Is he . . ." Taylor trailed off.

"Dead?" Steinert finished for her. "Yes."

"What about Max?" Taylor asked anxiously. "Is he okay?"

"He's fine." Steinert nodded. "Please, come with me. It will only take a minute to identify the body. Then we'll have someone take you to our office so you can give us a statement."

She took a deep breath and forced herself to step forward. When they rounded the corner of the building, she saw the parking lot filled with emergency vehicles, and several people were milling around on the sidewalk across the street. A local policeman was stringing out yellow crime scene tape, cordoning off the entire parking lot.

The other NCIS agent was standing on the upstairs walkway outside Taylor's apartment, talking to Max and another policeman, and yet another man was in the open doorway, snapping photographs of the crime scene. Steinert motioned to the man holding the camera. "O'Neill. Come here for a minute."

O'Neill nodded, jogged down the stairs, and crossed to where they were standing on the edge of the parking lot.

Steinert nodded at the camera. "Do you have a shot of his face we can use for identification?"

"Yeah," O'Neill nodded. He looked at the back of the digital camera and pressed a few buttons. Then he handed the camera to Steinert.

"Is this the man you called Gregorio?"

Taylor inhaled quickly, her stomach churning at the sight of the man's face, his eyes still open yet lifeless. Then she let out her breath, turned her eyes away from the photo, and nodded. "That's him."

"Thank you." Steinert handed the camera back to O'Neill, who immediately headed back upstairs. "It's going to be a little while before we wrap up here, and your manager said it's going to take a few hours before he can get your front door repaired. Is there someplace you can go for now?"

Riley nodded. "We can stay at my parents' place."

"Let me get your phone numbers, and then I'll have an officer take you over there."

"Thanks," Taylor managed to say as the coroner's van arrived. She dared to look back up at her apartment, still trying to grasp the reality that an armed man had followed her here. She thought of Quinn and hoped that his mission was going more smoothly.

37

THE EXTRACTION POINT WAS LESS than a quarter of a mile away when Quinn heard the subtle movement above him. He slowed, sniffing the air for any indication of whether the movement was from some desert rodent or an animal of a different kind—the kind that might be carrying guns. Unable to sense anything out of place, Quinn moved slowly forward.

The uneasy feeling that they were being set up hadn't dissipated since he had first looked down at Riesenour's hideout and seen that everything was dark. Again, he scanned the darkness, his night-vision goggles still in place to boost his perfect eyesight. Still, he saw nothing but the blackness of the night and the outcropping of rocks on either side of the path they were navigating on the way to their rendezvous spot.

He was on the left flank tonight with Tristan on point. He could see the outline of Tristan in front of him nearly forty yards away. Jay and Seth were bringing up the rear with Brent to his right. Quinn held up a hand to signal Brent his uneasiness. He half-expected Brent to signal him to push forward, but instead, he received a different signal. *Take cover.* Whatever reservation Quinn was feeling, Brent was feeling it too.

Quinn faded against a rock formation, watching as the rest of his squad did the same. Then, just as he heard the approaching helicopter, he saw it. A flash of movement and a glint of moonlight on metal. He lowered his voice and spoke quietly into his mouthpiece. "I've got movement. Twenty yards to the north up in the rocks."

"How many?" Brent's voice came over.

"Can't tell," Quinn said, keeping his voice low and the conversation brief.

"This is the perfect place for an ambush," Seth said now.

"Let's turn the surprise in our favor," Brent replied. "Seth, set off that little surprise at Riesenour's hideout."

A few seconds ticked by, and then Seth spoke again. "Tell me when."

"Everyone get ready. If there are unfriendlies out there, we're going to have to plow through them to get to the extraction point."

Quinn shifted the weapon in his hand and flipped off the safety. Then he pushed back the night-vision goggles for a moment before he heard Brent give Seth the go. A split second later, the ground rocked, light flashed in the sky, and complete chaos broke loose.

More than a dozen local mercenaries were instantly illuminated in the cliffs just above them, some fighting to maintain their footing, and others trying to shift back into the crevices of the rocks. A shout echoed through the canyon, and the firefight began.

Quinn squeezed the trigger of his own weapon, taking aim at the two men who had the best vantage point. He saw the first drop and then the second, but the moment those two threats were neutralized, three more men moved into their place and returned fire. Gunfire sparked all around them, and he heard Brent call for cover fire from the approaching helicopter.

Brent started rattling off orders to the rest of them. "Tristan and Jay, clear a path to the extraction point. We'll cover you."

The moment Quinn saw Tristan move forward once more, he held down the trigger, rapidly sending bullets into the ridge above him. He saw another man drop as a bullet whizzed by him and impacted the rock a few inches from his left ear. Squatting down, he took aim and dropped two more insurgents. He would think about the men he killed later, but for now survival was the only thing on his mind.

"Path is clear," Tristan told them a moment later.

"Let's go," Brent ordered.

Quinn put a fresh clip into his weapon and began edging toward the landing zone while still laying down cover fire to keep the unfriendlies at bay. He didn't look to see Seth and Brent, but he could see the sparks from their weapons as the whirring of the helicopter thundered in the canyon. A new spray of gunfire sparked from the chopper, giving Quinn, Brent, and Seth the opening to run the last fifty yards to clear the mouth of the canyon.

A moment later, the helicopter disappeared over the rocks and circled back to get them. The moment it was on the ground, all five men raced for the open doorways, their weapons still drawn in case anyone slipped through the canyon after them.

As soon as everyone was safely on board, Brent called out to the helicopter pilot, "Everybody's in. Let's go!"

"Yes, sir," the pilot said. They were only fifteen feet off the ground when the sky lit up and a projectile of some sort hurled from the darkness toward them.

"Incoming!" the copilot shouted tensely.

The helicopter pulled hard to the left and the projectile whizzed past them.

"Where's it coming from?" Brent asked over the radio.

"From the north," the copilot answered. "But I'm not reading anything on my instruments."

"It must be a rocket launcher," Brent responded and motioned to Quinn and Tristan to take position at the open doors.

As the pilot tried to gain altitude, Quinn lifted his weapon once more, shooting out into the darkness in a wide half circle as Tristan did the same on the other side. Then he saw the lights in the distance just as the copilot's voice sounded. "We've got a problem here. I'm seeing a lot of movement on the ground."

"Get those doors closed and strap in," the pilot ordered. "We've got to get out of here."

Quinn and Tristan both slammed the doors closed as another rocket speared up into the sky toward them, and the pilot evaded, sending them both skidding toward their seats.

"Buckle in!" Brent yelled as he clicked his own harness into place.

Quinn reached out and gripped his seat, quickly strapping himself in. Then he closed his eyes and prayed that he would make it out alive . . . and that he would find Taylor safely waiting for him in Virginia.

* * *

"Vernon Riesenour is dead?" Vanessa repeated over the phone.

"That's right," Graham said. "I just got the report from your husband's squad. Not only that, but it looks like we found the funding trail. It looks like Riesenour was willing to sell his soul to get his revenge, and it ended up costing him."

"What do you mean?"

"The funding was traced back to the group of insurgents in Abolstan I was telling you about. Apparently, they fronted Riesenour the money for his research with the expectation that they would eventually get that money back plus a whole lot more. They would also get the added bonus of seeing Riesenour create havoc for them in the United States."

Graham hesitated a moment and then continued. "According to the report and the computer records that were recovered from Riesenour's hideout, Riesenour missed a deadline. We think the insurgents thought he was double-crossing them."

"This sounds like it was more financial than political," Vanessa concluded.

"I think it was a combination of both," Graham told her. "If Riesenour had succeeded, rebels in Abolstan would have claimed credit as a showing of strength in their country. The extra funding and the likelihood that the US would stay out of their business for the foreseeable future almost guaranteed that they would be able to take control of their government."

"Any indications that we have any other missing links out there?" Vanessa asked. "Taylor Palmetta is understandably on edge after what happened yesterday."

"As far as we can tell, the problems have all been cleaned up," Graham said confidently. "The SEALs were able to recover Riesenour's computer, and we think his death was the Abolstani rebels' way of sending a message to his associates. I doubt they realized that most of them had already been neutralized."

"I think I'll have her stay at her parents' house for another day or two just to be sure."

"That's not a bad idea," Graham agreed. "And thanks for all of your help."

"You're welcome." Vanessa hung up the phone, praying that this threat really was over.

38

"I CAN'T BELIEVE THIS." TAYLOR gritted her teeth in frustration as she stood in the middle of her living room. Still perched on an easel was the canvas she had been working on before Gregorio Amici had shown up. Right above where she had painted the Jefferson Memorial was a single hole where a bullet had penetrated it. "Someone shot my painting."

"Better your painting than you," Vanessa said dryly. She put a hand on Taylor's shoulder. "Look on the bright side. Now that we know it really was Gregorio who was behind all of this, you're finally free to get back to your life."

"No more looking over my shoulder?"

"I didn't say that." Vanessa shrugged. "I have a feeling it may take a while before you stop doing that. And being involved with Quinn is bound to bring out any paranoid tendencies you might have."

"Are you speaking from experience?"

Vanessa laughed. "Actually, I'm the paranoid one in my family. Seth's pretty easygoing compared to me."

"Really?" Taylor turned to look at her. "You don't seem paranoid to me."

"If you saw the security system in our new house, you wouldn't say that," Vanessa told her. "Seth is still grumbling about how much it cost to put it in."

"Do you know when the guys are getting back?" Taylor asked.

"Not yet."

"But you know where they are, right?"

"You know I can't answer that," Vanessa said with compassion in her voice. "But I can promise you that I'll give you a call as soon as I know anything that I can tell you. Of course, Quinn will probably beat me to it."

"I hope so." Taylor managed a smile. "I'm going to feel so much better when he's home."

"I know." Vanessa nodded. "But at least now you know you'll be safe at your apartment."

"Actually, I think I'm going to pack up some supplies and stay at my parents' house with Riley until Quinn gets back. After yesterday, I really need an outlet, but I don't think I'm ready to be alone yet."

"I can understand that." Vanessa motioned to the shelves. "What can I help you with?"

Taylor began loading a variety of paints into a carrying case. She nodded toward the far side of the room. "If you can grab a couple of those canvases, I think I can get the rest."

"You got it." She picked up two blank canvases and carried them through the front door.

Taylor collected the last few supplies, turned on her alarm, locked her recently repaired door, and joined Vanessa outside. She glanced at Quinn's apartment and let out a little sigh. She wanted him home. And she wanted to be home when he got there.

* * *

Quinn hit speed dial the moment the transport plane landed in Virginia. He didn't look at the time, nor did he care that there were a dozen men close enough to hear his impending conversation. All he cared about was hearing her voice, hearing for himself that she was really okay.

"Hello?" Taylor's sleepy voice came over the line.

"Taylor," Quinn said and sighed with relief. "Are you okay?"

"I'm fine," Taylor said, but her voice sounded more awake now. "Are you home?"

"Just landed." Quinn watched a few of his teammates gather their gear and head for the exit, but he remained seated. "Where are you?"

"I'm at my parents' house with Riley," Taylor told him. "What time is it?"

"I don't know. About three-thirty," Quinn told her, now feeling a little guilty for waking her up. "I guess I should have waited a while to call you."

"Don't be silly. I'll be able to sleep better once I see for myself that you made it back in one piece," Taylor told him. "You did make it back in one piece, didn't you?"

Quinn glanced down at the gash on his arm from when he had rammed into his seat when the helicopter came under fire. "More or less."

"Any chance you're coming over here with Tristan?"

"Yeah," Quinn told her. "Go back to sleep. It'll probably be at least an hour before we get there."

"Okay," Taylor agreed easily. "Drive safe."

"We will." Quinn closed the phone and then looked up when a hand came down on his shoulder.

"I gather that was Taylor." Tristan handed Quinn's duffel bag to him.

"Yeah. If you don't mind, I'm going to come with you over to the Palmetta's house."

"No problem." Tristan shifted his own duffel bag over his shoulder. "Let's get going. I'm anxious to see my wife."

Quinn nodded, keying in on Tristan's words. The familiar ache was still there, the one that had been with him since Emily died, but for once it wasn't Emily's face that flashed into his mind at the mention of the words *my wife*. Instead, it was Taylor's. Not willing to analyze the changes in his thought process, he shouldered his duffel bag and hurried after Tristan.

* * *

"I guess it's true. The girlfriends are the first ones to hear when the guys are home," Riley said as she and Taylor stood together by their parents' front window.

"Maybe because the boyfriends don't care about who they're waking up." Taylor shrugged.

"I hate to break it to you, but Quinn has never been one to worry about what time it is when he picks up the phone."

"Does he usually call your house in the middle of the night?"

"Only if it's really important," Riley said. Then she seemed to reconsider. "He normally doesn't call after about eleven unless he's in emergency mode."

"Like when they're about to go on assignment."

Riley nodded. "Pretty much."

Headlights cut through the darkness and then flashed in the window as Tristan's truck parked in the driveway. "They're here!"

Taylor rushed to the front door, pulling it open as Quinn approached. His pace quickened the instant he saw her, and she could feel her heart racing. Quinn closed the distance between them before she could cross the threshold. He slipped his arms around her waist, picking her up as he walked inside.

Behind them Tristan followed Quinn inside and kicked the door closed. He dropped his duffel bag on the floor before pulling Riley close. Taylor was barely aware of her sister and brother-in-law or the greeting they exchanged. All she could think about was the man holding her right now and the warmth flowing through her as he held her close.

Quinn pulled back for a moment, his eyes dark. Then he lowered his lips to hers. "I missed you."

Her smile was instant. "I missed you too."

Before any more words were said between them, Tristan put a hand on her shoulder. "I hate to interrupt, but Riley and I are going to bed."

Taylor turned her head and smiled at him. "I'm glad you made it back okay."

"Thanks." Tristan hefted his duffel bag off of the ground and took Riley's hand to lead her toward the hall. Then he called out over his shoulder, "Quinn, you get the couch."

"I kind of figured." Quinn waited until they left the room before he looked back at Taylor. "I heard what happened at your apartment. Are you really okay?"

"A little freaked out by the whole thing, but other than that I'm fine." Taylor nodded. She motioned to the couch. "Did you want to sit down?"

"Sure." Quinn stepped away from her and led her over to the couch. He slipped off his jacket, and Taylor noticed the stark white bandage on his arm.

"What happened?"

"It's just a scratch," Quinn assured her. He sat down on the couch and pulled her down next to him. "Come here."

Taylor leaned closer as his arm slipped around her shoulders. "I'm so glad you're home."

"Me too." Quinn leaned his head back against the back of the couch and shifted so that Taylor could rest her head on his shoulder. "I've never been so glad to see a mission end."

"Now that you're back, maybe I'll try staying at my apartment again."

Quinn nodded. "I kind of like the idea of you living right next door to me, at least for now."

"What do you mean 'at least for now'?" Taylor sat up and looked at him. "You aren't planning on breaking up with me, are you?"

Quinn just rolled his eyes. "Not a chance."

39

TAYLOR STARED DOWN THE BEACH, barely taking the time to look down as her paintbrush moved from palette to canvas. The light was incredible, with the sunlight splashing through a thin layer of clouds down onto the nearly deserted beach. Over the past four days, she had recreated the buildings lining the beach, their varying heights, shapes, and colors providing the contrast she needed.

Now she was focused on the water. She dabbed her brush into a pale blue, hoping she could capture the curve of the waves washing up onto the sand. A sense of urgency rushed through her as she realized that her light was changing. Another fifteen minutes and she would have to stop.

Logically, she knew she could always come back tomorrow to finish, but part of her knew that the magic would fade by then. She found herself racing against time, reveling in the rush that always pulsed through her during those final moments of creation. The image was nearly complete, the pounding of the waves threatening the tranquility of the empty beach. Taylor leaned down, dabbing crests of white on the tops of the waves and adding the image of a few seagulls in the distance.

Despite her sense of urgency, she meticulously fiddled with the details for a few more minutes before she finally stepped back and stared.

"It's impressive."

Taylor whirled around to see Quinn standing behind her. "You startled me."

"Sorry." Quinn stepped forward to take a closer look.

"How long have you been standing there?"

"I don't know. Just a little while." Quinn leaned down and kissed her cheek. "I thought you might need some help loading up."

"That would be great." Taylor started cleaning her brushes, and then she looked at him suspiciously. "How did you know I was finishing up?"

"You've come home at the same time for the past few days. It's not rocket science."

"You've been spying on me?"

"Just a little." Quinn grinned. "Come on. If you want, we can go grab a late breakfast before I head over to the base."

"You have to go in to work today?" Taylor asked warily. "I thought you were off for the weekend."

"I am." Quinn picked up the protective case for Taylor's painting and handed it to her. "I'm actually going into the office to get your paintings. Vanessa wanted to take another look at them before she gives them back to you."

Taylor put the painting in its case and looked up at Quinn. "Is she still looking for the missing whatever it is?"

"Yep." Quinn picked up her easel and the case she kept her paints in. "It's out there somewhere, but we have no idea where."

"Do you think they'll ever find it?"

"I hope so. It would be nice to know that this rogue technology can't come back later to haunt us." Quinn took a step toward Taylor's car. "But for now, we can worry about more important things."

Taylor's eyebrows lifted. "Like where to go for breakfast?"

"Exactly."

* * *

"You're right, Quinn. They're all clean." Disappointed, Vanessa shook her head as she stared at the four paintings that were now propped against the wall of the base's security office. "Our best guess is that there's only one piece missing, but I can't figure out for the life of me where it could have disappeared to."

"I was talking to Taylor about that this morning. She doesn't know either." Quinn picked up one of the paintings and began packing it up the way he had seen Taylor do it earlier. "I'm starting to think that she either got rid of a canvas without realizing it or that Felicia sold one that we're missing."

"Maybe." Vanessa balled her hands into fists as she put them on her hips and considered. "The computer you recovered from Abolstan didn't have any of the designs on it?"

Quinn shook his head. "Riesenour probably figured that if his Abolstani friends found instructions on how to make the device, they wouldn't need him anymore."

"Then it's possible that the technology died with him."

"But the other pieces are out there somewhere," Quinn reminded her. "NCIS checked out Gregorio's apartment, and they didn't find anything. Same thing with the other two guys we eliminated." His eyes narrowed, and he looked back down at the paintings. "Do you think there could be someone else still out there who's involved?"

Vanessa let out a frustrated sigh. "There's no way of knowing."

"Maybe I should keep these here a while longer."

"That's a good idea," Vanessa agreed. "And I would have Taylor get a post office box, at least for now. She shouldn't start giving her address out for a while just to be sure."

"Maybe I should have you tell her that." Quinn gave her a wry smile. "She tends to think that I'm overprotective."

"You are." Vanessa laughed. "But I don't think Taylor really minds." Then she motioned to the paintings. "Why don't I help you hang those back up, and then I'll come with you to talk to her."

"That would be great."

Vanessa stared at him for a minute, still smiling.

Quinn's eyes narrowed. "What?"

"I was just trying to decide whether I should tell you that the guys have started a pool on how long it takes you to propose to Taylor." Vanessa's grin widened when Quinn goggled at her. "But I probably should just let you find that out on your own."

"You're kidding, right?" Quinn shook his head. "There's no way the guys would tell you about something like that."

"Unless they were asking if I want to put my vote in too." Vanessa lowered her voice as though sharing a secret. "Any advice on how far out I should be looking?"

Quinn considered a moment, both the question and the implications. Then the corners of his mouth lifted. "I'd go for sooner rather than later." He leaned closer and added, "Of course, you do know that this is top-secret information."

"Absolutely."

* * *

Taylor flipped through her sketches, wondering what she should work on next. She planned to take it easy tomorrow, but she wanted to start strong on Monday and knew that she didn't want to spend half the day deciding what project to tackle. Knowing that her parents and brother would be arriving in a matter of days made her even more anxious to get another painting completed. She knew that seeing Landon for the first time in two years would take priority over everything else, and after taking so much time off, she couldn't afford to get much further behind.

She was actually a little surprised that Felicia hadn't called to check up on her progress since she had left New York. Since signing with her six months before, Taylor had received weekly calls, sometimes asking what she was working on and other times putting in a request for a specific type or size of painting. Other than a quick call yesterday asking where Taylor wanted her latest sales contracts sent, Felicia had been oddly quiet.

Taylor turned the page again and smiled as she stared down at the sketch of Quinn and his dad. She considered the possibility of painting the scene as a Christmas gift and immediately wondered if that would be too over the top. After all, just because Quinn said he loved her didn't mean she was part of the family.

A knock at the door came before she had settled her self-imposed dilemma, and she got up to look out the peephole. Then she pulled the door open.

"Felicia." Taylor's voice was filled with surprise. "I was just thinking about you. What are you doing here?"

"I thought I would come down and make a friendly visit. I have some business to take care of in DC later in the week," Felicia said, clutching her purse that was the same canary yellow as her blouse.

"Oh, that's right. Suzanne mentioned that you were hired as a consultant for some redecorating up there," Taylor said. "At the Pentagon, right?"

Felicia nodded. "Do you mind if I come in?"

"No, not at all."

Taylor stepped back and motioned her inside. "I was actually just trying to decide what to work on next. Maybe you can help point me in the right direction."

"I certainly hope so." An odd expression crossed her face as she closed the door behind her. Then she opened her purse and pulled out a semiautomatic pistol. "The next thing you need to work on is telling me where the paintings are that didn't get shipped through my office."

"What?" Taylor stared at Felicia for a split second before she focused on the gun. She opened her mouth, at first unable to speak. Then she managed to stammer, "You were involved with the theft of my paintings? I don't understand. Why?"

"My brother is dead because of you." Cold fury vibrated through her voice.

"What are you talking about? I didn't even know you had a brother."

"Does the name Vernon Riesenour mean anything to you?"

Taylor shook her head even as she tried to place the vaguely familiar name. "I'm sorry, Felicia, but it doesn't. I've never met anyone by that name."

"No, you've never met him," Felicia snapped at her even as she appeared to fight back her own emotions. "But you and your boyfriend are responsible for getting him killed."

Taylor stared at Felicia, trying to clear the confusion out of her brain. "What are you talking about?"

"You know exactly what I'm talking about. That's why you called and asked about Gregorio. You and Quinn knew that he was involved." She shrugged. "And what better way to take care of that problem than to send him to visit you."

She felt numb, but still she managed to ask, "But how did you know where I was? I only gave you my address yesterday."

"I didn't know where you were. I gave him the address for your Navy SEAL boyfriend," Felicia told her.

Taylor's eyes widened. "You knew that he would die if he looked for me at Quinn's place."

"SEALs aren't known for negotiating, especially when someone is aiming a weapon in their direction." Felicia shrugged as she appeared to regain her composure. "Gregorio had become a liability. He never was much more than a puppet on a string anyway."

"I still don't understand why you blame me for any of this," Taylor said, trying fervently to make the connection. In the back of her mind, she also wondered how soon Quinn would return.

"Vernon was a brilliant man. He could have done anything with his life that he wanted to until his wife and sons were killed. Murdered by American soldiers."

A chill ran through her. "Your brother is the one behind everything that has been happening to me?"

"No, my brother has been hiding since some American spy found out about his invention." Felicia shook her head. "Your missing artwork is why this has been happening to you."

"Why me?"

"You were so naive, so trusting." Felicia apparently saw the hurt in Taylor's eyes because she let out a brittle laugh and added, "It was perfect.

Young American artist, talented enough for my bosses to want to sign you, but not so famous that your art would sell too quickly."

"What do you want, Felicia?" Taylor asked, forcing herself to look Felicia in the eye. "Why are you here?"

"I want the missing canvas."

"You always took care of the shipping," Taylor reminded her, confused. Then she remembered the day that Evan Bridgeton called her, requesting she ship some paintings out early. He had also had her send them directly to his warehouse. With a new sense of understanding, Taylor spoke calmly. "You may have chosen me because you thought I was too naive to figure out what you were doing, but you didn't count on me being talented enough to sell my work to anyone else so quickly. Evan Bridgeton messed up your system when he had me ship those paintings to him instead of you, didn't he?"

"It wasn't just Evan. I searched through your photos and knew that we were still missing another piece. You're the only one who can have it."

Taylor shook her head as she desperately hoped and prayed that Quinn would return soon. "I only kept four paintings. They've all been searched at least three times. Whatever you're looking for must be somewhere else."

Taylor stared down at the gun, trying to imagine what she should do until Quinn knocked on her door. Could she stall Felicia until then? Would Quinn even come to her apartment after he finished at the base with Vanessa?

The image of Vanessa clicked into her mind, the memory of the first time they met when Vanessa and Seth came to Italy. The day that she gave them their wedding gift—a painting.

"You remember," Felicia said, apparently seeing the awareness that flashed in Taylor's eyes.

"Maybe." Taylor motioned to her laptop computer, an idea forming in her mind. If she could just distract Felicia for a minute or two. "I gave a couple of paintings away as gifts. If you'll let me look at the photos of my art, I should be able to tell which one it was."

"Do it."

40

QUINN PULLED HIS PHONE FROM his pocket, wondering who would be sending him a text message. He clicked on the message to open the new picture mail, and his eyebrows drew together in concentration.

"Is something wrong?" Vanessa asked as they reached the parking lot outside of Quinn's office.

"This is weird." Quinn continued to stare at the image. "Taylor sent me a picture mail of one of her paintings."

"Maybe she just finished one and wanted to show you."

"She finished a painting this morning, but I was there when she did." Quinn held out his phone to show Vanessa. "And this isn't it."

Now Vanessa's eyes widened. "That's the painting she gave me and Seth for a wedding present."

Quinn looked at her and then studied the new message again. "This is from her e-mail account, not her cell phone."

Vanessa lifted a hand to her forehead, and Quinn saw the understanding in her eyes that matched his own. "It's been hanging on my wall this whole time."

"The missing painting!"

Vanessa nodded. "Gregorio must not have realized that she had used one of those canvases to create a gift."

Quinn nodded in agreement as confusion turned to worry. "But why is she sending this to me now? Why wouldn't she have just called me?"

"Call her right now. Make sure she's okay," Vanessa insisted.

Quinn's stomach clenched as he considered the possibility that Taylor hadn't called him because she couldn't. But how had she managed to send an e-mail to him? Surely if there was someone preventing her from using her phone, she wouldn't be permitted to use her computer. Worry consumed him as questions raced through his mind.

"She's not answering." Quinn hung up his phone, his eyes dark as he looked back up at Vanessa. "Is Seth home?"

"He should be."

Quinn punched in Seth's number.

"Hey, Quinn," Seth greeted him with humor in his voice. "I just got off of the phone with your other half."

Quinn's tone was no nonsense. "What did she say?"

Seth seemed to pick up on Quinn's tension, and his voice became serious. "She asked if she could come over to photograph the painting she did for me and Vanessa. I told her that was fine and gave her directions." He hesitated a moment. "Is something wrong?"

"Yeah, I don't think she's alone," Quinn told him. "And we think the missing piece of equipment is hanging on your wall."

"You're kidding!" Seth's voice was incredulous. "Where are you now?"

"Vanessa and I are just leaving our office."

"I'll call the rest of the squad," Seth told him. "If you let Vanessa drive, you can probably get here before Taylor."

"We're on our way."

* * *

Taylor took the long way, carefully keeping her speed right at the speed limit. She was behind the wheel of Felicia's rental car, a car that would undoubtedly disappear the moment Felicia had what she wanted.

She still couldn't believe that Felicia had fooled her so completely. Taylor had thought of Felicia as more than just her agent. She had thought they were friends. Now, after what had happened to Gregorio, Taylor had no delusions about who Felicia really was. She also understood what would happen once Felicia got her hands on that painting. She and anyone else in her path would be killed unless someone succeeded in stopping her. Taylor prayed that Quinn and his friends would do just that.

She had lucked out at her house when she had sorted through the photographs on her computer. When she had found the correct file, she had told Felicia that it had to either be in that painting or in one of the blank canvases she had brought home. Felicia had turned to search the canvases just long enough for Taylor to forward the photo to Quinn's cell phone. She only hoped that he saw it in time and that he would understand what her message meant.

"Can't you drive any faster?" Felicia asked tensely.

"I can, but I didn't think you'd want to get pulled over," Taylor told her. "The cops always set up speed traps through here, especially on the weekends."

"How much farther?"

"Five more minutes," Taylor said nervously.

"Just remember, you don't want to find out what will happen if I don't get that painting."

Taylor swallowed hard. "I know."

* * *

"Quinn and Tristan, you take the back of the house." Brent motioned to Seth's back gate. "Jay, I want you up on the roof across the street."

"Why are you sending Jay up there?" Quinn asked immediately. "I'm the best sniper in the unit."

"And I don't want you to have to take a shot when your girlfriend might be in the line of fire."

"I know the risks," Quinn told him, even as his stomach curled at the possibilities. "I can take the shot." His eyes met Brent's. "I need to take the shot."

Brent stared at him for a minute, and then he nodded. "Okay. Get in position."

"Where are you going to be?" Jay asked.

"I'll be inside in case Seth needs backup," Brent told him. "And Vanessa is parked down the street in case our plan works. She's coordinating with NCIS, assuming they can get here in time. Let's go. We don't have much time."

* * *

Taylor made the turn into Seth's neighborhood. It was one of the older neighborhoods in the area, situated along one of the inlets near Virginia Beach. The houses weren't large, but the trees in the yards were mature, and a handful of bicycles and kids' toys littered several of the front yards. In the back of her mind, Taylor wondered why there weren't any children outside playing despite the clear blue sky and the higher-than-normal temperatures.

"You know, you don't have to hurt anyone," Taylor said as she approached Seth's street. "There's a way for you to get the painting without Seth and Vanessa suspecting anything."

Felicia's eyebrows lifted skeptically. "I'm listening."

"You're my agent." Taylor barely suppressed the urge to roll her eyes. "If you tell them that you need to borrow the painting to catalogue it as an original painting by me, they would probably let you just take it."

"They're that gullible?"

"No, they're that trusting." Taylor sat up a little straighter. "I've never lied to them, so they wouldn't have any reason not to believe me."

Felicia didn't say anything for several seconds. Then when Taylor pulled up in front of Seth's house, she finally nodded slowly. "Okay, we'll try it your way." Felicia took her weapon and slipped it inside her jacket pocket so that she could keep her finger on the trigger without anyone seeing the gun. "But if you try anything funny, you'll be the first to die."

Taylor swallowed hard and nodded. Then with a prayer in her heart, she pushed open the driver's side door and stepped out of the car.

41

SETH HEARD THE CAR DRIVE up, and he spoke into the Bluetooth headset in his ear. "Do you see them?"

"I don't believe this," Quinn said from his position on the roof across the street. "It's her agent."

"I didn't see that one coming," Seth muttered.

Brent's voice came over the headset next. "Remember. No one takes a shot unless Seth gives the signal. This may be our best chance of getting Taylor away from her safely and finding the rest of the smuggled equipment."

A knock came at the door, and Seth looked down at the coffee table in front of him. A table covered with weapons. He didn't move toward the entryway but rather stayed seated as he yelled out. "Come on in!"

The door cracked open slowly. "Seth?"

"Hey, Taylor," Seth called out to her. "I'm in the living room."

Taylor walked in slowly, a blond woman of about forty standing slightly behind her, both of her hands in her pockets. "Hi, Seth. This is my agent, Felicia Davenport."

"Nice to meet you." Seth smiled up at her, even as he noticed Felicia's eyes focus on the weapons in front of him. "Sorry about the mess. I was in the middle of cleaning my guns when Taylor called."

He picked up one of his automatic pistols and rubbed at it with a cleaning cloth. He could sense Taylor's fear and knew he had to give her some indication that everything wasn't what it appeared. He thought of Quinn and smiled to himself. "Taylor probably told you that I work with her fiancé. I think you met him up in New York."

"You mean Quinn?" Felicia nodded, her body tense as her eyes remained on Seth's weapon. She glanced over at Taylor briefly. "I didn't realize that they were engaged."

"It's a pretty recent development," Taylor managed, her questioning eyes meeting Seth's. Then she gave him a subtle nod and pointed up at the painting on the wall. "Felicia, that's the painting I was telling you about. Do you think that it needs to be catalogued since I gave it as a gift?"

"Absolutely," Felicia nodded. "It's actually more important to catalogue paintings that didn't go through an agent or a brokerage house. Otherwise, the authenticity could be challenged down the road."

"I'm afraid you two lost me," Seth told them, focusing on Taylor.

"I hate to ask, but is there any way Felicia could borrow the painting I gave you?" Taylor looked at him hopefully. "Apparently since my artwork has been selling so well, her agency wants to catalogue all of my paintings, especially after what happened with the theft a few weeks ago."

"Is that really necessary?" Seth asked, trying to imagine how he would act if he really believed Felicia's request was genuine. "It's not like we would ever sell it."

"But its value will continue to increase," Felicia told him. "And you'll need it to be catalogued before you'll be able to insure it properly."

"I never even thought about that." Seth glanced over at the painting as though he were still considering the request. Then, finally, he nodded. "If you need to borrow it, I guess that's okay. How long do you think it will be before we can have it back?"

"Just a couple of days," Felicia told him, her shoulders relaxing slightly. "Come on, Taylor. I'll give you a lift back to your apartment."

"I thought you were staying over here for dinner. Remember? Everyone is coming over to celebrate your engagement." Seth looked at Taylor. Then he looked over at Felicia. "I'm sure Quinn can take her home later. He's supposed to be heading over here in another hour or so anyway."

"Oh, but Taylor and I have some business we need to discuss."

"It's the weekend." Seth smiled at her, rubbing the cleaning cloth over his weapon once more as though he didn't even remember that he was holding it. "I'm sure your business can wait until Monday."

"Let me get that painting down for you." Taylor moved forward slowly as though she were anxious to get away from Felicia but afraid of what might happen if she moved too fast. She only made it two steps before Felicia grabbed her arm.

"Why don't you let Seth get it down?" Felicia suggested, her voice eerily suspicious. "After all, he's a lot taller than you are."

Seth looked at Felicia, saw the flash of awareness in her eyes, and he knew. He reached up to scratch his left ear, prepared to resort to the backup plan, one that would include a bullet flying through his front window. Then suddenly Felicia shifted behind Taylor, reached an arm around her neck, and pulled her weapon free of her jacket pocket.

"I think the time for polite conversation is over." Felicia nodded at the painting. "Put down the gun and give me the painting."

"You can have the painting," Seth said, slowly lowering the gun in his hand. "Just let her go."

"I don't think so." Felicia shook her head vehemently. "The minute I let her go, you or one of your friends will put a bullet through my head."

"Just let her go, and no one will get hurt."

Felicia's tone turned venomous. "This is about more than one person getting hurt."

Seth looked at Taylor's panic-stricken face and calculated the angle from the roof across the street. Felicia had positioned herself so that there was no way a sniper could get a clean shot. He took a deep breath as he set the weapon down on the table and reached up to take the medium-sized painting off of the wall.

"Here's the painting. Now, please, let her go."

Felicia shook her head. "You already know why I want the painting." Fury flashed in her eyes, and her grip on Taylor tightened. "And you already found the piece of equipment I'm looking for. Where is it?"

Seth looked at Taylor, pleased that there wasn't just fear in her eyes now. He could also see her determination. She was going to fight back when the time came. Seth was sure of it. He pulled a plain black flash drive from his pocket and held it out to her. "It's right here."

"Take it from him." Felicia nudged Taylor closer, still holding her as a shield.

Taylor reached her hand out and took it from Seth and then stumbled backward as Felicia dragged her toward the kitchen. Felicia must have sensed Brent's presence because just as she reached the doorway, she flattened herself against the doorjamb and pressed the gun firmly against Taylor's head.

"Tell your friends to let me go. And give me your car keys."

"You heard her," Seth called out as he reached into his pocket and pulled out his keys. Seth edged forward to hand the keys to Taylor as Brent stepped out of his hiding place and lowered his weapon onto the kitchen counter. Then both men watched helplessly as Felicia pulled Taylor toward the side door and disappeared with her into the garage.

* * *

"Can anyone tell who's driving?" Quinn asked anxiously from his position on top of the neighbor's roof. The garage door had opened, and Seth's car backed out with a squeal of the tires. For the first time since Felicia had grabbed Taylor, he could get a clean shot, but now he couldn't tell which of the two women was behind the wheel.

"Negative," Tristan said as Quinn saw him peering over Seth's back fence. "I can't see past the glare on the windows."

"Seth's having Steinert pull up the GPS tracker on his car," Brent told them as the car picked up speed and turned at the first street corner. "Let's move. We've got to get Taylor away from her before she realizes that the flash drive has been erased."

"They just passed Vanessa," Seth announced as he ran out of his house and raced toward Brent's car. "She said they're headed for Independence Boulevard."

Quinn shouldered his sniper's rifle and shimmied down to the ground as he tried desperately to bank down the panic rising up in him. He saw Brent and Seth take off in pursuit as he headed for Tristan's truck. From across the street, Tristan raced toward the driver's side.

"I've got a direct line to Steinert." Seth's voice came over the headset again. "My car is headed for the freeway. Apparently, Felicia Davenport flew into Norfolk this morning so our best guess is that they're headed for the airport."

"We can beat them there if we take a chopper," Quinn said urgently as Tristan gunned the engine to life.

"You and Tristan head for base. I'll call in and get you clearance," Brent told them. "We'll try to catch up to them."

"Roger that," Tristan responded and turned toward base. He spared Quinn a quick glance. "We're going to find her."

42

TAYLOR TRIED TO KEEP HER breathing steady, even though her heart was still beating rapidly. They had been driving for forty-five minutes, but when Felicia instructed Taylor to turn toward the airport, she realized that she was running out of time. *Think!* Taylor ordered herself. Clearly, Felicia had insisted on bringing her along as protection from the Saint Squad, but given the history of how Felicia normally dealt with liabilities, she was somewhat surprised that she hadn't tried to get rid of her yet.

Her hands grew moist on the steering wheel as she tried to let logic overcome her fear. For whatever reason, Felicia still needed something from her, but that couldn't last for long. Her gun would be identified if she tried to get through airport security, and surely Felicia didn't think that Taylor would go along as a willing hostage once she ditched her weapon. No, whatever Felicia had planned, it was going to happen before they reached the airport. And it was going to happen soon.

Taylor glanced over at the flash drive in Felicia's hand, and suddenly she understood why she was still breathing. Felicia needed to make sure that what Seth had given her was really what she had been searching for.

"Are you going to tell me where we're going?"

"Take a left at the next light."

Taylor looked at her speculatively. "I thought you were heading for the airport."

"That's what your friends will think." Felicia looked at her knowingly. Then she pointed to a park just ahead. "Park next to the white car over there."

Taylor looked at the park, at the nearly vacant lot. Two young mothers were standing on the edge of the playground on the far side of a wide grassy area, while several children played on the swing set. She tried to remember the lessons from the self-defense classes her father had forced her to take so many years ago. Be alert, check out your environment, look for someone to help.

The help she had been praying for didn't appear to be forthcoming, and all Taylor was sure of was that she didn't want to run toward the children. The closest trees were about twenty yards away. Could she break away from Felicia and make it over there safely? And if so, what would she do then? She thought of the action movies Quinn liked, wishing that she could stage everything to play out perfectly. Of course, real life didn't work that way.

Taylor parked Seth's vehicle next to the car Felicia had indicated, leaving an extra space between them. She heard a squadron of navy planes fly overhead, and in the distance, she could hear the thrumming sound of a helicopter. The navy base was practically around the corner from her, the same base where her father had spent the better part of his career. How ironic was it that she might very well die so close to where she had spent most of her life? Or that such a thing could happen when she had finally found happiness?

She squeezed her eyes closed for a moment, uttering a silent prayer that she would survive the day. She thought of the way Quinn looked standing over Emily's grave and knew that she had to do everything she could to keep him from being in that position for a second time.

"Turn off the car, and give me the keys," Felicia instructed, holding out one hand.

Taylor opened her eyes, feeling an unexpected sense of calm. Slowly, she did as she was told. "What are we doing here?"

"Making sure your friends didn't double-cross me."

"I don't understand," Taylor said, even though she understood perfectly. Knowing how devastating the attack on the US's financial systems could be, Taylor had to assume that Seth had given her something other than the item Felicia was so desperate to find. "Whose car is this?"

"It's another rental," Felicia admitted. "I didn't trust your friends to make this easy so I rented this car this morning and parked it here. Then I took a taxi to rent another car just in case someone tried to track the GPS signals. Besides, I couldn't very well drive around with what could be the most valuable piece of equipment ever invented."

"So you left it here in a parked car?"

"Where no one would ever think to look for it," Felicia nodded. Then she waved the gun toward Taylor. "Stay right there."

Taylor stared at her as she climbed out of Seth's car and backed toward the rental car. She mapped out her plan in her mind, ready to spring at the first opportunity. She watched as Felicia dug out a set of keys, clicked the button to pop the trunk, and, while still keeping her eyes on Taylor, reached into the trunk. The piece of equipment she pulled out looked like a series of electrical cords attached to what looked like a mini version of a computer motherboard.

Felicia held up the flash drive and took off the cap. The moment she looked down to plug it into the appropriate slot, Taylor pushed her door open, rushed from the car, and raced for the trees. *Run in a zigzag pattern,* she remembered her self-defense instructor saying. She dodged to the right as a shot rang out. Then she ducked to the left and sprinted for the nearest tree.

A second shot rang out, and Taylor heard herself cry out as she tripped over a tree root and stumbled to the ground. She could hear the screams of the mothers at the playground in the distance and hoped that they were ushering their children to safety.

Breathing heavily, Taylor scampered around the base of the tree and pressed her back against it. Terrified, she looked at the next cluster of trees. They were more than forty yards away, too far for her to make a run for it safely.

Staying close to the ground, she peeked around the base of the tree to see Felicia's face alight with fury as she threw the flash drive to the ground. Then she gripped her weapon and started toward Taylor.

Taylor's heartbeat quickened, and she debated whether to run now or take the daring option of trying to disarm Felicia. She took a deep breath and offered up another silent prayer. She had to do something. Staring across the field, she knew that she wasn't willing to go down without a fight. Forty yards would give Felicia too much time to take aim. She had to face her. She had to fight.

Quickly and quietly, she scrambled to her feet and prepared to lash out. She vaguely heard the approaching helicopter, annoyed that she could no longer tell how close Felicia was to her. The sound intensified, as did her pulse. She thought back to those self-defense classes, wondering if it was even possible for her to win this confrontation. Then she saw the glimpse of yellow to her right. Taylor shifted to her left until the gun Felicia was holding came into view. Then Taylor uttered yet another silent prayer and kicked at Felicia's hand.

Felicia cried out, and the gun went flying in the opposite direction. Taylor dove for Felicia, knocking her to the ground before she could scramble for her weapon. Felicia kicked at her, crawling forward and reaching for the gun that was only a few yards away.

Taylor grabbed at her legs only to have Felicia kick her hands away. Lunging forward again, Taylor grabbed her ankle, but Felicia managed to wriggle out of the hold and continue forward. Taylor could only stare. She was still lying on the ground, only now Felicia was just out of her reach with the gun once again in her hand and once again pointing right at her.

Taylor saw the fury in Felicia's eyes, saw the intent even as she tried to scramble backward. Just then a shot rang out. Taylor screamed, and Felicia's body jerked in pain as the gun fell to the ground once more. Instinctively, Taylor scooped up the weapon that now lay practically at her feet. She sucked in a ragged breath and stared down at Felicia, who was now holding a hand against her wounded shoulder. Then footsteps pounded toward her, and all she could see was Quinn's chest as he pulled her close.

"It's okay," he said, his own breathing sounding as ragged as Taylor's. Gently, he eased the gun out of Taylor's hand and handed it to Tristan, who was tending to Felicia. Quinn's voice lowered to a whisper as he added, "You're safe now."

Taylor's hands came around him, clinging to his shirt. She felt herself tremble, felt the tears welling up inside her. Then, as sirens sounded in the distance, Quinn scooped her up in his arms and carried her away from the woman who had come so close to taking her life.

43

"HOLD STILL," QUINN SAID, DABBING some hydrogen peroxide on the scratch on Taylor's forehead. She was sitting on the single bar stool next to his kitchen counter, her face still paler than normal.

Taylor winced as he pressed the cotton ball to her face but didn't say anything.

Quinn dropped his hand and looked at her again. He still couldn't get the image of Taylor grappling with Felicia out of his mind, especially that moment when Felicia broke free and aimed her pistol at Taylor. His heart had stopped beating in that instant. His fear of being too late had nearly prevented him from doing his job, from pulling the trigger and taking the shot that had disarmed Felicia and ultimately saved Taylor's life.

He reached for her hand, felt it tremble. "You're still shaking."

"I know." Taylor took a breath and let it out. "I can't seem to stop."

"I'm sorry." Quinn leaned forward and kissed her gently. "I'm so sorry about everything that happened."

"It wasn't your fault." Taylor squeezed his hand. "And if it weren't for you, I wouldn't be sitting here right now."

"I don't think I've ever been so scared in my life."

"That's hard to believe." Taylor managed a small smile. "But I'm glad you were there when I needed you."

"Me too." He leaned down as though he were going to kiss her, but then a knock sounded at the door. "I wonder who that is."

"I just hope it isn't another unexpected visitor looking for me. I haven't done so well with those lately."

"Isn't that the truth," Quinn muttered. He glanced through the front window and then pulled the door open wide to reveal Seth standing outside.

"Hey, Seth. What brings you by?"

"I came to invite you both over for dinner. We're having the whole squad over to celebrate the end of Taylor's nightmare." Seth nodded a greeting to Taylor. "Besides, I told Taylor we were going to have everyone over for an engagement party."

Quinn couldn't help but smile. He turned to look at Taylor. "I think they like you."

"That's convenient." Taylor's face lit up. "I like them too."

"Are you up for going out tonight?"

Taylor hesitated for a moment, and then she nodded. "Actually, yeah. I think I'd like that. Hanging out with a bunch of armed men sounds very soothing right now."

"Great." Seth grinned at her. "Come on by whenever. We'll eat around six."

"Sounds good," Quinn agreed. He closed the door and turned to face Taylor, his voice hesitant. "You know, everyone will understand if you need some time alone."

"I know." Taylor gave him a timid smile. Then she glanced around the somewhat barren room before looking back at Quinn. "You don't have any pictures up, not even of Emily."

Quinn looked at her, not quite sure what she expected him to say.

Then she shrugged a shoulder. "After you told me about her, I thought maybe that was why you'd never invited me inside your apartment before, because you didn't want me to see pictures of her."

"Did you want to see a picture of her?"

Taylor stared at him for a moment and then nodded. "She was important to you. I guess I just want to be able to visualize who she was in my mind."

Quinn was surprised that he had the urge to smile. He moved to the bookcase and pulled one of the photo albums off of the shelf. Then he set it down on the kitchen counter in front of Taylor.

She hesitated briefly before she opened it up and stared down at a photo of Emily on their wedding day. Taylor's eyes were damp when she looked up at Quinn. "She's beautiful."

Quinn nodded, leaning against the counter. He looked down at the picture of him and Emily standing in front of the temple, and suddenly he was able to imagine himself standing in that scene again, only now he could see it in the future as well as the past.

"It's funny how I could fall in love with two such completely different women," Quinn said. When Taylor looked up at him, he continued. "Emily was pretty quiet and preferred to stay at home. With you, just walking out the door can be an adventure."

"That wasn't my fault," Taylor began.

Quinn laughed now. "I don't mean the stuff that's been going on since you got home. You love being with people, you're artistic, and you're always up for a new adventure. Not to mention that you tend to be a bit unconventional."

Taylor seemed to consider his words, and she nodded. "I guess that's true."

Quinn reached for her hand, lacing his fingers with hers. "I'm just saying that I've been very blessed. I was fortunate that Emily loved me for as long as we had. And I'm incredibly lucky to have found you."

Taylor smiled and reached up to kiss him.

Quinn closed the photo album and slid it back on the counter. "We can look at that later." He looked down at Taylor skeptically. "Are you sure you're up for going to Seth's house tonight?"

"Yeah. I'd like the chance to thank everyone for all they've done for me."

"In that case, I think we have an errand to run before we head over there." Quinn stood up and nodded toward the door. "Come on."

"Where are we going?"

"Ring shopping." Quinn smiled at her now. "If they're going to throw an engagement party for us, the least we can do is get engaged before it starts."

Before Taylor could respond, he pulled her through the door. They were nearly to the stairs before Taylor finally stopped walking and waited for him to turn to face her. "Did you just ask me to marry you?"

"I don't think I actually asked the question." Quinn's eyebrows lifted, a combination of humor and uncertainty showing in his eyes. "I'm not sure I want to give you the chance to say no."

Taylor stared at him for a minute and nodded. "Oh, okay."

"Okay what?"

"Okay, I'll go shopping with you." Taylor took a step forward, but now Quinn stopped her.

"You will?"

Taylor's smile bloomed. "Yeah, I will."

Quinn grinned back at her and let out a short laugh. "I love you, you know."

"Good. I love you too." Taylor leaned forward and kissed him. "And I always will."

ABOUT THE AUTHOR

ORIGINALLY FROM ARIZONA, Traci Hunter Abramson has spent the past two decades living in Virginia. After graduating from Brigham Young University, she worked for the Central Intelligence Agency for six years before choosing to stay at home with her children and indulge in her love of writing.

Traci also coaches the North Stafford High School swim team. She currently resides in Stafford, Virginia, with her husband, Jonathan, and their four children.